# Lands *of* Eden

# Lands of Eden

## *the* Remnant *of* Candor

written by M. Gabreyl Scrolls
edited by April Shefield
illustrated by Mykle A. Lee

Leeway Literary Works
Published by Leeway Artisans, Inc.
PO Box 1577, Laurel, MD 20707

Book & Cover Design Mykle Lee

ISBN: 978-0-9744929-9-5

Copyright © 05/2003 by Leeway Artisans.

No parts of this book may be reproduced or utilized in any form or by any means, electronic or mechanical, including photocopying, recording, or by any information storage or retrieval system, without permission from the Publisher. All inquires should be addressed to:
P.O. Box 1577, Laurel, MD 20707.
ALL RIGHTS RESERVED

Minor portions of John Milton's Paradise Lost are excerpt in this novel under the fair use clause.

First Edition
Printed in the United States of America.

## CHAPTER ONE

The Realm of Enduring Peace 11
The Return of the Hunters 31
The Rim 41
The Night Presence 60

## CHAPTER TWO

The Seed 73
A Design and Purpose 84
The Sacrifice 103
The Night Scatter 118
The Fall of Candor 125

## CHAPTER THREE

The North Refuge 155
Plots of Evil 168
There Remains Hope 179
The Message 200
The Abomination of Pfiax 208
The Rebellion 216
A Dismal Escape 228

## CHAPTER FOUR

The Remnant of Candor 245

Sedonna

Ga

Pfiere

Cush

Eden

Barba

"And a river went out of Eden to water the garden; and from thence it was parted, and became into four heads. The name of the first [is] Pison: that [is] it which compasseth the whole land of Havilah, where [there is] gold; And the name of the second river [is] Gihon: the same [is] it that compasseth the whole land of Cush. And the name of the third river [is] Hiddekel: that [is] it which goeth toward the east of Assyria. And the fourth river [is] Euphrates."

-Genesis 2:10 – 14

# The 1656 years of Biblical Eden before the Flood

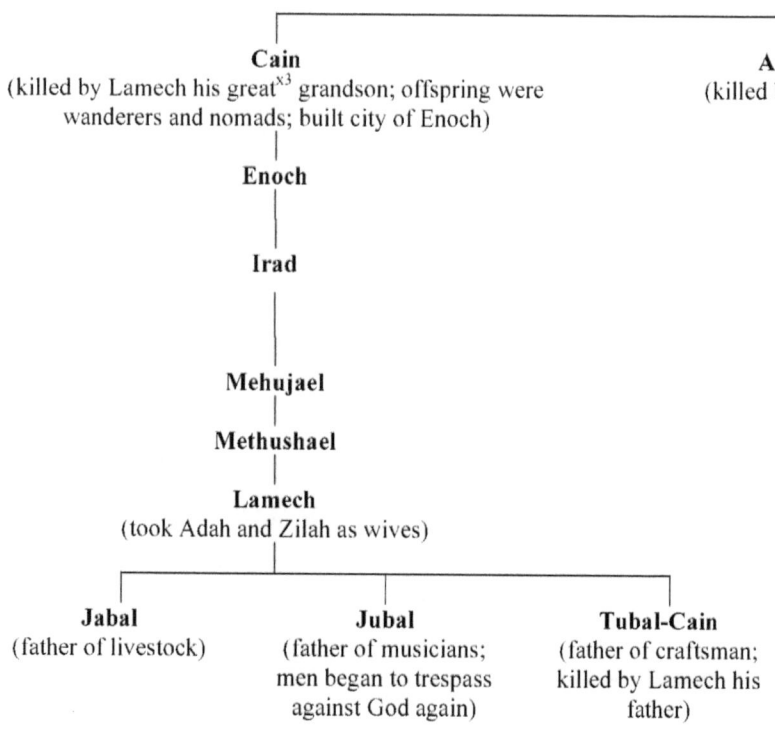

**Adam** (lived 930 yrs)

**Cain**
(killed by Lamech his great$^{x3}$ grandson; offspring were wanderers and nomads; built city of Enoch)

**Able**
(killed by C

**Enoch**

**Irad**

**Mehujael**

**Methushael**

**Lamech**
(took Adah and Zilah as wives)

**Jabal**
(father of livestock)

**Jubal**
(father of musicians; men began to trespass against God again)

**Tubal-Cain**
(father of craftsman; killed by Lamech his father)

"And the LORD God took the man, and put him into the garden of Eden to dress it and to keep it. And the LORD God commanded the man, saying, Of every tree of the garden thou mayest freely eat: But of the tree of the knowledge of good and evil, thou shalt not eat of it: for in the day that thou eatest thereof thou shalt **surely die**."

- Genesis 2:15-17

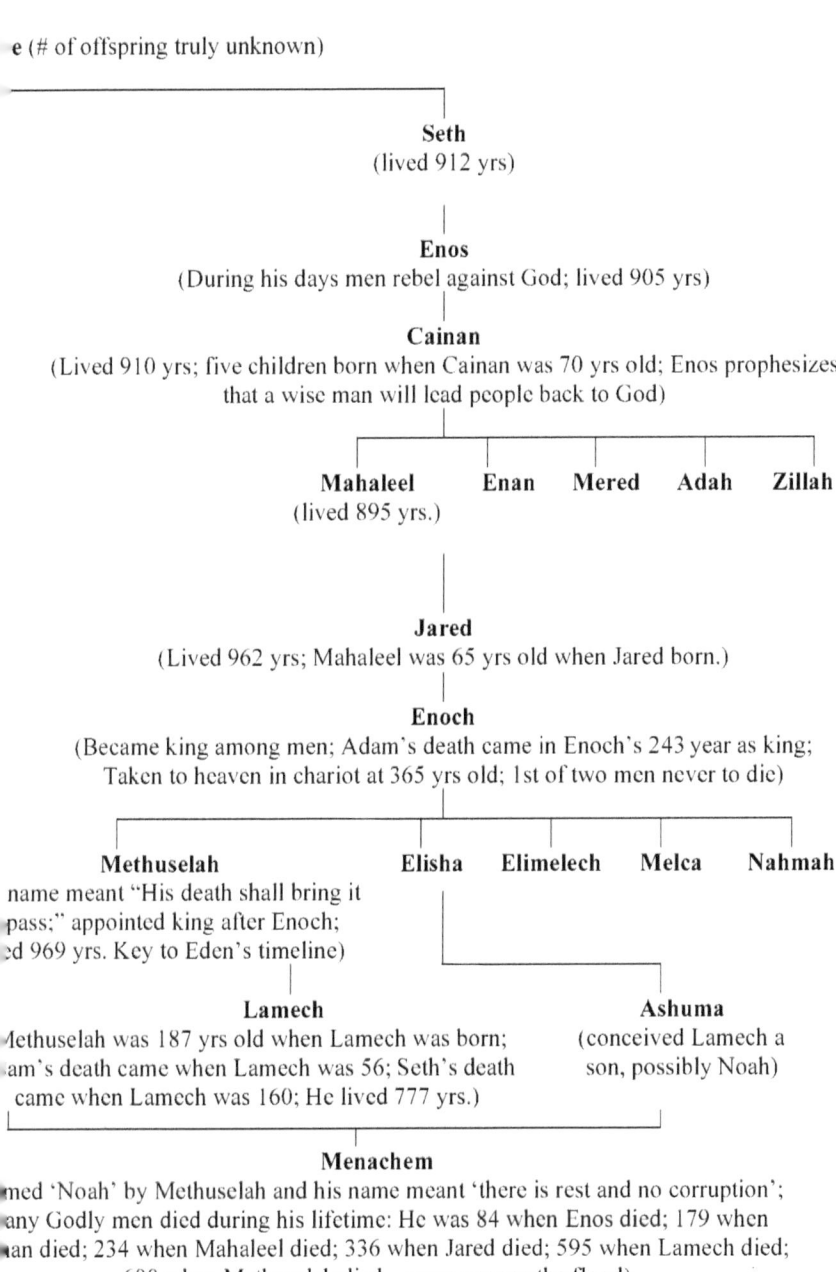

# Characters in Alphabetical Order

**Aman** – youngest son of Jebas, shepherd of Candor
**Apayim** – descendant of Mehujael, dellamy, barter of Candor
**Barra** – father of Ezra, spear-bearing hunter
**Benjin** – second son of Jebas, 'Jin', archer for the hunt
**Cephas** – descendant of Tubal-Cain
**Dolan** – first son of Jebas, Benjin's twin brother, spear-bearing hunter
**Elias** – elder shepherd, second of the eight sons of Enos, Warrior
**Ephese** – father of Lathan, dellamy, archer and spear-bearing hunter
**Ezra** – son of Barra, spear-bearing hunter
**Hala** – daughter of Uriah, knitter of Candor
**Jebas** – chief hunter of Candor, father of Jebas, Dolan and Benjin
**Jodia** – elder grappler, sixth of the eight sons of Enos, Warrior
**Lathan** – only son and child of Ephese, planter of Candor
**Lórcephoene** – possessed being
**Melhazur** – descendant of Mehujael, dellamy, barter of Candor
**Mered** – elder archer, third of the five sons of Cainan, Warrior
**Morcial** – elder healer, descendant of Seth's lesser sons
**Seth the III** – elder spear-bearer, third of the eight sons of Enos, Warrior
**Udell** – elder fielder, descendant of Seth's lesser sons
**Uriah** – father of Hala, archer, spear-bearing, and grappling hunter

## Reference for terms in Alphabetical Order

**gonya** – flower that bloomed along the southern border of the rgêeda valley

**ō** – weapon used by the warriors of Adam, in appearance a seven ɪot staff roughly two inches in diameter.

**oncauct** – buds which grew from flaxel branches; bloomed with dark reen stained **moisture**

**ellamy** – the word itself meant 'wanderer', used to describe Cain's escendants

**ɪhi** – ancient majestic bird known to fly from plain to plain without ease; possible source pterodactyl fossil

**axel** – tall trees with deathly green leaves and pale bark; trees were elieved to have grown from seeds which Adam cursed

**inya** – spicy root, modern day ginger

**ooky** – balm that was created from mix of balsam beans, used as ealing cream

**ɔ** – weapon used by the warriors of Adam, in appearance a four foot ɪpered staff roughly two and a half inches in diameter

**onoa** – **modern-day** sap, used to gloss crafts and weapons to mprove grip

**eah** – pasture, rest

**ɔbita** – treasured beetle-like insects; trilobites

**ɔhania** – small tree with thick, porous bark

**ɪ☐konops** – the name means 'tiny bitters'; **modern-day** mosquitos

**uct** – horse; animal used by elder men to plow the grounds

**e`em** – ancient scavengers of the plains, hyenas stem from these reatures

**aquara** – vast plain of forest and fertile oasis **where** men spread ivilization; much of the Saquara was swallowed into the Atlantic and the remaining forest wilted to become the **modern-day** Sahara and Saudi desserts

**scaffles** – ancient buffalo that was the source for much clothing, food, shelter, and weaponry

**schudora** – smelly spice, smelled as sulfur, and the aroma was flammable

**sefíya** – fallen seraph by closest definition, the word means 'swine' in modern tongue, in ancient tongue it was equivalent to a curse

**topac** – ancient herb similar to **modern-day** garlic

**tryton** – giant amphibious breeds of lizards which dwelt in the southern borders and lower hills of Eden; source of **modern-day** dinosaur fossils

# Prologue

There was a purpose and beginning for all occurrences in the ages of man that holds claim to the truth of his pre-destiny. What begot these ages is found in that which was bred long before the sapphire waters, the emerald plains of the Northlands, and blooming scents of the great garden in Eden. That which was bred in the time before earthly times, the only essence not created from the Alpha, would set the course for the abundant heavens, still waters, beasts, fowls, and flora of the field… that fateful tree which would forever taint mans' heart… and the mystical battles of that lost paradise, fuelled by the wrath of the fallen prince and waged against the first-fruits of Adam. These are untold chronicles of the lands of Eden, pavers of the honored age that fathered mankind.

\*        \*        \*

In the beginning was nothing but the overseers of the void, known as the Trinity. The Trinity was alone, above the void, for unparalleled lengths of time still unknown by any that were to come. Little was known of the mysteries of the Trinity. What was known was the Trinity was the beginning of loneliness. And loneliness was the reason for all things made.

The first created things were the inhabitants of the early kingdom. Of these were the Cherubim, the Sarim, the Archs, and the Seraph. Cherubim remain as the fastest of all beings ever created. Cherubim were given six adjoining wings made of the purest pallid and feathers un-breaching to the wind. In their wings was the melody of chimes, and their flight was an aerial dance of rhythm and sinuous peace. Their tongues were trained only for singing, which they would do seven times a day during flights in unison around the throne of the Trinity. Seven hundred of these beings were created by the hand of the Father.

The Sarim were the most magnificent of all beings inhabiting the kingdom. A Sarim's skin glowed eternally with brilliant cascades of all colors in existence. Still each separate Sarim possessed one central hue that fashioned more radiant than others. These were the great musicians and singers whose very bodies were instruments that produced the most heavenly harmonies. Most important were the pure colorless crystals given to them by the Trinity, measuring five cubits in width and eight cubits in length and placed as ornaments around their necks. This was the second most priceless gift the Trinity would give any being, for it gave the Sarim the power to bring the highest joy to the Trinity, and in turn brought them the highest favor. Sarim were giants among all other beings to be created, and twenty-eight were created by the word of the Son.

Archs were created as the strongest and fiercest of all beings. Archs were given wings the average span of 25 cubits with feathers that shimmered as silver in light, and that clasped with the resonance of thunder. These beings were skilled in aerial acrobatics and champions of guard and battle. Each was given swords made from the ashen flame that burned only at the voice of the Son. Their bodies were fortified with unyielding armor, and their speech carried as the sound of trumpets, louder than all other beings could voice. Arches were charged with the message in the Father's voice, which was quite powerful and only to be heard by a purified soul. They used their tongue to proclaim triumph. In all, one thousand were created by the breath of the Spirit.

Seraph were peculiar beings, the tiniest of all kingdom inhabitants, measuring five cubits but standing only three cubits in height. The backs of all Seraph were hunched and their legs remained bent at their knee as they walked. Like the Archs, these were skilled guards and battlers but with tremendous leaping ability, drawing their strength from endless wisdom. The Seraph were given bows and arrows by reason of keen vision. When in flight, their arrows scrolled the mysteries of the character of the Trinity across the sky. Four hundred fifty Seraph were created collectively by the Trinity's hand.

At the breath of the Father these beings came to life and all immediately proclaimed Him "the Alpha." These were the first beings created, and the Father named them collectively "Angels," because they were exceptionally holy beings of good spirit.

    \*    \*    \*

Loneliness was the beginning of all things, the Fall of the Angels was no exception. The Trinity was pleased with His Angels, yet found favor among each tribe of them. A decree from the Trinity went throughout the kingdom, "I will choose from each tribe certain leaders to establish an order." Of the Cherubim, 14 were selected and each given charge over their choruses. The Trinity declared, "I have endowed you Cherubim with the ability to make peace at the very sound of your voices. Use it to proclaim love and mercy, for I love my creation endlessly." The only name known among these leaders is Gabriel, who found great prominence in the Trinity's kingdom after the Fall.

Ten were chosen from the Archs and each given their centurion league. Of these were Betheal, Vestual, Uriel, Phanuel, Raphael, Metranon, Baal, Peniel, Sariel, and Michael. These were the least of the Archs, but the Trinity blessed them. "I bestow upon each of you certain strengths in angelic powers and abilities of omnipresence, for I am a source of endless strength for all beings from the East and West." The full abilities of the Archs remain a mystery. Yet prophecy foretold that one, a privileged scribe in exile, would witness their full abilities upon the isle of Patmos where the end of things would be revealed.

Among the Sarim was an angel most esteemed in the eye of the Trinity whom many of the other inhabitants of the kingdom also adored. His name was Lucifer, and he was chosen by all other angels to be the sole leader of the Sarim. The Trinity instead decided to make Lucifer a supreme angel among Angels. "Lucifer, my morning star, you have abundant favor in my eyes. I grant you the order of a prince. You are endowed with wisdom, love, strength, beauty, and powers unlike any angel, for I give grace freely to all who seek." Encompassed in Lucifer was the wisdom of the Seraph, the vigor of the Archs, and the melody of the Cherubim. And the order of the Seraph was placed in Lucifer's keep. At the appointment of Lucifer, there was a great parade in the kingdom in which all the Angels praised the Trinity for their prince.

When this happened, Lucifer's heart was turned to cold and loneliness. Immediately, he spread whispers of his rights to the tribute and honor of the angels. Very few relented to him, and so he was secluded from the kingdom for a time without fulfilling his charge to appoint the leaders of the Seraph. None sought the prince's absence and this angered him into hatred and rivalry. Upon his return, Lucifer found the throne of the Trinity more fitful than his role as prince. When the angels called forth the morning, Lucifer sat himself upon that throne and decreed his glory to the Angels. He performed miraculous powers the Angels had never seen another perform. His beauty enchanted all who watched, as he demanded the same praise as the Alpha. Of the Angels, all the Seraph and Sarim bowed and praised him. Nevertheless, many of the other Angels were reluctant to join in his adoration.

Of the Archs were Baal and Vestual who were most impressed by Lucifer and his graceful presence on the throne. The two persuaded many in their leagues to adore the prince. Noticing how vast a multitude Lucifer amassed, fellow Archs Sariel, Betheal, Phanuel, and Metranon believed him to be a destined leader. None of the Cherubim would praise the prince, instead they sang in unison that their tongues were trained only for the glory of the Trinity. In all, 726 Angels bowed in praise at the return of prince Lucifer.

The remaining Angels proclaimed heaping sorrows and wept at the sight of the boasts, this was the first instance of weeping and sorrow known to any living being. The volumes of their sobs pierced deeply through the heart of the Trinity, causing Him great pain. When the Father found the 726 Angels bowing to Lucifer, He was enraged and gathered the Son and the Spirit to make a decree. "Lucifer has consumed himself in pride, he has exalted himself above the Holy Trinity and thus will be humbled for all eternities. And all who bow to worship the prince will be swallowed in humility with him." But Lucifer scorned him hysterically, proclaiming that the Trinity had made him greater than all the Angels, even greater than the Trinity himself. He promised to take the kingdom from the Trinity and rule the Angels greater than their creator.

The 726 were suddenly filled with fortitude at his words and with a trembling ovation charged the throne. A great battle waged in the kingdom for a grand amount of time and as the rebellion swelled toward the throne, Lucifer declared that he would empower all to be just like the Trinity.

At that very moment, the Trinity cried thunderously, "Who is like God?" His voice rumbled throughout the kingdom and charged Michael the Arch with great power. At the Trinity's command Michael rushed the throne and hurled Lucifer into darkness. Then the entire relic of steadfast Angels gathered under Michael's order and overcame those who had bowed to the prince. The battle silenced as a horrendous wail, like no other, surged from amidst the gloom. Instantly, the 726 were enthralled as Lucifer emerged with skin of crimson and eyes of endless shadows. Before all the Angels in the kingdom, Lucifer began to morph into a gruesome beast. The instruments of his body contorted into a single tail stemming from his hind, he hunched, and fell to his knees as his growls echoed with his pelt hardened into scales. The splendor of his countenance vanished in the darkness that engulfed his face.

Lucifer proclaimed the Trinity marred him and must be brought down so their morning would again shine. "I am the Light of creation!" shouted the Trinity. And the thunder of His voice charged Uriel's sword with abundant light. As Uriel the Arch raised his sword its radiance illuminated the entire kingdom, flushing the 726 to Lucifer's side where they too began to morph into hideous gloomy creatures. The winds of the kingdom flourished with fouls of sulfur as ash mounted at the feet of the rebellious. The bodies of the Seraph flared in dark green un-quenching flame. Each Sarim roared in agony as their bodies were chained and morphed into monstrous creatures with hideous skins, tongues struck mute and darkness hiding them. The flame from the bodies of the Seraph singed the feathers of the Archs and turned them thin and leathery as their flesh melted from their faces. Lucifer again rallied his praises, decreeing he would purge the throne of the kingdom for all the Angels.

And at those words the Trinity shouted, "My work is just, you will be humbled for all ages, for I will purge the darkness!"

Instantly the wings of Rapheal the Arch extended and lifted him towering into flight. With one flap of his mighty wings, a forceful gale swept the 726 from the kingdom and plummeted them into the Abyss. As they fell, silence reigned in heaven for several moments. Finally, the Trinity spoke.

"My kingdom has suffered a tremendous loss at what prince Lucifer has bred. A grave darkness, an evil has been created today that threatens everlasting morning." After the Trinity spoke the Angels began to mourn over the battle that transpired and the new existence of evil. But the Spirit moved among them and quieted their tears. "Do not mourn, this will not be allowed to exist. We will create another being who will be destined to overcome this evil... Come, let us make man in our own image and our likeness..."

# Chapter One

## *The Realm of Enduring Peace*

One hundred years after the burial of Adam, Earth's first descendants inhabit the vast tropics of the Saquara, centered along the equator of Eden. Men manage to thrive throughout the tropical tundra building widespread civilizations that span the rich lands of Havilah and reach the southern banks of the Gihon River. All cities, townships, and villages live harmoniously under the rule of the great prophet and king Enoch, fifth generation son of Seth. Yet men's hearts have turned silent to the teachings of Adam, the father of mankind. Many of the prophets of old seclude themselves from man who has begun to revel in the pleasures of dark desire. The roving descendants of Cain build endless citadels to constellations, natural forms, and foreign beings and craft tools of brutality as they spread wild seed through the line of offspring. None take heed to the prophecy of the king, written in the very name of his son as time tests the patience of the great wrath to come.

    Centered in the midst of all civilizations is the land of Candor where the glow of the mighty flame guarding the Garden can be held in the night halo. This is the land which the Alpha promised Adam and held to those of his blood line.

Here men live prosperously, spared from the smite of drought which drains the land and hardens the soil. Here men are nourished by the abundant wildlife and fertile land brought in from the Pison and Euphrates rivers. It is here where the first age of men was molded by hearts of purity and threat of taint.

A heavy mist settled over the emerald grasslands and rolling hills of Candor, blocking the morning sunlight. The sullen mist glided over the hills with a chilly wind lifting and swaying through the breeze. The trees and meadows stirred with an unwelcomed presence. Shadows loomed along the horizon, and groaned forth where sun rays pressed. Chilling winds swept forth along the barriers summoning darkness as it wrestled through the Rim Forest. Nevertheless, this lurking shadow would not remain unseen.

Just outside the fences of the village stood a lone figure, robed in tapered wool, carelessly letting the cool breeze lift the cloth in its gusts. His eyes peered along the border as the mist drifted solemnly into the shadow which culminated among the trees. He pealed through the cover to sighting the appearance of strange figures dancing in ash.

A sudden cold hand and presence of a darkness gazing back at him with engaging anticipation ruffled, but did not break him. Strapped to his back rested a seven foot staff smoothed and blunted to perfection, marked at its center with the victories of countless engagements. He stepped forward, perhaps to give such presence a better view of him. With arms crossed, he stood tall and confident, prepared to draw out this weapon in the swiftest fashion and spoke softly his vow to Candor and to the truths passed down by his forebearer.

"I am Seth the third, son of Adam, son of Seth, and son of Enosh my father. I am held to this land and to the truth passed down from my grandfather. Let any enemy of man… and every enemy of the Alpha, remain fallen by the strength the Creator has instilled in me."

At those words the gloom groaned with aggravation. Seth felt the darkness awakened and irritated at his presence. Still he stood as stone and dared the gloom onward.

Seth the III was the fourth of the eight sons of Enos, and Adam was his great grandfather. He remembered much of Adam. The father of mankind was not too far aged to impart much to him. He spent many years in Adams way and swore his hand to protect his forefather's promised soil. And while age slipped the focused warrior's count, courageous skill had not, and he guarded Candor with great honor.

The winds increased with unsettle. Faintly heard were the whispers and chants of darkness that licked their chill at Seth's ears. The forest whined as if in labor from the gusts. A brief silence then gave birth to an ominous grumble that would beckon fear in the hearts of most. But Seth remained fortified, repeating his vow, praying his words to carry deep into the forest.

Mere seconds passed before he perceived a luminous pair of green eyes glaring at him. He squinted back, then gripped his staff just as a ray of sunlight climbed the horizon. A sudden scatter and the distant specter was gone. He stood still, waiting, questioning, searching the borders, still at his guard. As the sunlight illuminated the entire forest, a herd of foals fixed their eyes back on him.

Seth released his grip on his staff and watched as the foals scampered across the fields. He closed his eyes as the wind shifted westward, bringing with it the warmth of the morning sun, and the hope-filled laughter of three unsuspecting children.

\* \* \*

The bright ginger of the awakening sun gleamed off the settled morning dew. A delicate silence kept calm the dawn

# Chapter One — *The Realm of Enduring Peace*

drifting through the village with the warmth of early morning. Centered in the village stood a towering trunk, dead to its root and yet blooming with the glow of rays slowly descending toward its base. Beacon to all in the village, but to three fully awakened rascals, a place to grab the first beams of breaking sun.

Aman appeared first, he popped his head out of his tent and was forced to squint at the bright orange globe gleaming back at him. He seeped further out of the weathered cloth, quietly. Seeing no one he crouched low, setting his sight on the tower. Hala peered out second, snatching Aman into sight. He looked back at her, doe-eyed and smiling. Hala jolted forward and the chase ensued. Aman's legs flurried him into flight down a path created between tents.

Lathan, the third accomplice, bounded out from the rear of his tent at the prey, nearly catching Aman's heel in his grip. The attempt shook Aman's pace, but he held his balance knowing Hala kept pursuit.

Aman checked his shoulder, Hala was gaining, effortlessly gaining, so he would have to use evasion to win the morning.

Hala stretched her stride moving her ever so close to his catch. Aman looked back, smirked and snapped around a tent, hurdled and twirled parallel to the ground and was off in another direction. Her chase, faded, still rounded tent after tent finally leaving Hala lost.

Aman chuckled with success then halted remembering Lathan was still to be contended, and Lathan was a much harder stalker to shake. Aman searched around sensing no sign. He situated himself for the tower, but the snap of a twig sent him crouching behind a pile of lamb's wool.

Meanwhile, Hala spun feverishly in circles, darting in and out of the paths between the village tents. Aman was in arm's reach before his wild acrobatics that now placed him nowhere within her sight. Ahead soared the pole, the suns rays now traveled down the center of the trunk. Aman would make a dash for it soon. She charged its base and stood in preparation.

"That's against the rules!"

The faint shout sent her sprinting forth toward its origin. She silently peeked behind a tent only to see nothing and sighed in exasperation. Upon turning, she was snatched to the ground by Lathan.

"You know the rules. No guarding the base."

"So how are we going to catch him?" Hala responded.

Lathan shushed her, "Follow me…"

Aman's anxiety grew with the moments of silence between each roll and tuck behind the tents. He moved cautiously, with his toes set to spring him. Each shift from tent to tent brought him closer to his goal. A trill of laughter ahead indicated Hala's presence. He spotted her scarf slip just behind the tents ahead as it fluttered in the drafts of her chase. He glanced behind believing he spotted Lathan's shadow. They were cornering him, so he had only one chance. Aman bolted out into the open at the next nuance of Hala's giggles. She spotted him and quickly began to cut short his distance.

"I've got you, I've got you," Hala shouted with triumph.

"No you don't, no way, no way!" Aman pleaded. But Hala's speed was indeed closing out his opportunity. She had made her way behind him and was within snatching length of his shirt. Aman felt her fingertips inch closer and instantly tumbled to his left. Hala sneered and charged forward to brink his ground. Aman paused to double back just in time to be tackled to the ground by Lathan who followed his triumph with cheer.

"And once again the hunter marks his prey!"

Aman whined in false agony, "Get off, get off…Let me up!"

"You have to say it first Aman," Hala reminded.

# Chapter One             *The Realm of Enduring Peace*

"No way, you two cheated, you normally don't work together…You would not have caught me if you hadn't."

"Nevertheless 'reushamim', you still have to say it…'first to rise…'" Lathan propped his weight onto Aman, pinning him down. As Aman struggled endlessly, he endlessly caused himself less freedom under Lathan's grip.

"C'mon Aman, you know you won't be able to break free, Lathan's too strong." At that Lathan smiled, lifted one arm and flexed, to which Aman responded with a series of squirms only again to find himself more entrapped.

"I'm not saying it! Besides Hala, you can still make the base…He can't stop us both…" Aman exclaimed. Hala appeared to ponder the thought for a moment before catching Lathan's warning eye.

"It's not the rules, you have to play by the rules. No one can go for the base until he says it." Lathan demanded with application of more pressure to Aman's forearm.

"C'mon Aman…'first to rise…'"

"Fine, fine, 'first to rise, first to fall,' now let me up!" With that Lathan was up on his feet, straddling over Aman with Hala's leg in his hand. As soon as she took a glance at the pole, Lathan yanked back and sent her face first into the dirt. He then stumbled forward and strolled triumphantly to the base. Upon tagging the pole he basked in the warmth of the morning sun.

"Ah yes, champion again, no one can compare!" As Lathan paraded around the pole, Aman assisted Hala to her feet.

"Are you okay Hala," he spoke softly.

"Yeah I'm okay… I just never get to win…"

"You'll never beat me to the sunrise Hala. Just face it both of you…I can't be beaten, I was meant to bask in the sun…" Lathan proceeded to boast in proclamation, "… because I'm the oldest, strongest, and wisest, and one day, I'll be the greatest hunter ever!" He roared and beat his chest sending his voice bellowing across the south plains and deep into the forest where they each paused and gazed. What they saw was instantly ironed in their minds. The three glanced harmoniously at each other, then rushed forward toward the pasture fences to get a better glimpse.

Far in the distance appeared a black smoke dancing through the trees of the border. The three youths stood awestruck as each perceived the sounds of blissful music stemming from the dark fog droving ominous shadow as it moved with the west wind. Aman squinted questioningly at the model of a human figure absorbed in the haze. Instantly the three froze at the sound of a ruffling robe behind.

"There are still some resting beyond the morning's first light, young ones." Hala was the first to turn and catch Seth's gaze upon her wide-eyed expression. Aman turned next and sighed his fright away. Lathan remained transfixed until the disappearance of the smoke, which drifted deeper into the trees. Seth crossed his arms shifting the bō strapped to his back. He raised his left brow slightly and caught their attention with a chill that tickled their spines. His thin stormy beard hugged his strong square chin like a coat and would not shift in the gust of the wind. None of the youths said a word, each struck silent at his commanding presence.

Seth hummed, stepped forward and parted them, and set his back toward them as he gazed across the flat. Lathan was the first to run off, followed by Hala who dimly called after Aman. Aman stared at Seth's back for a moment before finally responding to the unified calls of his accomplices. The morning was quickly approaching and none of the three wished to be caught with the charge of waking the elders. The wind howled a final whisper as the trio left Seth's sight. He nodded with a smile that was seldom seen by any in Candor and repeated his vow before heading off to monitor the morning labor.

# Chapter One                    The Realm of Enduring Peace

\*          \*          \*

The warm morning met with subtle laughter and conversation as Candor awakened. Young men, women, boys and girls gathered outside the tents, greeting each other with wide smiles and warm embraces. Eden had never seen a land more tranquil than that of Candor. Throughout the countries it was known as *hetaqua pac vendragen*, or "the Realm of Enduring Peace." Stepping onto the very grounds of Candor brought joy to any travelers.

Candor had not seen the vile elements that shattered villages and scattered peoples in earlier ages, such dark times were yet to breach the peaceful grounds. Dark works searched through the lands of Eden with destructive effect. Candor long remained free from the root of dark inspiration. But the grounds surrounding the village grew gloomier as forces threatened the borders.

Aman, Hala, and Lathan each made their separate way in preparation for morning work. Aman rushed to the grassland pastures with his short staff, which actually towered over the boy, tucked tightly under one arm and a tan crumb sack strapped from his shoulder, spilling scraps through a split in its cloth. The lad was quite a humorous sight, nearly toppling sideways from the weight of the sack upon him. Still he ran with inspiration, for this day he, like all others in the village, had a job to do.

Life in Candor was simplistic, every man, woman, boy and girl completed the necessary tasks toward the central goal of flourishing. The women of the land focused most on the preparation of foods from herbs and crops tilled from the land. When the hunters returned, they would prepare animal skins and wool knits set aside for tent housing and clothes. Hala, like all other girls, would spend her days among the knitting tents

# Lands of Eden

*by M. Gabreyl Scrolls*

learning knit methods by teacher and inventing speedier methods of her own. She dreaded each day in the knitting tents, longing to be taught more about the field and hunters' way.

Village boys raised grains and vines of exotic fruits, herbs, and vegetables and shepherd lambs, mules, buffalo, and the most treasured of animals, *scaffles*. Each family owned its own crops and small herds. Young males were responsible for raising the livestock and fields, and once they reached the age of knowledge and understanding, they would pass the task onto another family member or offspring in exchange for the duties of a hunter.

Hunters were held in the highest esteem throughout the lands. Fortified with strength and skill, they were the providers often filled with boasts and prideful manners that aided the pull of darkness in its conquests. Candor's hunters were perhaps the strongest and most skilled in all of Eden. They journeyed for weeks and at times months to return with bountiful hide for the Candorian feasts. Yet with the vast famine that plagued other lands of Eden, game begun to diminish and was often harder to catch as a result of unknown frights among the expanse that sprawled the animals. This led to hunters journeying further into foreign lands and becoming enthralled with the ways of unfamiliar civilizations where idol relics, elaborate jewels, and temple grounds incited unnatural devotion. Jebas, chief hunter and father to Aman, kept close to the teachings of the prophets and did his best to hold many of Candor's hunters in moral standing. Still the temptations of foreign wonders lured many hearts as their eyes harvested seeds sown to shade and hindered wisdom.

As the youngest of a family of four, a father and twin brothers, Aman faced many more duties at a much earlier age than most boys in the village. He learned the ways of the field along with the tent and was quite capable in knitting clothes

# Chapter One — The Realm of Enduring Peace

and food preparation. His brothers, Dolan and Benjin, often called "Jin", were taught the way of the hunter soon after Aman's birth. They held twelve years over Aman but were not to become hunters so early. The circumstance of the death of Aman's mother, Mariah, brought the need for Jebas to train his sons at earlier age. Aman never quite understood the meaning of his mother's death, why life came to him at birth but went from his mother in the same moment. His brothers cursed his birth in their sorrow and called him *Achan-Jebaz*, which meant 'he caused travial and sorrow,' even while their own births brought upon the death of their mother, Juleah. Yet Jebas refused to have his son marred as he by this name, and called him Aman-du`Lana, after Mariah's wishes. His name meant 'he is faithful and will be a fortress.'

Aman believed that his mother's life was taken into him and this was why he was so fit for both field and tent. The boy soon would learn that more abided in him to surge seeds in willful warriors and encompass the evil threat throughout all of Eden.

Lathan joined his younger friend on his way into the pasture. The sturdy lad boasted two sacks of equal weight on each shoulder. He trotted alongside Aman effortlessly with a mischievous grin. This was not abnormal as Lathan was well known as a rascal among the camps. He carried with him the haughtiness of his father Ephese, champion spear bearer and mason of the *Dellamy* tribe. Though not cursed in fashion, Eden knew the hunter and his son as "anilo dellamis Thetandras" because they were descendants of Huveel, son of Jabal. The phrase was grimly based and meant "not of Adam's blood." There were very few in Candor of dellamy, so scarce that most developed enough in Candors' way that there was no distinction nor need for disguise.

Like his father, Lathan commanded attention among his peers, and attention was given as his stature and prowess outmeasured many boys his age.

"What are you smiling about?" Aman asked sensing something devious in Lathan's high spirits.

"My duties today Aman, Sachal gave me his sack this morning at the call of his father." In all likelihood this meant double duty for Lathan during the day.

"And you're happy,that means you'll be planting till dusk."

"No my friend, this means that I'm planting in the southern crops."

With that short response Aman felt a cold current glide up his neck and lift his hairs with a tickle that revealed the scheme hidden behind Lathan's grin. The crops of Candor spanned out in six-cubits along the west and southwest bend of the village where the east sun beamed rays from early dawn till dusk. The southernmost point of the crops opened to a vast russet wheat field where few in the village journeyed. The plush green crops grew tall with lavish vegetation and wild leaves, and bordered the village from view of the existence beyond the meadows. For beyond laid an ominous valley where tall *flaxel* trees huddled together in a shield to the light of day to cast the endless shadow on the inhabiting ground, and massive jagged stone formations glistening with lucid ooze did ward away the outside world from the veiled nature existing within. The Rim.

The Rim, the darkest hold of the Caspian forest and gateway to the blackened, haunted ground. Once guarded by the embattled elders of Candor, this was a tumultuous place where untold forms and creatures tramped for hundreds of years before leaving in wake of Adam's death. These creatures were believed to come in existence when all animals were scattered from the garden and driven vicious by the darkness that entered that fateful day. Early civilizations were terrorized by these creatures which roamed ravenous and untamed.

# Chapter One — The Realm of Enduring Peace

Many were struck dead under the hand of great prophets and warriors, others were finally driven from the lands and into the deepest depths of the Rim by Candors' forefathers. Though the years saw the beasts of the Rim succumb to man's dominance, the grounds along the dark forest were never to be touched by any of the inhabitants of Candor, particularly after nightfall.

The journey to the Rim from the southern crops was across a long tree barren land of treacherous nature all its own. Ripe with wild ravenous animals and shallow dens deep enough to entrap ones small enough. A morning journey would mean twilight upon entrance into the dark forest for feet so young. Twilight was when the animals of the field grew wild and cruel forces teased the helpless stock.

"Lathan, you know we are not to go out to the Rim, it is dangerous, and we could be—"

"—Who said anything about 'we,'" Lathan interrupted with a frown. "I'll go wherever I wish, I know the plains very well, and I'm strong enough to fight any animal if I have to." Aman struggled to keep his balance as Lathan managed to reach over and steady the crumb sack on the small boy's back. Though help was needed, Aman masked his gratitude.

"What about your sacks, it will be night before you have emptied them both, you won't have the time."

Lathan looked away as the two slowed their pace. "I'm not going to plant any seed today. I'll take Sachal's normal duty, but once the field hand is turned, I'll dump the seed and be off."

"Lathan, you know the field hand will be angry if you have not planted."

"Elder Udell is the chieftain, he won't even be able to see enough to know that I am gone." Lathan spoke nothing more true of the aged field hand whose eyesight had failed greatly. "I'll leave early and be back in time enough to finish my job through until morning."

"The Rim is a long way, there is no way you could make it back here in time. Everyone will know you're missing."

Lathan halted entirely. He let his sacks drop to the ground and looked at Aman with a stern impression. "Everyone won't know I'm missing because no one will find out...will they?"

Aman looked up at his companion with great protest in his heart, yet the daring response in Lathan's eye made him back down and look at his feet. He shook his head then looked off into the distance where the crops bent to the south. The shadow there peeked over the tall crops with a delightful stare upon the village. Yet whatever was there would remain in place for the moment.

"Look, we'll be back just before dawn and no one will know. Our fathers will not return until the day's end. Think of all we can boast to others. All we have to do is run fast. And I'm plenty fast. Now do you wanna come?"

The invitation was not as itching as would normally be for other youths throughout Candor. Aman's brothers had frightened him all too often with the images of ferocious animals and fowls traipsing the Rim moors, driven unnaturally mad from the darkness that retreated there.

"No, I'm not coming."

"You're afraid!" Lathan mocked.

"I'm not, I just...I don't want to get into trouble out there."

"We won't get caught and just think of the fun, and what we will be able to tell everyone."

Aman did not hesitate a second and shook his head, "You shouldn't go Lathan, it's going to get dark by the time—"

"—You're afraid." Lathan interrupted as he sucked through his teeth and rolled his eyes. He hoisted the sacks back onto his shoulder and headed away. "If you wanna come, meet me at the south bend. You'll have to skip your duties today if you're

## Chapter One — The Realm of Enduring Peace

not too afraid. Otherwise, you can't tell anyone. I'll be the first and only boy to ever enter the Rim. See ya reushamim."

Lathan ran off toward the crops, bouncing with his sacks jostling on each shoulder. Aman stared curiously as Lathan joined the other young croppers headed toward the southern fields.

Aman slid his sack off his shoulder to relieve the stress the weight had caused him as he stared. Lathan took a quick glance back just in time to see Aman hoist his sack back upon his shoulder, then turned away just in time to miss Aman fall over from the weight.

When Aman regained composure and control of his staff and crumb sack, he continued toward the pasture.

Candor possessed one pasture where all herded animals grazed under the tending of elder shepherds, most of whom were hunters unable to hunt any longer as a result of age. The pasture stretched in a grand oval centered among the tents of Candor. Broad hills and long olive blades distinguished the pasture grasslands from the level paths padded between the tents. Within four cubits of the pasture, a whiff of the animals aroused the senses with tear pulling putrid. Thus the pasture was called *Leahsham*, meaning 'odorous pasture,' and boys who worked in the pasture were called *reushamim* or 'smelly shepherd boy,' a phrase Aman grew ill of.

Several sheep dispersed in front of Aman, 'baa-ing' at his entrance as they scuffled. No animal was more precious to the people of Candor than the sheep. Custom in Candor was for every family to raise and breed herds of seven sheep, and no more, to be used as a source of clothing, shelter, and food. Offspring of the herds were passed down through generations. Jebas often taught his sons that the lamb was the most treasured animal in all of Eden. Aman did not fully understand but would soon learn this and more as instruction from the

# Lands of Eden
## by M. Gabreyl Scrolls

messengers would find Elias, head shepherd of Candor, as the one to guide the young shepherd in wisdom and valor. Elias was truly the sole shepherd of all the herds. He uniquely knew all the names of the sheep, horses, mules, and scaffles in the pastures and would take special care naming every birthed animal. The pasture was his home, he rested there, he woke there, he meditated there. Long years of lying among the animals caused the elder to appear and smell quite unpleasant.

Of the elders living in Candor were Morcial and Udell, sons of Lemuel, first daughter of Seth; Seth the III and Jodia, sons of Enos; Mered son of Cainan of Enos as well; and finally Elias, brother to Seth and Jodia. Elias was the oldest elder in Candor, and he too, like Seth, had long lost count of his age. He was the second of the eight sons of Enos, Adam was his great grandfather. He was hinted around the age of 690, gruff in speech and mannerism with shadowed eyes that told sorrow and fatigue. Still, his physical prominence was fortified with broad shoulders, thick muscle and powerful legs, a physique that fooled some to believing he was much younger.

Once a great warrior, Elias became subdued in the midst of a brutal struggle with a most heinous being spawned from supernatural villainy. He was forever hindered at his knee and could not swift through air or upon ground as the other elders. Put away by his loss, Elias grew silent among the people. Few dared speak of his combatant days. Few dare speak of the old man at all. But he found comfort in the young lad Aman, and quickly found his belly full of wisdom to impart and sharpen his youthful mind.

Aman was about to call out to the elder when he noticed the old shepherd's back turned to his approach. The boy decided to quietly approach Elias from behind and prepared to claw his leg and growl with surprise. He placed his crumb sack and staff on the ground, his face beaming with fun, and crept

# Chapter One — The Realm of Enduring Peace

nearer. The old man appeared to be transfixed with the morning sky as he leaned his weight upon a jō gripped under his right hand. Once close enough, Aman leaped forward with a joyful scream. Elias quickly turned with his eyes wide and caught the boy's small frame in his arms. He hoisted Aman up with the momentum, upon his shoulder, up higher over his head, growling the entire time. Aman laughed as he ascended, surprised that Elias caught him in the act of attack.

"Did you really think you could sneak up on me, am I truly as old as I reflect!?" Elias snorted as he feigned dropping the boy. Aman screamed and shut his eyes tight, he kept them closed until he realized his feet were planted. When he opened his eyes Elias was looking down at him, smiling warmly. Aman smiled back, embarrassed but reassured.

"Now then, I don't believe running up and frightening an elder is the proper way." Elias smirked with a lifted eyebrow.

"Oh um… sorry," Aman chuckled, "Good morning elder Elias."

"Good morning indeed young reu, and how are you this morning?"

"I am well."

"Well, staying out of mischief?" Aman looked up and nodded. Elias studied the boy's face taking all of five seconds to decipher what the boy hid. "Hmm…who won this morning?"

Aman shot a glance in wonder. He smiled shyly, "It wasn't me…Lathan won…Lathan always wins."

"Ah…I take it you would like to win every time like Lathan?"

"No, not all the time, I just wish I could win sometimes, but I can't because I'm not strong enough."

Elias cocked his head in questionable fashion, "Strong enough?"

Aman sighed and looked at his feet, his shoulders slumped. "I just wish I was bigger than Lathan, he's bigger and stronger than all of us. If I were bigger, maybe I could win at least once." Elias drummed his jō with a roll of his fingers and chuckled, he then knelt to Aman's level and rested his weight upon his knee.

"My young reu, do you have your scroll with you?" Aman pointed to his sack, "Retrieve it, quickly now."

Aman hurried to his sack on the ground. Nearly his entire torso scampered into the bag before he scuffled out with a disheveled stack of white leaves wrapped in thin brown animal skin. He brushed off a few crumbs, which were quickly gathered up by a few sheep. A thin, rounded scriber made of red ochre, pointed at its tip and kept moist by a damp lambs cloth wrapped around it, was attached to the animal skin by a nimble strand of horse hair sown into a spine that held the leaves together. The scriber dangled helplessly as if ready to snap free as Aman hurried back to Elias' side.

More lambs crowded Aman's sack as the smell of the food crumbs attracted them. Elias slid his short staff through the hide strap set round his waist and began.

"Now then, record this and listen carefully young boy...A victor is claimed so only from his completion of a task, not when and how he completes it." Aman scrolled speedily upon the thick canvas, Elias slowed him by lifting his head. "Young shepherd, you will grow strong and mighty, but your strength and size will soon mean nothing in the face of great trials. Your heart...that will be proof of your victory."

Aman fell quiet as he scribbled the last letters on his scribe. He peered up at the elder whose pupils rested in the corner of his eyes. "Stand here beside me young one." The boy remained still as Elias stood with hand rested on the boy's shoulder with a smile and full breath of relaxation. "Do you know what you see?"

## Chapter One — The Realm of Enduring Peace

Aman looked out from the tall hill on which he stood and could see the full village of Candor. Tall tan tents spanned out from the pasture center to the prairie fields and broad wheat borders, even to the north gates of the village. Women milled about from tent to tent, some carrying baskets, some carrying fruits, vegetables, and foods, some carrying babes clenched to their chests. Young boys and men tended to pasture animals, shearing sheep, grooming horses and feeding herbs to the herds. The morning sun illuminated the village with bright blonde halos and the warm Euphrates coast shimmered yellow and white reflections as the morning sunlight danced across the river surface.

"What you see is a land of seemingly endless tranquility, something these eyes have seen for only a few hundred years." Aman turned his attention back to Elias who stared ahead solemnly. His warm hand lifted from Aman's shoulder and came to rest behind the elder's back as a cool breeze glinted the whites of his aged eyes. "We have been able to flourish under peace here for so long Aman. Something many my age hope against fear will endure."

Aman's face formed with questions building.

"Why wouldn't peace flourish on Elias, everyone here is happy?"

Elias smirked and looked down at the boy. "You are right, everyone here is quite happy and thankfully so. But there exists a darkness, an evil that despises the joy of men." Aman frowned with more confusion. "Are you yet too young to understand *evil* young one? All of us lack true understanding of what evil is…even more lack the judgment to accept its existence. This is why many of us fear, the very threat of Candor's peace rests in the denial of existing evil."

Aman looked over the village again, noting the smiling faces and laughter found in each person. "Elias, what does it take to understand evil?"

The elder paused with a deep breath and closed eyes before responding with a squinting search over Candor. "To understand evil, one must gain wisdom. And for some, wisdom as such demands too much."

"You mean learning how to shepherd and hunt and things like—?"

"—Ha ha…No,no young one," Elias quieted, "you see that is knowledge, the knowledge to do, to have, to get… Wisdom is much more, it is understanding more than just what you see, feel, and hear before you."

Aman blinked several times before continuing his intrigue. "Do you have wisdom?"

"Of course I have wisdom," the elder grumbled with a smirk, "I have acquired more than sufficient amount over my years." Aman smiled and looked off again. "Still, there is much that I lack, and I do not connect with my people as I have been charged to."

Aman looked up at the elder whose face held sadness. "Will I get wisdom when I become as old as you?"

Elias let out a loud snorting laugh nearly causing Aman to shutter where he stood. "As old as me, ha-ha…! Well, when you become as old as me, you should have a good amount of wisdom yes, but wisdom has nothing to do with age, Aman." he chuckled. "You see, there are some things that require much more than physical effort could ever allow one to understand. Wisdom comes to those who are ready and willing to test beyond physical realms to attain it."

The young boy looked around questioningly as he puzzled meanings together. "Elder Elias, do you suppose I will be ready to test beyond physical effort?"

Elias smiled delightfully and knelt by the youth, "My boy, you shine with great understanding, and wisdom is very swift

# Chapter One

## The Realm of Enduring Peace

upon you. You may no doubt find full wisdom in your youth, as I said before, just be willing."

Aman was struck silent and filled with warmth where he stood. His youthful face brightened with a polished smile as Elias grunted and rose upright.

"Now then, enough with these conversations, how careless you've been with your sack boy…do you intend to feed my entire pasture today?"

Aman looked at his sack which was quickly being swarmed by the herds of the pasture. He lurched forward but was quickly halted by Elias' hand.

"Ah aah, young reu, stay by my side and watch." Elias squinted. His dark pupils were completely hid from Aman as he peered along the encircled pasture. The elder then nodded with an 'aha' and produced a peculiar sound from deep within his throat. His mouth opened wide as if he was yawning. Instead he resonated a series of *'aahs.'* Aman looked up at Elias and frowned, Elias simply winked back at him and produced the sound again. The next moment, the sheep rummaging his sack dispersed and a small pack of innocent eyed lambs began to shuffle through the herds toward Elias. Their coats were ripe with clean white wool, and they trotted gaily toward the figures.

"How did you do that Elias?" Aman wondered as the sheep obeyed the elder's voice.

"One lesson at a time child," he barked, "now then, these sheep are ready to be sheared. I took the liberty of washing their coats gingerly just last night. Terrible time they gave me, specially the little one." Among the sheep was a precious runt, half the size of the other lambs, but twice as feisty. "Yes, you have a new count reu boy, no longer seven now eight, let's see there's Adjure, Ceasal, Ceasar, Uyla, Delilah, Bethel, Becca, and…" Elias pointed at the small lamb then looked at Aman.

He waited quietly, "What do you think Aman…A name for this little one?"

Aman stared at the lamb for several moments as it pushed against the wool of another.

"Speak up boy, don't waste time."

Aman smirked at Elias, unable to hold the humor he found in the elder's impatience. " Mariah…after my mother."

Elias paused with a gentle grin. " Mariah, that's a fine name." With that the small boy ran to his sack, shoved his scriber into it and tossed the sack onto his shoulder.

"Elder, I have one last question." Elias nodded in response. "Was evil the reason for my mother not living to be happy like the rest of us?"

Elias' face grew solemn. He walked toward the boy and knelt near him. "Aman, even unto your birth your mother lived with a love and joy for you, so powerful that nothing could take away. Never mistake, there was no end to your mother's happiness." Aman nodded proudly, turned and grabbed his staff to lead his herd off.

The elder rose and turned his face to the early sun, basking quietly in its warmth. A cool hum brushed past his ears bringing with it an unsettling whisper. Elias turned quickly and gazed into the far distance where Candor's land met the thick dark forest of Caspian. A deafening hush met him as the cool hum subsided.

## The Return of the Hunters

Mariah continued to ram her head into her mother's belly as Aman knelt by shearing the thick wool. Adjure, Mariah's mother, appeared undisturbed by either Mariah or Aman's small fingers pulling at her fur.

## Chapter One — The Realm of Enduring Peace

"Please Mariah, that's enough…" Aman begged, as each jostle unbalanced his progress. Beside him sat a large wooden bucket he retrieved from the knitting tents. It acted as a tub for the mounds of wool piling into it. Aman would later trade a full bucket of wool for woven gowns in the village once he finished. That was if Mariah would ever let him finish. She rammed time and time again into Adjure's side, producing nothing more than a ruffle in her mother's stance and occasional aggravation for the young shepherd. Once she finally got her chance at grooming, she was calm in Aman's hands. He barely combed through a quarter of her coat before she was sound asleep.

Shearing his herd was truly Aman's most favorite activity. The soft hair melted through his fingers as he drew out handfuls trimmed perfectly from the skin. The fully sheared lambs sparkled with bright curly locks that would grow thick and strong for the next cut and produce warm robes and cloths for the township.

When Aman first began his reu duties, he found the *slith*, a wooden shear tool used by most shepherds, sheared poorly. He ventured to the clear flowing waters of the Pison and found a smooth black river stone graded by the waters. With its fine point it functioned superbly as a shear. He offered its use to others, but few of the reus took to the tool. Yet his father followed Aman's lead and found the river stones useful for hunts.

Aman finished his duties much earlier than he expected given the amount of wool he managed to collect. He left his herd to graze the morning pasture as he carried his bucket toward the village tents. Hala came running excitedly toward Aman with her eyes sparkling bright hazel.

"Aman the hunters are returning…cmon' hurry." Aman barely caught a single note of her message before being yanked in her grip and sent sprinting alongside. Hala was nearly three-quarters of Aman's size but was plenty strong and equally fast. She was playful and persuasive in her manner. In Hala was the heart of the lioness, strength, courage, and skill, contrary not only to other girls of the village, but unlike any youth known through the ages of Candor. A predestined valor was instilled in the child as she was perhaps the only one who would fortify Aman in the time that was to come.

Aman tried to keep pace with Hala but once she released his arm, he watched her speed ahead toward the stone fences with not a single glance back. Aman was assured she would spare him a spot along the stone border, and she did.

Upon reaching the stones, Aman peered out across the northern tundra and listened as the ground rumbled with the romp of a herd. Within moments the crowd gasped as scaffles took the horizon. Their fur flurried with shimmers of brown in the breeze gliding over their bodies as they bellowed in unison. No amount of dirt or cloud of dust stemmed from their swift stampede and their hooves graced as if they ran upon the wind. Their bodies were elegant and proud as they chased onward with unburdened speed.

An exalted hunter sprinted commandingly ahead of the herd, losing no ground to the thin-legged creatures. His hair flocked behind his neck and caught the gail of his sprint which he balanced with arms spread as if prepared to take flight. His cloak tied round his waist gathered the breeze as he forged the lead.

The hunter halted suddenly, several meters ahead of the flock, and turned to face the stampede. His arms still, outstretched at shoulder height. The scaffles rushed closer and closer. Aman felt his heart pounding with anticipation imagining the hunter felt even greater fear at the stampede about to trample him.

With immediate motion, a loud clasp echoed from the force of the hunter's clapped hands. The herd shifted in flight and

# Chapter One — The Realm of Enduring Peace

headed toward the crowd. Everyone gasped, mothers clenched their children back from the stones. With a shout and second clasp of his hands, the hunter established his command and reassured those gathered. The herd slowed into a steady trot as the hunter guided them with his hovering hands toward the pasture.

The crowd whispered softly as the strong figure paraded amidst the scaffles, shepherding them effortlessly. Everyone recognized him, Uriah, the champion of the hunters. Not another moment's silence passed as the crowd erupted with cheer and applause. Over the horizon appeared Candor's men, marching with proud triumph. Hala stared intently at the spectacle, never blinking, never moving from her spot. Uriah shot a quick wink at her. "Papa!" she responded with a radiant smile.

Hala's father was Candor's best hunter, a title which Hala made sure everyone knew. Uriah possessed trademarks that all skilled hunters desired. Like Elias and other elders in Candor, Uriah managed to learn the bellows, squeals, and moans of several of Eden's animals. This was quite peculiar for a man of Uriah's youth. Adam passed this skill on to very few elders and much had been forgotten through many years. At 67 years of age, he possessed mighty strength. He was known to project his spear farther than any man had capability and bound over 30 cubits, much like the elders. He often scouted for the hunters by leaping onto towering tree branches from the ground. What was most remarkable about Uriah were his swift feet. He appeared to run almost tirelessly and with untamable speed. Many had seen him out run the vicious prairie cats and wild re`em. Others witnessed him leap to catch air fowl after chasing them upon the ground. Uriah appeared unbound by most natural constraints.

Hala dreamed of joining her father on a fierce hunt, but Candor observed the traditional law and forbid women to venture to the field. Secretly, her father trained her by night, teaching her the animal language, and hunting skills of great value. Uriah even gave her a new hunting tool he invented which he called a *flear*. Hala had yet possessed the strength to lift a full spear, so Uriah carved dozens of thin rods from tree wood. The cusp of a flear was pointed finely enough to pierce through animal skin and its tail slightly wider and weighed with a bulk of animal fur that allowed firm grip and better projection when handled. The tail fit perfectly when mounted into the thin sling of an archer's bow. When shot, the flear flew through the air with greater force and speed even greater than that of a hunter jolting a spear. It cut through the air with no traces of sound, unlike the whining arrows of an archer. This eliminated the misfire that often occurred when a hunter or arrow startled an animal.

Uriah demanded that Hala keep the tool and her training secret, not even Aman or Lathan were to know of her keen abilities. Yet she was greatly skilled, swift as her father, and growing with tremendous strength.

Unlike other young boys in the village, Aman did not have the great desire to become a hunter. He did not admire the murky slate scars, remnants of the brutal claws of unyielding beasts that marred his brothers' and father's faces, nor the foul odors that soiled their clothes after weeks of hunting. Scars would diminish in a matter of days, but the repugnance of animal hide would linger for weeks.

Candor's hunt festivals would last for several days but always started with the grand parade of the hunters. Their return was highly anticipated and praised by the women and children of the village. The hunters would be gone for weeks at a time and were always treated as long lost strangers upon return. Their presence in the village was greatly welcomed and deeply missed when they journeyed again.

# Chapter One  *The Realm of Enduring Peace*

Aman began to clap along with the crowd which sang with shouts, laughter, and the calls of mothers and children to their husbands, sons, brothers, and fathers. Aman spotted his father waving excitedly at him as Jin and Dolan trailed behind wrestling. His father led their young colt which carried two piles of animal hide that had been won from the hunt.

Aman would have to gain help to store the hides in the freezing waters of the Candora forest. As the chief hunter, Jebas was also renowned for his skill. He tamed the animals even without full knowledge of their tongue and exercised abilities that kept the more predatory animals from the hunts and camps. Rarely did he brag about his methods, but he was known to wrestle away she-sabers and the wild re`em, the most territorial field creatures of the hound order.

As the crowd hurried to the hunters' welcome, Aman found his joy realized against Lathan's mischief. His companion's father, Ephese, returned long before Lathan believed, and he would be found missing. Moreover, Aman would be found knowing of Lathan's mischief. He wondered what his father would do if Aman kept his silence as promised. He glanced back to the south grains to see if Lathan truly had ventured to the forbidden grounds. There was no sight of his friend, only empty soil cleared of laborers from the edge to the wheat borders.

\*     \*     \*

In spite of the commotion at the northern gate of Candor, Elias continued to glare over the fields leading to the Caspian forest in solitude. Seth approached his elder brother upon the hill carrying nearly the same bewilderment and worry upon his shoulders.

# Lands of Eden

by M. Gabreyl Scrolls

"The return of the hunters has always been a joyous spectacle, even for a grumpy-haired man like you Elias. Not like you to meet such an occasion with face full of dread."

Elias cleared the heaviness in his throat, "Not like you to wander Candor with your bow fixed to your back as if for battle, old man."

Seth smiled and gripped the tail of his weapon. "Something compelled me to stay with it after dawn, just a notion of something eerie."

"Perhaps it is the same notion that sets my eyes to the horizon." He shot Seth a glance from the corner of his eye, "Something through the forest troubles me."

Seth squared his shoulders and peered out across the eastern praries. A flat silence crept on them as they watched the forest lean with a gentle breeze. A bright flock of *fahi* took to the clear air with broad shadows cast from their vast blond feathered wings. The calm birds ignored the roars that echoed from the Candor gates and traveled over the pasture with tremendous speed. Their smooth majestic glide brought no exchange in the men's demeanor.

"Though beauty comes with the morning light, how deadly creeps the western night and swallows this world in darkness," Elias moaned.

"Not so brother, yes I'll admit that I've seen the gathering shadows, but they dare not threat here, they just pass through, as they've done long before knowing they cannot enter. Adam blessed this ground, and we have kept to his ways. Even through our generations. To come here would mean their destruction."

Elias shook his head and sighed softly, "Adam may have blessed this ground, but men have so easily forgotten our father's way." The elder turned and faced the parade, "We don't keep to his instruction. We've prided ourselves in life, in what's here, what's now, what our hands have built and

# Chapter One

## The Realm of Enduring Peace

sustained. Well, is anything sustained but by the higher Creator? And since, where is our pride and homage then? Not on things that keep the blessing Adam placed on this ground. You've heard the men. They whisper. 'We've not seen this Abba, we've not heard as Adam heard. He takes no concern in our sweat and blisters, nor the wails of our women.' The great rivers bank and run from dawn to night and fertilize our ground so that our labor is reduced much greater than any other land in Eden. We had no hand in their flow. The sun warms our skin and the moon ignites our harvest, we added no torch for their shine. We remain here, in this great village as people trained to look above, living daily in grace undeserved, to see our sustainer. But where is our pride and homage?"

The elder paused for several moments as more cheers lifted from the crowd. The fahi turned uniformly to reclaim their origin with descent more effortless and magnificent than their start. This time neither man could keep their focus from the beauty the birds displayed.

"Such is the way Seth, we know," Elias continued with a look at his brother. "Candor knows. The nomads deny the Abba out of ignorance and polluted minds that cloud their vision. But we here see clearly yet neglect the bond that existed before the ground was cursed, and bones ached from daily toil. So which is worse? To be ignorant and deny, or understand and disregard?

"Perhaps one is no more than the other. But to see how men indulge in their own nature, taking no look to the ways that glowed through our father's very countenance. Such causes me fear. Nothing of our nature is righteous or unrighteous, everything is simple, complacent. That is what diminishes the blessing, and welcomes darkness."

Wisdom was the spirit that Candor was built around from the very day that Adam dug his fingers into the fertile soil. The father of mankind did not walk the earth as damned or

# Lands of Eden
### by M. Gabreyl Scrolls

ashamed, but with thankful heart. Man had been spared the full justice superseded by love. So Adam taught his sons, grandsons and daughters to be grateful for even the short freedom given. For hundreds of years his offspring held to his instruction, their father's wisdom was revered and treasured. He was the only man touched by the very hand of the Abba, a process that caused his body to glow, at times immensely, through all the days he walked the earth. Age struck Adam harshly. Being unable to speak to men and hear anyone's voice clearly, the father became solemn as he watched the decent of his offspring.

Upon his death, Eden mourned for thirty years then suddenly all was forgotten. Adam's sons took to foreign lands, strange beings, and dark practices. Only few held righteousness, many the very elders who were passing with ongoing time.

Seth's arms were folded tightly to his chest as he explored the crowd with keen sight. Men embraced their spouses and children with grand hugs. Children played at the hunters' legs with unsuspecting joy and rhythm intrinsic to the peace that engulfed the village.

"There is hope brother," Elias continued, "perhaps not in these men whose hearts are unwilling to be directed, even if for a second time. But I do hope in us, men of faith, in our youth, where there is still promise. I hope and I fear. Of which be greater I am unsure."

Seth stretched the skin of his face as he pulled his chin and lifted his eyelids knowingly. Children jostled vigorously with the hunters without care. How could ones so lowly be chosen from the tribe to continue Candor's honor. In particular the lowly Aman, whom Elias favored of great promise. Seth knew his brother's heart, yet wondered how much in it was blind hope.

# Chapter One  *The Realm of Enduring Peace*

"Just what did the arch tell you of this young Aman that I should be so enthralled as well?"

Elias dropped his hand onto his chest and curled his cloth into his fist. "The messenger told me nothing of Aman," he responded "'A youth will spur the journey of these hundreds, and will lead men victoriously for mankind. You must stand firm and guide him in Candor's way.' This could mean any among these young."

"Yet why do you focus so on the chief's youngest?"

Elias grinned with a confident sniff, "My heart binds me to him. If not the curiosity, the quest for understanding, the simple glint of his keen eye. He speaks as one ready. And indeed have you too not seen this in our young nephew?"

At that Seth nodded and glanced over the festival at the gate of the village. He hummed softly with the cheers of the people, "I wish to see hope in these aged and wayward men, yet find none. Let's hope for the sake of these hundred that *our* hearts are right about…our youth." Elias and Seth looked at each other for a brief moment before Seth grabbed his staff again and walked calmly down the pasture hill.

Before Seth was fully from his sight, Elias called to him, "Brother, should Candor spies become threats yonder, will you be ready?"

Seth smiled and responded as he continued on his way, "I sense from the chucks strapped to your waist that either one, or both of us will be, dare that time come." Elias grinned and pulled his robe tighter around him. A subtle breeze grazed his neck with haunting cool. He kept his back to the taunts of the Caspian and fixed his eyes on the joy ahead.

"Dare that time come, let this peace be remembered as hope to spring back civil. And let them revel in this time's peace should darkness spring none but evil. Let these words spoken here on this hill find mediation in greater planes, that You would protect these people, if not their land, keep their lives from evil's hands."

Elias relinquished his guard upon the hill and headed toward the village pools where the remaining elders were gathering the first meats of the hunt for the night feast.

## The Rim

The Rim lurches with darkness at its thresholds and swallows men whole that dare to enter. Pale barked trees shiver with sinful delight to the answer of the deep lures of twilight. Shrubs and vines cradle swarming shadows hovered at ankles and guides gloomy fog into blind eyes and gasping lungs. What hex enchanted the vast Rim forest was rarely indulged by Candor's forefathers and the elders who knew. Such mystery greatly spurred the foolish curiosity of youthful minds.

This curiosity tingled through Lathan's bones as he breached the forbidden branch-laden borders and burdened ground of leaves and thick shrubs. He carelessly bent long pale stalks and snapped twigs to make way, carrying with him a sense of bravery and accomplishment that no other of Candor's youth would experience without first noting his triumphant entrance and all that his eyes would behold. Sallow trees towering overhead with broad sable leaf crowns hurling the dark canopy onto the forest floor that rendered ferns and shrubs left ashen from days of diminished sunlight. Hushed echoes of leaves, detached from limbs, fluttering as ember to the vacant ground. Quiet creatures camouflaged in the blind, blanketed by the dark grounds yet lured to curiosity at the new scent the boy offered. From within, a deep hum, carried upon a cool wind that engulfed, caressed and drowned him, then just as ghostly as it came, drew back toward its origin.

# Chapter One                      *The Realm of Enduring Peace*

And suddenly his bravery turned, doubt seeped inside as trickling anxiety through his belly. Something was amiss.

As he trekked through the wood, Lathan recognized what tickled his spine, drummed his chest, quivered his arms, loins, and feet. A silent heavy fear built from an invisible something among the evident endless shadow. But he would not stop, for the same fear that chilled him inside begged him onto discovery.

Rhythms of endless silence came from every direction as Lathan ventured deeper, his eyes glancing left, right, ahead, upward, and around in unsteady sequence. This same silence met him upon his very entry, as if the forest did barricade itself from all outside influence in that single moment. Eerie quiet birthed the sensation of an empty wasteland, yet Lathan could not resist the suspicion of something chasing, and more threatening was the suspicion of something hunting. Glances to-and-fro smacked his eyes with dreary onslaught of hollow gloom and empty air. But something had to be here, burning its eyes on his neck, stretching to prick his skin and capture him with creeping bony fingers.

Lathan hasted his pace while fear hammered at his heart and wrought frosty strokes along his hair-raised skin. Silence still overwhelmed every ensuing stride the boy managed as he ventured. He could no longer view his feet pounding onto the black earth. The ground softened with each step, soles slipped deeper into the thick soil underneath. His hurry, hindered by the turbulent forest floor, found sluggish progress as his shins were mounted by thick mud. The canopy of shadow descended as branches began to sway with growing drones of unearthly laughter. Fog quickly thickened around the young boy, it slithered across his cheeks then gripped round his neck and chest. His breath was cut and pressure weighed upon his lungs with unimaginable force. The ground tugged his legs as Lathan struggled to break free, his head became light and lungs

# Lands of Eden                           by M.Gabreyl Scrolls

scrapped for air. Tears streamed from the boy's heavy eyelids as he heaved and heaved and, with mouth opened wide, sucked all manageable air he could. And as he gathered the final gasps of chilling air, he shut his eyes, and with lifted arms howled in fear.

Suddenly, the Rim shrieked with a resonance that trembled the grounds as a mighty stampede. An immersing light scattered the shadow into hasty retreat, illuminating the entire forest with glowing indigo. The wail weighed Lathan's ears with incredible force and vibration causing him to cringe with sealed eyes and clenched jaw. And not moments before he felt his lungs empty a final breath was the boy engulfed in brilliant light.

*       *       *

Mists hovered with pleasant scents as all in Candor were put in preparation for a grand feast. Plants, herbs, and crops were being brought to the warm Candor pools as the elders of the village gathered in meditated unison over the meat prepared. The river pools more ordinarily were used as baths for the women and young children as they often steamed with warm mists during the morning. Yet during feasts, these pools were filled with glowing smelt, hot pebbles, and boulders smoldering in bond fires few meters from the riverbeds. These kept the pools boiling hot for the evening, when the meats and crops were to be prepared in them. The pleasant smell of the cooking stew enveloped the entire village with an auspicious aroma that none could resist.

Aman and Hala joined with dozens of other children of the village throwing smooth pebbles from the riverbed into the fire while keeping their eyes for the elders' signal for the feast.

"My papa caught all the scaffles herded into the pastures today, by himself!" Hala held back no detail in her boasts of her

# Chapter One  *The Realm of Enduring Peace*

father's triumphs, and rightfully so. Scaffles were the pride of Candor, their sturdy hides provided thick tents and strong ropes for the village and the full hairs of their fur rendered softer cloths, much softer than those sheathed from lambs, adorned by women and used as bedding and swaddling for babies. These also provided good trading for the village barters as the fur of a scaffle was considered lavish. The hoofs of a scaffle were solid with gruff bottoms that allowed these animals to keep their grip on steep grounds. Men created shears from them to smooth spears, tools and various wood carvings. Scaffles possessed thick pearl tusks of forearm length and width that provided ivory spearheads, tent anchors, and sharp shears for some. But most enjoyable was the animal's tender meat, which released delightful scents, melted warmly on the tongue, and brought with each bite sweet flavor like that from fruit.

As Aman soaked more of the smell, it took all his self-control to keep from sneaking a quick taste of the stew while the elders gathered more pebbles for the boil.

Hala, still remarking on her father, continued, "He says that they were the wildest scaffles he had ever caught."

"I can't wait to taste them, we have to keep watch so that we can be the first in line," Aman responded. He watched closely as Jodia, elder and village warrior, stirred the vegetables and meat together in the pools with a long wooden rod. The Euphrates and Pison rivers blended full of nutrients and spices that not only flavored the meats but purified the contents throughout the process. Water filled into the pools from hot vents deep below the surface at the bottom of the pools. The pools then returned to the river during the high tide afternoons. The entire process daily cleaned the pools and kept fresh nutrients flowing over and into the fertile banks.

Crops thrown into the stew included barley and wheat grains, *ginya* seeds and *topac*, potatoes and brown maize. The meat would be cleaned and heated in the flames before being added into the bubbling pools. A single scaffle could feed a multitude of up to 15 for five full days. Thus, whenever the meat of a scaffle was being prepared, everyone in the village was informed so that the meat would be consumed to completion by the feast, as was taught by Adam. During the grand feast, three scaffles were prepared for the entire township and any left over meat would be thrown to the prairie hounds to avoid the lure of roaming scavengers. Bowls were hollowed from *lohania* tree bark and filled with spices that were gathered from the river with cupped ivory saucers and dried over a cool flame. When combined with the stew, the spices produced a thick red color in the soup and added the extra season to all its contents, season that might have been lost in the large pools. The youth often cut out the bottom of the bowls and sucked the lohania wood to savor the fresh flavor the porous bark absorbed from the meal.

All the children were lined by the pools by age, Aman and Hala stood patiently as the elders went through the lines washing everyone's hands. Jodia made his way steadily through the line, turning each of the children's hands over and studying them as he hummed an unknown song. He took his place in front of Aman and Hala and grunted, "Hands."

Aman shot his hands out, turned them over and back then smiled widely. "Clean as lambs wool young boy, and you Hala?" Hala looked down and slowly produced her hands from behind her back. They were spotted with mud and grass. "Oh my, how do such pretty little hands become so filthy?" Jodia lifted Hala's hands as Morcial laid a pitcher of warm water at his feet. He dipped the sleeve of his cloth in the water, then spun the soaked sleeve around his palm. "Now let's polish these little fingers."

As Jodia wiped Hala's hands clean, a tall gray man crept behind Aman with a mischievous grin hiding behind his thick

# Chapter One — The Realm of Enduring Peace

beard. He rolled his sleeves and gave Hala a quick wink once she spotted him. It was a signal for her not to give him away. Still Hala shouted with cheer.

"Ephese!"

With a growl Ephese gripped Aman's sides and massaged, sending the boy into wiggling laughter. He lifted and spun Hala in the air with an effortless toss before he lowered her and rubbed the boy's head with a deep chuckle.

"Good evening Aman, Hala. How are you two?"

Aman's joy quickly ran as he realized the sun had fully set. Lathan must not have abandoned his mischief. He did not respond as a sudden twinge of guilt tickled his belly.

Hala's face glinted with a smile as Jodia finished, "I can't wait to eat… my papa says he caught the scaffles that we are eating today."

"Ha, ha, yes he did, Hala, your papa showed us quite a hunt," Ephese answered.

"He did?"

"He did. I saw with my own eyes him chase the beasts on bare feet. Uriah is quite the hunter. Candor is very fortunate to have him. Now then young ones, have you seen my boy? I've been looking for him since our return. He was not at the rock gate today." Aman looked at his feet and made no attempt to show any knowledge of Lathan's whereabouts. His hidden manner would have given him away even to an old blind man.

"I haven't seen him since this morning, he usually beats us to the feast." Hala responded as she searched the line for their older companion. The boy wanted to hide in her response to avoid all question but would not escape Ephese's searching eye.

"Aman, let's have it." Aman glanced up at Ephese with a frightened stare. He then shot a quick glance at Hala and looked away with a shrug. "Don't tell me you don't know where he is. I know no doubt he's into mischief, and it is not like him to work without an accomplice."

Aman kept his head down feeling the tingle of Ephese's eye's weigh upon his conscience. Hala waited as well, with suspicious ambition as the boy mustered his response. "The last time I saw him he told me he would be in the fields this morning, near the south gate."

As Hala's eyes widened Aman knew that she deciphered more, though she would ask him into confession. Ephese stood upright as if he too deciphered what Aman was hiding. The joy of the feast was suddenly dwindled from the father's face. "The south gate..." Aman nodded, "Son, did he tell you anything more?"

Aman felt his audience study his expression with desperation. Hala out of excitement for the mystery, Ephese from sheer doubt and anxiety.

"Aman, did he tell you more?!" Ephese's pressed.

Aman gasped and finally looked at his companion's father, but only stutters could proceed from his lips. The tension was quickly interrupted by Udell. "Ephese, come quickly, something I must show you."

Ephese made his way off without a second guess as to the whereabouts of his son. Hala however, would not keep her curiosity quiet.

"So where is Lathan?" Hala demanded.

Aman frowned and shook his head as Jodia sounded the call for the meal. "I bet you know where he is. I know you do." Aman attempted to step around Hala as the line moved ahead of her. Hala pushed him back and stood eye to eye in front of him. "Lathan would only tell you where he was planting if..." Aman gave her an aggravated scold. Hala easily interpreted his frowns. "He went into the Rim!"

# Chapter One           *The Realm of Enduring Peace*

Aman quickly covered Hala's mouth. The young girl shoved his hand away and gave Aman a harsh poke at his shoulder. "I can't believe you two were planning on going to the Rim without me—"

"—Quiet!" Aman sighed as he looked in the direction of the south gate. "We weren't going into the Rim, I tried to tell him not to go."

"Not to go!? Do you know how fun it would be out there? C'mon'!" Hala turned with readied sprint just as Aman snagged her arm in his hand.

"No! We can't go Hala, it is too dangerous out there, and we'll get in trouble."

Hala huffed, "We'll only get into trouble if you tell," she responded, "you're just afraid."

"I am not afraid!" The young shepherd shouted as nearby ears alarmed to their tiny commotion. He hurried her away and softened his tone. "I am not afraid Hala, it is just too dark to go out there now, we could get lost."

"I won't get lost, I'm not afraid of the Rim, so I'm going!" Hala snatched her wrist from Aman's hand, chuckled softly and without delay dashed toward the Caspian fields. Aman ran instinctively after her.

He sprinted madly behind Hala hoping for her to slow her pace. With all the excitement of the feast, Aman and Hala appeared as if at play and by the time they made it into the fields, they were out of view for any of those gathered at the pools to find them.

Grand stalks of wheat hid the bobbing children in the brush as they carved narrow trails toward the prairie opening. The busy feast noise diminished as they sped further along. Aman's urgent calls met no response as Hala sprinted onward with excitement.

"Hala!"

# Lands of Eden — by M. Gabreyl Scrolls

She cheered with laughter as if she was startled at Aman's voice. "Hala! Wait, slow down, wait!" Aman panted and panted as he steadily lost momentum in his chase. He waved vigorously, guiding the thick stalks apart as he made way. Hala's trail became untraceable. Yet the boy continued forward without guide. He sunk deeper into the vast field as the dusk glow yielded to the dark night of the east. Grains slapped his face and hindered his line of sight, stalks wrapped round his ankles and tugged his clothes as he shoved through the span. With a final desperate jostle, Aman suddenly found himself tripping out the edge of the wheat field onto the clear grassland that looked directly into the black gate of the Rim.

All fell silent. Aman froze completely, stared across the vast plain at the dark verge of the mystic forest. Its soaring silhouette swayed in the sinister wind with a canopy of limbs and claws stretched outward to snag him in their clutches. Mellow hums and monstrous grumbles met the subtle scent of *schudora* spice which oozed up his nostrils, and down into his lungs with prickly discomfort. Air was struck cold and short. An eerie tickle in his belly shivered him as all around recoiled under the growth and swallowing abyss of the Rim forest.

"Yaah!" Hala shouted from behind. Aman howled in fear as Hala's tiny fingers jabbed at his sides. He fell to his knee as his heart throbbed. Hala simply cackled, holding her belly and pointing at his colorless face. "I knew you were afraid, slow poke!"

Red quickly flushed Aman's face, yet his embarrassment did not remove his fear gripped expression. He turned and looked back at the Rim. Darkness released a moan from the towering trees that lurched at him with shadows cast temptingly at his feet. Aman jumped to his stance. "That wasn't funny, I'm going back, you wanna go, fine, I'm not getting in trouble out here."

# Chapter One

## The Realm of Enduring Peace

Hala swiftly pulled at Aman's arm, "C'mon' Aman, don't go back, it will be fun."

"No, Hala, look out there, I am not afraid, but look at it. Doesn't it look bad to you?"

A cool breeze met the soft skin of Hala's plump cheeks as she turned and faced the gloomy vision. Her eyes widened and studied the Rim intensely until she found herself breathing hastily. She hugged herself from the chill, turned away and shut her eyes with regret.

"You see? I don't like it here, we need to go back."

"We can't go back yet, " Hala responded, "What about Lathan?"

Aman looked at the deep forest with regret. Darkness had come and their companion was missing amidst animals driven wild in the night. What could Aman do to help Lathan if he was too afraid to venture out himself? The boy shook his head.

"We have to tell Jebas, " Aman said with confidence. Hala looked back at the forest with worry. "We must tell my father, Hala, c'mon!" Instantly he gripped Hala's wrist and pulled her with his sprint.

"Aman!" came a loud shout from the fields.

The children could hear the ruffling of stalks as the shouts making way towards them. Each panicked and scrambled without thought into the fields. They were quickly scooped into arms before they could make it much further. Not knowing what was happening, they screamed and kicked in fear. They were carried out of the tall wheat and placed on their feet.

"Young ones, young ones you must hush please... It's okay Hala, Aman be calm." The two youths quieted their pants as they looked into Uriah's face. He nodded assuring at both. Ephese frantically rushed out from the field, he held Lathan's satchel in his hand. Jebas was soon joined by Aman's brothers who guided Udell behind them.

Uriah nodded at them and continued, "Okay, you two must listen to me carefully, you must be honest. You know where Lathan is, yes?" Hala glanced at Aman's guilt flushed face. "Aman, please tell us where he is," Uriah pressed. Aman's eyes moved from face to face as he felt his stomach tremble.

His father's voice quickly eased him, "My son, listen to Uriah, you will have no trouble, I know you came out here to retrieve Lathan, but it's important you tell us where he went." Aman nodded, looked at Ephese and pointed toward the Rim.

"As suspected," Udell remarked with strangled speech.

Ephese cursed and hurled Lathan's satchel before he sprinted off toward the dark forest. "Ephese!" Jebas called out as he watched him dash into the darkness. "Uriah, please take my boy home, Dolan, Jin, with me."

"Papa! wait—" Aman shouted but to no avail. Jebas was off without a second look and his brothers were in quick pursuit.

"Come on Aman, they will be fine, Hala come, it's too dark and dangerous for you out here, come let's go eat."

Aman stared after his father for a long moment until he and his brothers vanished over the hills of the prairie. He whispered a subtle call for their return before he turned his back. There was no mistaking the bone-chilling response that painfully screeched from the forest depths.

\*       \*       \*

Ephese ran with the wind leaving Jebas and his sons much ground to catch before they would reach him. The dark menacing forest mounting at their approach appeared to fortify the closer they neared. The tall pale trees, being quickly

# Chapter One — The Realm of Enduring Peace

enveloped in thick fog and blinding darkness, portrayed a mystical manifestation beckoning from within. Jebas searched the sky above attempting to peer through a thick cover that blocked the orange glow of the evening moon. Yet the fog flushed the canopy and formed a thick hedge against all forms of nature's light.

Angry howls searched the four for fear as ruffled pine gave notice of restless re`em hounds and lurking sabers seething strikes. Above clapped carnivorous tetras, dragon-like fowls with cold outer skeleton used to blunt their prey. Ephese ran with no eye on theirs, which glowed back with clear vision and sensing the heat of the men's lungs. Jebas marked them, however, counting until the predators diminished into three tetras circling overhead and eight other beasts stalked along the ground. And he without his spear, would pray for strength in his hands to fend them away.

Worn pace kept the journey long. Jin and Dolan held their urges to watch in alarm of the predatory animals. By twilight many of their prowlers yielded. And their focus became the great gloom of the Rim gate upon them.

"Ephese wait!" Jebas called out, rattling all anxieties in his stride. When the three finally caught up to him, Ephese stood with his hands on his knees, panting heavily.

"We have to go…now." His voice quivered with choked tears of terror and troubled thoughts. Try as he might, Ephese could not keep still long enough to focus on the treachery that threatened round them. While beasts were nearing, the dark gap threatened with greater fright, so much greater that these animals were kept back from vicious growls calling from the emitting darkness. Wild beasts awakened even more to scents of potential prey outside the dark borders of the forest. "We have to go now!" Ephese repeated as he lurched forward.

"Wait!" Jebas demanded. His voice boomed against the fog and brought Ephese to a halt. "We are hunted…"

Ephese looked around and noted the reflecting eyes.

Jebas continued, "Even now we are hunted, yet we are not attacked. Look deep into that chasm and see why." The men gazed into the black wall before them which seemed to swell with anticipation. The sight could produce no greater terror, no wider eyes or pounding hearts. "If even these vicious animals hold off in fright, how are we to blindly enter, without arms against what might be greater predators yonder?"

Ephese moaned, "What of the predators, am I to hold in fear so that my son be taken by them?"

"You know the perils of this place…" Jebas answered, "Indeed we must be after young Lathan. But we must also journey with calm enough that we are not lost ourselves."

Ephese frowned and shook his head, his shoulders dropped with relent. "Venturing blind will not do for us well in this night. My sons are best among us for tracking. Dolan and Jin, find a path to follow," Jebas commanded.

Ephese shut his eyes and cursed repeatedly before looking into the abyss. "Hurry, find his path, please, we do not have much time."

Dolan and Jin searched cautiously for any sign of broken twigs or branches along the Rim borders. Yet as they neared the borders, the more frightful the dark forest seemed to each man. The shrubs thickened as darkness climbed the bark barriers. Each branch along the edge threatened at snagging the young men's cloth, yanking them into the dark.

Finally, Jin found a narrow breach marked by several broken twigs and bent stalks. "Here! Up ahead!" Jin needed little strength to call Ephese who found the entry in short moment. "Up ahead, he entered here."

Ephese sighed heavily and looked into Jebas' eyes, "We must hurry."

# Chapter One — *The Realm of Enduring Peace*

"Right, Jin well done," he gasped, "You two must stay outside of this place until our return..."

"Pap no, you'll need us to serve with the trail." Dolan interrupted.

"Father, we are not afraid to journey within the Rim, we are ready," Jin continued.

"No sons, look around you, listen to these woods," Myriads of monstrous snarls, shrills, and howls flooded the air as the men stood, cast in dark at the helm. "These woods are treacherous. Ready as you are, there are too many mysteries existing within." Dolan and Jin both frowned angrily yet hid their faces from their father's eyes. Jebas placed his hands on their shoulders, "My sons, Candor will not lose four men to this place tonight. Lathan may find his way back, and if so, then may only one of you come retrieve us. But until then, you must not enter, please obey me."

Dolan nodded, but Jin kept his face hidden. A dim shade covered the young man's face which was held in the visage of contempt. Whether this went unnoticed by Jebas was unknown, but the shadows within hastily leeched on the seed developing inside. As the two watched Jebas and Ephese disappear into the forest, a cold gust pushed cruelly across their faces with the full fury of the Rim's breath. Their eyes gazed down the path and each was brought to brief shutters at the sense of a presence, sinister and grave, staring back at them. Jin could not turn his eye away.

\* \* \*

Quivering cries cascaded from the canopy reigning with a host of inhuman yelps and growls, threats from marauding creatures hidden in the night. Ephese ignored the terrors and pushed through each branch and shrub as if his very life were

# Lands of Eden  by M. Gabreyl Scrolls

sourced in his task. Jebas followed, deeper into the forest, keeping his eyes on the dim rays which pierced through the dark shade thwarting the glow of the moon overhead. The deeper into the forest they pressed, the darker their journey grew. Jebas would not admit that without his sons, Lathan's trail would become trackless, that the two men would create an aimless path in the thick darkness. His sons were excellent trackers even in such circumstances. The darkness might have hindered the speed of search, but the trail would be followed without question. Still he would not admit, for fear that what might overtake him and Ephese would also claim his eldest sons and leave Aman by his lonesome.

Jebas learned well of the wild creatures inhabiting the forest, but had never experienced the heinous sounds nor felt the blinding thick he faced. The frightful warnings that met them before at the breach brought forth anxiety unlike any. Perhaps the elders' warnings were correct and one must pursue more than physical strength and ability to overcome the Rim perils. Jebas found his senses easily tricked inside the pitch-black wall bordering his eyes and mind. Leaves tickled his cheeks, branches poked his neck and spine with chilled fingers. Mists whispered taunts as the forest reveled in its dark deception. Every stride renewed images of the scarred backs, grim faces, and wearied limbs of those who drove the supposed darkness into the forest.

"Ephese!?" Jebas called as he griped that he could no longer see through the thick fog and brush. "Ephese, are you ahead of me, make noise for me!"

Ephese found himself frozen with confusion. He turned and strained to see, yet could barely distinguish his very hands before his face. "Jebas, are you still with me?" The two were mere meters from each other yet could scarcely hear each other's voice. The fog thickened, muffled their voicesand suppressed all other sounds within the forest in dense matter.

# Chapter One — The Realm of Enduring Peace

Jebas felt his stomach turn and body halt with fear. Ephese's eyes tensed to comb through the dark with tears that streamed down his cheeks. The gloomy burden weighed down upon them and broke the heavy silence with maniacal laughter. Neither man could interpret the sounds as a multitude of beings groaned in resonance with evil murmurs and eerie swears. Whispers grew louder as screeches stroked the hair of their necks. A violent horn shook the ground with impeccable force. Jebas clenched his teeth and fell to his knees as the sound overpowered him.

Ephese too fell from the force of the horn. His stomach churned with anxiety as he glanced into the distance where a faint light glided among the shadows. "Jebas, if you see what I do, head toward that light…"

Before Ephese took his first step, the ground beneath him shifted suddenly. The men were hurled forward by unseen force as the ground raced with untimely speed toward the light. Dirt and mud compiled against their bodies and trapped them to the rushing floor. The forest howled mightily as they clawed and lurched helplessly against the pull. Sable leaves scattered round them, some disintegrating into ash and landing as smudge on their faces as coarse shrubs severed their clothes and sliced flesh. Each slammed painfully through dead twigs and leaf mounds that obstructed the journey.

Jebas caught a glimpse of Ephese, who clung to a tree root with clenched eyes. The forest floor continued to drag them as prey. Jebas yelled out but was overpowered by the vast chaos. The light grew brighter as the earth brought them rapidly into the mouth of a clearing deep within the Rim. A sudden halt catapulted Jebas as a pebble from a sling. His body flew limply through the clearing and caught every whip as branches lashed his chest, arms, and face. He slammed into a broad trunk, flopped onto the ground, and consciousness slipped by the moment.

Ephese struggled to his feet with heavy breathing and fright-riddled eyes basking in the mighty glow before him. He glanced around for Jebas, but could not hear nor see him. "Jebas… brother where are you?!" Suddenly the light flared and dispersed more darkness with an illuminating hum. Ephese held his hand to his brow to shade his eyes from the brilliant radiance.

Jebas roused to a putrid scent that invaded his nostrils with singeing effect. He groused as he lifted his wounded leg to his chest and snapped free the twig that extended from his calf. Once on his feet, he felt warm breath upon his neck. He turned and gazed into the cerulean glow, believing to see a tall human-shaped figure silhouetted in the light. Yet as the light dimmed, more of the figure was revealed and Jebas' heart pounded with intense fear.

The enormous crimson colored being stood fiercely ahead of him, straddling the root of an ebon tree. The creature's feet clawed the forest floor with sharp spines protruding from its heels and shins. Its scaled skin shimmered in the blue light and revealed a chiseled muscle frame riddled with gruesome scars that oozed black substance. The creature's head was masked with grey smoke that rose from its neck and shoulders and only green eyes that glowed through the ash gave detection of its face. Its arms morphed at the elbows into dozens of hissing vipers and millipedes. The creature breathed menacingly and filled the air with soot. Jebas' body shook with terror as the being lifted a small body coiled and constricted to lifeless form among the deadly vipers. A small boy, eyes shut, arms and legs immobile, chest motionless.

"My son…" cried Ephese as he ran toward the creature.

"Ephese…" Jebas grunted. He tried to inch forward but could not move. Something held him in place. When he cried out again and struggled free, he hasted into the clearing. Without warning, a powerful impact lifted Jebas into the air.

# Chapter One — The Realm of Enduring Peace

He was held stiff, with his feet dangling inches above the ground. Great pressure closed around his neck and shortened his breath. He felt a sharp claw dig into the flesh of his neckline as an inhuman figure manifested in front of him. Jebas panted desperately for air as the creature squeezed and held him above ground with one arm.

Ephese approached the spiny beast as it began to grumble deeply. A single snake perched at Lathan's head hissed with venom dripping from its fangs, its tongue slithered amidst his hair. Ephese crept slowly as the viper looked at him with a hint of a smirk. Suddenly, the viper plunged its fangs into the arm of the young boy and an evil hiss was sung among all the snakes. Ephese reached for his son and several snakes snapped at his arm, sinking their teeth into his flesh. Yet neither Ephese nor Lathan showed any reaction to the stings. Ephese lifted his son from the creature's coil and fell backward.

Jebas' eyes rolled and head spun from the monsters vice round his neck. Tears of agony streamed down his cheeks as the creature in front of him came into the full scope of the light. Its thin body was completely dark with slime dripping from every crevice and eyes aglow with piercing jade. Jebas struggled against the beast's grip with even greater fear after seeing him. He finally rammed his heel into the creature's head. The monster snarled and released its grip. Jebas stumbled onto the ground and coughed uncontrollably. The being stumbled back steadily, regained its ground and roared wide-mouthed, spewing strings of yellow spit in Jebas' direction.

Jebas stood in awe as the creature glowered at him. It crouched low, and before Jebas could make another call to Ephese, the brute lunged forward and slammed into Jebas' chest with incredible force. It careened onward for several feet, then stopped and used its leathery wing to thrust Jebas through the air. The hunter soared into another trunk. His body throbbed and legs gave way as he slouched at the tree base. He could feel the rumble of the beast stomping towards him. Jebas searched the ground for something to use against the mighty creature but found only dark soil. His back ached with anguish. His legs would not budge. The dark figure sprinted toward him with a howl of deadly intention spurred by the fiendish laughter of the crimson beast. The snakes sneered with proclamation as the evil being leaped forward with pointed claws glazing in the mighty glow and Jebas' eyes widened with terror.

Suddenly, a second horn blasted from among the trees. The creature faltered in mid air with chaotic fashion and crashed onto the ground mere inches from Jebas feet. The animal looked upward and cowered in fear. Then with a gasp the creature vanished into nothing. Jebas panted hastily. The thick darkness that enveloped them lifted and he could see the dim white moon of the morning sky. He gazed into the canopy and searched for several moments. What frightened the creatures off mystified the hunter, and frightened him even more. His head swayed with the shock of his wounds and before they overcame him, he managed one final call to his companion, and collapsed into unconscious.

Ephese cradled his son in his arms with a rocking motion. He mumbled quietly before peering through the shrubbery mounted along the stems of the trees. Amazingly, he could see a clearing through the Rim forest, even more remarkable was that the men were only several steps from the border.

"Jebas..." The excited father called, "we are here!" Tears continued to stream down Ephese's face as he began to laugh with joy. "We are here, at the border! He kept his promise, he helped us! Jebas. Do you hear me?" Ephese searched the grounds as the groans from the chief hunter met his ears. Lathan remained limp in his father's arms. The boy showed no hint of life in his cheeks, still Ephese showed no panic. He

# Chapter One *The Realm of Enduring Peace*

found Jebas slumped against a tree base closer to the border of the forest. Jin and Dolan woke within earshot and instantly came to their father's aid at Ephese's call. The sky hazed with blue as morning breached from the east sky. Ahead their path was laden with the eight carcasses of re`em and sabers driven so wild from the men's scent that they ravaged each other in the night. Dolan and Jin's eyes were humbled with shock and fear. They were grateful their slumber was spared, yet desperate to return before dark brought more.

"Do not fear," Ephese mumbled, "we will return safely, this he promised." The brothers looked puzzled at each other as the man rambled to himself. After several moments he continued, "Gather your father, we must hurry back to Candor."

The three then raced across the vast fields as the morning light began to break. "We must hurry, there is much from here to tell our people, so much to prepare," Ephese exclaimed.

## *The Night Presence*

Aman stared curiously through the thin gap of the veil that covered Lathan's quarters of Morcial's tent. He studied his friend's vacant appearance. Dozens of incense and spices were lit and placed around the boy's body, their haze sent nose itching aromas circulating throughout the tent. His chest was covered with powdered herbs which upon waking would send Lathan into chronic sneezing. Yet he rested without motion, the occasional moist cloth pressed against his temple would release warm droplets to travel down his lobes. But rendered no response.

Aman found no assurance in the steady rise and fall of Lathan's chest. He watched intently for the slightest twitch in his friend's hands or feet. His brave companion's eyes were

# Lands of Eden

*by M. Gabreyl Scrolls*

partly opened. The slight curve of his mouth under flared nostrils suggested subtle elation.

Aman made attempts to rouse him with steady pokes at his ribs while Morcial was not looking. "Leave him be son," grumbled the healer from behind the small kettle set over a kindling fire centered in the tent. Aman withdrew his fingers and stared through the flame at his father's blank and similar expression. Jebas sat still and upright and gazed into the kettle with wide eyes and not a sound from his belly, only occasionally he rubbed his neck and squinted with anger. Morcial wrapped Jebas' torso with *gooky* speckled with balsam beans taken from the creamy liquid boiling in the pot. Jebas' back was tendered with thick maroon bruises and open cuts stretched from shoulder to shoulder. He could not yet stand on his leg which ached from the deep puncture in his calf. Morcial had removed the fragment lodged in the muscle. The process would ordinarily produce agonizing pain heard throughout the village. But Jebas simply grunted and shook in pain calmly until Morcial finished. Morcial dressed the wound with the thick cream gathered from the balsam and would soon pinch the puncture with scaffle thread. Jebas certainly did not show complete apathy to the pain, yet his indifference displayed he was troubled by something more. Morcial pressed him for what caused such injury, yet in frustration Jebas could not recall.

Dolan and Jin offered very little description of the Rim, and neither indulged Aman's questions as to their father's wounds or the horrendous sounds heard from the field. Ephese too said very little as he paced outside Morcial's tent. He did not seem affected with the same terror that riddled Jebas with anxiety. Instead he mumbled to himself, methodically rubbed his left arm, and chuckled occasionally from underneath a clueless grin. Dolan and Jin stood outside the tent believing the man

# Chapter One  The Realm of Enduring Peace

was driven mad, yet both waited eagerly for him to relay his story.

Curiosity had also overcome Aman. He too anticipated an end to the silence. Yet something more intrigued his eye through the thin gap of the veil. While Morcial stitched his father's wound, Aman crept through the veil with set gaze upon a faint glimmer emitted from Lathan's arm. He squinted and inched closer to catch the sounds of soft chimes seemingly voicing from the twinkle. As it dimmed, Aman noticed four punctures in Lathan's flesh. Each oozed with shiny thick black liquid. He glanced back through the veil, Morcial continued to knead Jebas' calf with creamy pale substance. He turned and looked again at the breaks in the skin. The ooze seeped from the punctures and pooled round the wound. Aman stretched his finger over the substance. The prints of his index reflected off the glossy surface of the ooze which eerily swelled toward his finger.

"Aman," Morcial called. The boy jumped with alarm and withdrew his finger. The dark matter quickly retreated into the ruptures with a dark whisper. "Go now little shepherd, don't worry about your friend, I'll take good care of him and your father." Aman nodded, but took one final look at Lathan's arm. The wound had completely vanished and no hint of the ooze remained. He frowned with great confusion as he headed from the tent. A final look at his father's blank expression offered no solace to his uncertainty.

With his sheep sheared, there was no work for the young shepherd in the pasture. His brothers would make plenty work for him however, with appetites that would demand a recreation of the stew missed the night before. The two would surely be upset and Aman was fully prepared to calm their anger with a decent meal. But upon entering his father's tent, the boy was forcefully snatched into Jin's grasp.

"Well, well, little brother, what a fine heap you caused last night, huh!?" Jin mocked as he wrestled Aman onto his shoulder.

"Put me down," Aman grunted, pounding his fist onto Jin's back and kicking aggressively.

Jin swayed at his hips causing Aman to feel dizzy and cease kicking. "And after all the heap you caused last night, I believe I'll drop you in the scaffle dung, maybe you'll feel more at home in the stench!"

Jin charged toward the pasture hedge, with Aman struggling to free himself from his grip. Dolan immediately followed with flared nostrils reigning over a mischievous grin. When they reached the fence, Jin flung Aman effortlessly from his shoulder, caught his legs in mid-air and held the boy upside-down over a heap of steaming scaffle waste. Aman dangled from Jin's grip, screaming wildly with tears of fear dropping from his eyes.

"Brother, don't," Dolan warned though unable to disguise his amusement, "you know Jebas will throttle us if you do this."

Jin frowned with agitation, "That he may, but still, don't you suppose its time this little runt gain some manners?" Tears continued to fall from Aman's eyes as he pleaded for Jin to release him. Jin obliged and released Aman's legs. Aman screamed and shut his eyes just as Jin gripped his ankle with one hand in time to spare the shepherd a hair above the smelly pile.

Aman now heaved with pitiful wails. He begged against Jin's intentions but carefully chose the words "not in the waste." The amusement rapidly escaped Dolan's expression as he stared at Jin, whose face budded with focused ferocity and even more frightful hint of delight in their younger brother's torturous howls.

"Brother, that's enough, put him down."

# Chapter One — The Realm of Enduring Peace

Jin glared at Dolan as he dangled Aman over the swell several seconds more. The two stared each other down with intense silence as Aman uselessly squirmed. Dolan finally intervened, offered Aman his arm and hoisted him away from the heap and forced Jin's grip. He then placed Aman on his feet.

The two stood in front of the fence as Aman panted and cleaned his face. Jin fixed his hateful eyes on Dolan, "You baby him like your father." Jin spat and looked at Aman with a squint. "You caused all of this you little runt."

At those words Aman plunged his fist into Jin's stomach. "It was not my fault!"

Jin bellowed over, Aman took the opportunity, shoved Jin's shoulders and sent him toppling through the fence and into the pile of scaffle waste. Jin squirmed out of the pile. The putrid smell engulfed him quickly as he slopped off chunks from his hands and fingers. Aman was already in mad sprint from the scene as Jin rose to his feet.

"You can run with a fire at your heels you little runt, but I'm going to catch you! Hear me! This is all your fault!" Dolan hollered with laughter as Jin smeared dung from his cheek. "You think it funny brother, why not try some?!" Jin lurched with his arms forward in attempt to shove him into the steaming stench and even the score. Dolan shifted and only kept his foot out which caught Jin by surprise. He tripped and fell face first into the dung for a second time. Dolan roared with thunderous laughter as Jin squirmed out and ran straight away to the Euphrates' pools.

\*   \*   \*

Aman hid near the wide wool tents along the east side of the center pasture with his face buried in his arms. His sleeve darkened from tears, his eyes refused to hold as he wondered if Jin's anger was just. Could he have prevented the chaos if he had chosen not to hold his tongue? Aman wanted to avoid the alarm Lathan's Rim journey would cause. Yet in not wanting to bring trouble, he caused such for his brothers, for Lathan and Ephese, and believed he was the reason for his father's wounds. Moreover, his father's distressed demeanor provided no solace for Aman's guilt.

As he sat with tears melding his face to his soaked cloth, his quieted whimpers met with a low grumbled echoe from a distance. His heart raced and he immediately sprang to his feet, fearing Jin was close by. He peeked round the wool tent and gazed into the village lit with small fires kindling along the paths. Neither of his brothers was in sight. The grumble ended. All turned still as Aman stepped from the tent and searched the wide hills that opened to the north lands. He rubbed his eyes and blinked several times at the sight of a distant grass peak lit with a diffused glow. The gusto cast a long single shadow down the hill toward the base where a figure stood statuesque. 'What was this brilliant specter,' the boy wondered.

The green blades bent toward the hill and reflected a shimmering dance of light though no wind angled their bow. Their ruffles hummed softly as melody and grew more distinct with each step the small boy made toward the glow. But this was the only sound to be heard, not a tree swayed, not a bird chirped or animal called. Even Aman's steps fell silent as he approached.

Eden's evening canopy seemed to fade into morning gray the more Aman neared. And the beam rendered warmth as the sun upon his feet and hands. The appearance became more definitive as he neared the tall hill. At the base the figure stood with bō at guard, back turned to the light. Still distant but advancing, Aman began to distinguish the face, eyes shut at rest, foggy beard and strong jaw set. Atop the hill, the

# Chapter One — The Realm of Enduring Peace

silhouette prostrated arms and hands forward on bended knees with head tucked to the ground. An occasional lift and nod were all the boy could gather from the hilltop swallowed in the brilliant incandescence.

Dizziness met the warmth with unexpected strength as Aman halted his progression. His moans found ears as he swayed where he stood. The guard at the base caught the child in sight with concerned alert. Aman stared back into the open eyes, touched his head and fell to his knee. "Seth?" The boy called with question as if the elder could provide answer to his sudden stupor. Seth instantly dropped his staff, relented his wonder, and rushed toward the boy. Aman turned and look toward the hill. "Elias?" He pondered again. Suddenly, the light swelled down the hill toward him. Radiance blinded all, yet just as quickly faded to black as the boy fainted.

\*     \*     \*

Glitters of orange and red danced along the Euphrates banks as the sun was ending the quiet day. No other in the village witnessed the bright halo to the north where Seth and Elias had retreated for meditation. Aman was nearly forgotten even by his brothers. Jin's frustration with his stench and wrestles with the heat of the scalding pools provided endless amusement for his older twin. Along the forest borders, haunted shadowed predators with vigil watch on the gates of the village, else unseen by the peaceful villagers. The plot was set and all pieces gathered and ready, but Candor would rest another night before the evil feasted.

Dolan stared into the distance and studied the southern border as Jin came to his side. "We should have gone in after him, we could have helped them," Jin stated.

"Jebas told us not to go, we did the right thing in obeying him."

"Obeying him? We looked dastardly because of this... because of him."

"Benjin, he gave us the right warning, we could have come from that forest just like him, or Ephese. He warned us, we were not ready—"

"—Enough," Jin interrupted, "You want so much to sound like our father but don't believe what your saying anymore than I do." Dolan attempted to mask his admitting expression but Jin knew his flesh all the same. "Brother, we are men. Jebas wants to keep training us but we are trained well enough. We know how to stand on our own feet. Yet when he calls, we jump to his command. We spear at his word not our instinct. We track paths for his hunt and carry his game on our shoulders like servants. All the things he taught us, but he allows us to prove none of them. How much more ready do we need be?" Dolan flared his nostrils and looked away with grievance. "You know as well as I, we are more than ready and could have faced whatever threat that forest offered, better even than those two old fools."

"Old fools?" Dolan and Jin turned at the objection to see Ephese glaring at them both with question. Dolan lifted his head and Jin squinted back with aggression as Ephese strolled toward them. "Young man, do not assume you know so much that you cannot learn more from those around you. Even from an old fool can one learn the perils of folly."

Ephese turned and folded his arms behind his back. He resumed mumbling in similar fashion as was seen outside Morcial's tent.

"Is that what we should make of your rambles?" Jin mocked. "Did the *perils* of the Rim bring more fool out of you?" Ephese paused and glared at Jin who continued his ridicule. "Or maybe you're trying to teach us something of *folly*."

Dolan chuckled nervously while Jin held a humorless stare. Ephese smirked and strolled confidently toward the two. The

# Chapter One — The Realm of Enduring Peace

tall hunter towered head and shoulders over the two young men. He kept his hands behind his back and stopped few inches from Jin with a commanding stance.

"You of such short age believe you know the world of Eden because of what you have been taught and trained. But if you follow in the training and beliefs of old fools, how much of a wise man does that make you?" Jin swallowed heavy and Dolan's amusement quickly retreated. "Perhaps the question you should ask is, 'what this *old fool* can show you of your own folly that might perhaps make wise of you?'" Ephese stated sharply.

Jin looked away briefly with apparent shame-flushed visage. Dolan frowned and responded, "Just what is making you mumble as such hunter? What was in the Rim that could hold your fear so greatly?"

Ephese smirked again and glanced out the corner of his eye toward the southern border. "Not what was in the Rim, what was not in the Rim." He looked back at the two. "You speak of perils and fear from what you've been told. I tell you do not believe what you have heard about the dark forest." Ephese said excitedly as he shook his head. "The only perils there are those impressed upon us by the false fables of our trusted protectors."

Jin squinted at the hunter as he glanced again over the horizon. "What makes them false?" he pressed. "Forget what you didn't see, what did you see?"

"What I saw, young man, was the truth behind the mysteries of the forbidden Rim. With my very eyes, I saw what they've hidden from us for centuries. I've heard from his lips, from his voice, I saw... I saw no darkness in the Rim, the elders have been deceiving us. I cannot explain everything, my thoughts run together like a stampede, but I know I felt no fear, only an incredible comfort in that forest. To believe I was blinded by these teachings—"

" — Ahh," Jin scoffed, "You accuse us of foolishness but ramble from anger. Do you even know what you're saying? You accuse Candor's forefathers of — "

" — Brother," Dolan interrupted with raised hand as he turned and looked at Ephese with more wonder in his face, "Sir, just tell us, what did you see in the Rim?"

Ephese glanced away with a sigh. He huddled the two together and spoke softly. "I saw a being of immaculate light that gleamed and towered above me like a *tryton*. Its face glowed with unspeakable beauty. It had the body of a man, but its voice hummed with a melody not to be found in a human tone."

"Brother, don't listen to this, this man is crazed." Jin stated as he pulled away.

"I know what I'm saying young man, and you would be wise to listen. Or keep believing the lies of these elders. Nevertheless, I tell you the truth. He spoke with music, he cradled my son in his arms and called me forward. He told me not to be afraid, and that he meant no harm for my son nor me. As I took my son from his arms he said, 'Verily, I am the son of the dawn. Kneel and sing my name.' Listen when I tell you that when he is revealed all of Candor will sing his praise and know his triumph."

Jin shook his head, "You are senseless, I won't be foolish enough to listen any longer. Come brother, we've got better purposes."

Jin started off, but Dolan was far too intrigued by Ephese's discourse to dismiss him so easily. He glanced at Jin momentarily, then turned and questioned further. "Do you speak the truth hunter?" Ephese nodded with sincerity. "You say you sang his name, what was his name?"

"Lucifer."

# Chapter One

## The Realm of Enduring Peace

## Chapter Two

# The Seed

Few men of Eden had come to learn the full embrace of the dark seed transferred through Adam. The time of righteous warriors and prophets was forgotten as fallen angles, supernatural beings, and vile spirits masked themselves within men's revelry. As the cruel acts of Cain's descendants were vanquished in the struggles that drove wicked men to the far corners of earth, civilizations grew passive to the ways of godly prophets, allowing their hearts to stray further from truth and deeper into the harvest of a venomous enemy. An enemy that lurked in continual darkness, long awaiting the decent of shadowed hearts to fill its quiver.

Since the dawn of breath, this enemy was known to spur the evils that dwelt within. With cunning deception, enchantment and temptation, did this fiend toy shield away from guard, pluck the strings of the defenseless heart, and puppet the soul into ruin. When guile was not enough to turn one's mettle, fear and tyranny became the only aim to fulfill the brute's intent. Revered among the fallen as the great musician, Lucifer, bright and morning star. Yet the prophets and elders,who stood in the statutes of Adam, knew him cursed as 'Sëtan', the everlasting adversary.

# Chapter Two

## The Fall of Candor

In the day when hearts were simplistically turned from righteous ways, few could withstand the strong deception of the fallen dragon. His clever craft confounded even his minions in the smooth song sung on his lips. No greater deceit could come from any being known to man. The beast embodied night like no other fallen forlorn, yet could shine more glorious than the saffron bronze of an Eden morning. His strengths and abilities, though yet witnessed, were unmatched among angels and celestial creatures spawned at the dawn of existence. Lucifer swore to unleash his power upon the cursed ground which he was doomed. The shamed sarim grew more impatient with each auburn sunset. The knowledge of evil only disrupted the course of man's existence. And his desire to bring destruction was to be carved faster and harsher than any living beast could fathom, faster than any human could recover.

Still Lucifer was not to be mistook as a vengeful conqueror with meticulous ploy pottering at every parcel of man's essence. His actions were based solely upon tantrum and no other aim than anarchy. Lament and shame were the endless emotions that sowed the being's hatred. Not even by thought was Eden a comparison to the effervescent majesty of his former residence. And so cursed to its ground, the adversary roamed with no more to gain than spoils in this unwelcome paradise. How he longed for the Creator's merit, cursed his rebellion and loathed his fellow deviants who plucked his heart strings onto futile fury, offering no appeasement of his jealousy for those, lowly in origin and order, granted grace which he would never obtain.

Vestual inhaled the puffed jade smoke blooming from the *concauct* buds which soaked the moisture of the thick fog swarming through the forest. His eyes rolled with euphoric rise at the rotted scent of their bloom. Night descended upon the peaceful town he surveyed. His eyes were yellow and dull as the wicked spirit of his heart. He salivated with blue tongue drawn along his lips which dripped the dark ooze of grubs and millipedes. The arch slurped and turned toward Lucifer, who glared into the west through his shadowed mug of vacant expression.

"Night descends again, are you not pleased my prince?"

Lucifer sighed slowly with no dismiss of his gaze. The beast had assumed the form of a Sarim, only in size and shape as human. Still his countenance, shrouded by relentless specter, distinguished his darkness in the moonlight.

"How fallen, how changed from this, that, in happy realms of light clothed with transcendent brightness, did outshine Myriads. And now, misery," Lucifer scoffed as his lower body morphed into the tail of a black serpent. "Joined in equal ruin, into this pit unable to see from where he's fallen."

The Sarim glanced at Vestual who turned in disgust. Lucifer's eyes caved with black emptiness. Teeth, rotted with holes, seeped from his dark gums and rested in crooked fashion upon his jaw. "What purposed served here Vestual?" he bade, "Does twilight terror upon this town make any good of evil, does captured peace in fleeting feet of fear gripped hearts, raining down this fire, reign and ravaging pitiless defeated, make slightest good of evil?" The beast searched Vestual with full expectance of his command.

The fallen arch kept his eyes from the gruesome appearance of the black serpent. "What can make good of evil!?" Lucifer grumbled with eyes flared bright red as if to command Vestual's sight upon him. The serpent then turned and shut its eyes as if in pain. The rumble of his anger subsided as he looked over the Candor glow.

"To be weak is miserable, and so I am. By change in outward luster? No. By disdain from He, who could inflict no harsher levy than denial of grace. So never can any make this evil good!"

# Chapter Two — The Fall of Candor

The beast swiped his tail at the arch narrowly missing him. His mighty tail slammed into a tree trunk and sent course vibrations up the grey bark and caused loose leaves and twigs to snap and fall to the dark forest floor.

Vestual hissed as more flames engulfed Lucifer's face. The arch flapped its thin, fleshly wings and glided round the fallen star. He gently pressed his scoured palms upon Lucifer's shoulders. Lucifer calmed and hummed softly before recoiling from Vestual's comfort.

Still Vestual prodded, "But my prince, our tally is not for that Celestial plane. My star, that light is long dimmed. Keep to the course, for ours is mans' end."

"The course is mans' end, what course then do we serve these men? Either life in Eden, tilling the ground and women's pain, or the Celestial plane? Our tally brings them glory, so is that to be our joy?"

Vestual recoiled at the aggression in Lucifer's voice yet soon found his way into his ear. "My prince, consider these. These, His meagr`st creation. And these he's given subjection? Did not their father, given that great garden with shade and abundant ruby, crystal springs and fertile sands and perfumes of jasmine, hyssop, and magnolia, given daily communion with the great Creator, yet did not he turn at the slightest savour? And with that tongue do these desecrate His thunderous name, and as we did the same. Yet, we, the higher beings not given gracious fall, but doom, with these the ones to beguile us. Do you find that truly just?"

Now what was known among the fallen was the weakness of the adversary's dark heart, which could be tuned with the slightest stroke to manipulate the prince to desired ends. Vestual was perhaps the most cunning of the demons to toy with the perverse prince. The fallen arch could inflict venom with his soothing tongue that enticed lustful hearts. He commanded a legion of demons named by Adam as the "Ya'goviah," unskilled at the hand yet profound in the art of deception. Though not full with the tremendous power and combat as most Archs, Vestual was a vile, ruthless demon with a heart to destroy mercilessly. He, like most among the fallen, sought more than simple havoc upon the inhabitants of Eden. He desired power and praise among demons and believed they could reclaim the lost kingdom from man's desolation in spite of the lament filled prince.

But Vestual had to bide his time under Lucifer's authority, just as all awaited the former morning star's hatred to spawn destruction.

"No, you do not find this just," the arch continued. "And thus must we do ill His plan among all lands and forth their wickedness."

Lucifer grumbled with anger as the dark winds howled round the hosts gathered at the border. "There calls the blood of mark'd flesh ' pon the winds. My bowels hunger and tongue savors its scent. What can make good of evil? Not this place. For even when it seeks refuge 'mong pointed men, it finds me." Lucifer hissed again as Vestual's eyes flared with animation. The monster gazed into the stars and mocked, "You cannot take that flesh which you mark'd for my direction, such men belong to these minions, to my fangs."

"It exists here, my star," Vestual chimed, "to be claimed back to your hand."

Suddenly, the host jostled restlessly. The vicious villains hung harsh hisses on the black weighed canopy as the detection of a wayward presence pressing through the moors caught their eyes. The thin figure was covered by shadows and approached from the jagged gate, eyes glowing blue with curiosity. The figure was human.

# Chapter Two

*The Fall of Candor*

Lucifer snarled with immense anger as hatred bubbled with murderous intention. He clenched his claw and salivated over the taste of a pending gouge and the relish of warm red. The human would be obliterated instantly at the solid swipe of his claw or impact of his tail. How dare one threat his ground with unwelcome presence? Lucifer was poised for the kill and dozens of demons mounted upon his arm in curious cravings for the violence to take place.

"Hold off your hand prince," Vestual hastily pleaded, "and entreat me to have this visits ground."

Lucifer glared ferociously into the frightened eyes of the demon arch. None were to hold off the prince's intentions and such meant brutal battering. Yet Lucifer relinquished his grip on his sharp nails and settled his rage. The great adversary rocked backward as if dazed by reminiscence and unseen control. He closed his eyes and held his temple as his crooked claws recoiled. In the same moment, he stared into the sky with wonder as if something demanded his attention. As the demons round him yelped like jackals upon warm meat, the dark prince regained composure. With a wave of his hand, the demons vanished into the curtain of darkness provided by the hollows.

Lucifer licked his nails and awaited reason from the legion's leader. "Why does this being bid my senses greatly? Speak your halt seducer, quicken your tongue to keep back my hand."

The figure wandered aimlessly as if not to be found among the grim bark. His eyes searched as invisible creatures lurked round him with snickers and taunts. Vestual hasted reason as he approached.

"Nights ago, do you not recall, the venom sunk into the pale weak flesh? This be he, who wayward roamed into the lair of the mighty serpentine. Do you not recall his scent and taste upon your fangs? This be one of the descendants strewn aimless...You hold you hand as you scent him too. My prince, lessen hatred for remembrance and do not raze him, for he is your intended, returned for puppetry."

Lucifer scoffed and dug his nails into the bark of a nearby branch. The vile villain sniffed as his eyes rolled with pleasure. "Look at his eyes Vestual, look how veiled and blind he strolls. Fool! And I too fool to use such a mind so easily moved." Lucifer snickered and looked upward. Through a dim clearing in the canopy that opened to clear night sky littered with bright stars. With a mocking squint, he hissed with spit. "Even so, such is *Your* creation."

His mockery was not without quiet tremble. The fallen prince, held still with upward gaze, seemed to cringe with doubt as to the implication of his ridicule. When nothing occurred, he puffed his chest and focused back on the human.

The figure wandered with a mass of bewilderment on his face. His blank expression only frustrated the demons more as they prepared to pounce upon him with ravaging effect. Lucifer commanded them away with a grumble. Within moments, the woods cleared and the dark adversary was alone with the human. He set his jaw and ripped the bark from the branch.

"Off fiends of aimless decent, and let me to play as his mind thus dictates me..."

\*     \*     \*

Ephese shielded his eyes from the sudden spark of blinding ray that shot from the dark and hummed softly a monotone melody of comforting warmth. The ashen leaves above captured the light from escape into the night sky and returned dulled reflection enough to illuminate the clearing where soot-

## Chapter Two — The Fall of Candor

stained earth, jade bark, and pale ferns littered the forest floor. Ephese stood, mouth agape, with awestruck fascination.

The misconception among the prophets of old was that the dark prince could alter into benevolent varieties. Yet this was not so. Lucifer could assume no forms other than those from and into which he was changed. He could assume the form of a sarim though this no longer bore the brilliant light that glowed through his body. The radiance that did shine from him was sourced from the glory of his Creator, a shine that could not be removed no matter how grim Lucifer's spirit. Few men have come to see Lucifer in this form. Still, this manifestation was Lucifer's most common as it reminded the fallen of what was lost in their fool-hearted allegiance.

Before the fall of man, Lucifer's powers were still abundant and allowed him to take the shape of beasts and fowl. After his curse in the garden, he could only assume the serpentine form, which caused many to revile him and revealed how weak and low he had fallen. In this form Lucifer disguised his tempts of those who followed in Adam's way.

His final form was most sinister and vicious that it struck great fear in the heart of any being who dared look upon it. Jagged scales of dull crimson that scored the land and cut red any flesh that dared touch. Towering claws which dripped black poison from deep grooves and cavities filled with pestilence. Enormous jaws that opened to an abyss in its belly which puffed with putrid soot which engulfed air and sky in vast darkness. And most terrifying was the formidable great tail, whipped to and fro with careless destruction and paralyzing strength. This was the great red dragon that appeared in Sëtan's unquenchable fury.

These were the forms of the fallen prince and no other images of him prove true.

What was true was Lucifer's embodiment of relentless deception which allows the prince control over how men witnessed him. Wayward and frightened hearts could not view this devil in dutiful existence. Such was the case for the visitor who shook with fright in Lucifer's presence.

Ephese stared with hesitance for several moments as the appearance towered before him with menacing light. Through quick gasps and shaken lungs he managed to finally speak.

"I have returned, 'son of the dawn' to hear more truths from you, to sing more of your name as you request." No response came as the twinges of courage began to swell in the fooled hunter. "I've returned so that you will grant me the greatness as you promised. I am ready to serve you."

Lucifer appeared to Ephese as a tall fortified human with bright radiance blooming from his face. His head bald and skin bright cream as if his entire being glowed with spirited essence. Behind the manifestation hissed the serpent with aim to engulf the visitor and vice the life within him.

"I have informed only few of you," Ephese continued, "but those who listened wish to come and kneel before you as I have." Lucifer snarled as drool dangled from his fangs, still unresponsive and threatening. "Please, you must reveal yourself to them as you have to me. You must let my people know of who you are, and the truth of our being."

The illumined appearance shut its eyes with a grin. When it fixed its eyes back on the man, a subtle chill flowed through the trees with a wild shriek. Its voice chimed strings and flutes of mesmeric merry. "Before you stands the bright morning star, dare not address me but upon your knees. Know me with your face upon the earth."

At that Ephese instantly fell to his knees. In stupor, he pressed his forehead into the cold black dirt. The hunter shook violently for unknown reason and though the light filled the

# Chapter Two — The Fall of Candor

atmosphere with warmth, his body felt cold and motionless, as if the very heat of his inner core was drawn from him.

The being hummed with colorful tone and continued, "Of those who have heard my name in these inhabited lands are few, thus graced are you this name and in present to view my countenance. Soon will this reveal to men abroad and beneath so they will know him that holds power unlike any. Still to bear your witness, more must be at your side. Since none abide, wonder bids me how great your pattern on my behalf has bore. What is your purpose here since not the charge I gave, to tell men of me, and before my feet bring them to bow? Only when such has happened will I grant your every desire and so too theirs."

Ephese shivered tremendously yet managed to lift his gaze upon the being, "Bright being, I so desire to bring my men to you. But the elders of Candor have swayed many to never venture here. These are considered cursed lands, dark and condemned. To come here implies danger in their eyes."

Lucifer refrained from lunging at the human to tear his limbs. This being was not of the order and did not know the great prince's commands were never to be questioned. He thundered through the specter the human witnessed, in part to convince, but mostly to frighten.

"Take you the words of your men above the words of he that exist a great lord?!" The boom of his voice shook the man with intense vigor and pounded his body with such force that Ephese felt his lungs hit with suffocating power. Lucifer mercilessly rumbled with more force, "Twice, this border have you ventured, and into what danger did you fall, and twice I bid you to these grounds, outstretched and inviting. Is it these, elders, who tell you forward and move you? Or this way, then that, and you go? Perhaps should I then end you and choose another more fitful? No? Then to your elders, to your men, to these with my command and dare not return alone again."

# Lands of Eden
### by M. Gabreyl Scrolls

The light dimmed from the being's face as it turned away. A sudden flash and the being vanished in the same fashion as it appeared. Ephese felt warmth returning to his body and slowly lifted his head. His bones trembled, though he could not fathom why as he kept his eyes fixed on the present darkness that fronted him. He struggled to his feet as the terror gripped. Why such fear was caused by the vision of the benevolent being troubled him. But he had his command, and would do for Candor what was needed for fortune.

He waited for several moments as if the being would reappear with more instruction, But nothing. With a quiet whisper he repeated Lucifer's name, turned, and sauntered back to the forest border.

\*       \*       \*

As the human left the dark nest, Lucifer fixed his gaze on the canopy. Dawn approached and the light of the sun would threaten to break through with view of sky. A legion of devils cackled round the serpent's jagged tail as they morphed from the forest shadow. Vestual settled near Lucifer's head, veiled in pluming ash as the adversary relented into the shape of a sarim. His voice nearly sang with sadness.

"Marvel they at the sky lit with rose and ivory hue, do they honor Him for sultry morn? This creation mocks His prowess, indeed turns way His grace to the sea and tramples it under sand. Yet none cast down to dismal depths, none removed from form and likeness. Bright as the light from He who formed these hills where we now stand, richer than the chasm where no torch flames. A rebellious act and hundreds descend onto this, Eden. A rebellious act and one innocent lamb slain." The great beast paused in thought. "No Vestual, I do not find this just."

# Chapter Two

## The Fall of Candor

At that the fallen arch grinned with delight as hatred surged the prince's body. The seed of deception planted. The wayward dellamy set to ploy. The annihilation was to begin, and he would lead the rage of deadly menaces against the throngs of mankind. Only left were the commands of the great prince to spark the demons orchestra.

## *A Design and Purpose*

Stirs of echoes rippled over Aman's eardrum as the haze scattered and vision came. Clouded thoughts and curious wonder kept him from fathoming his state and comprehension of the voices swimming through his mind. The bright glimmer that engulfed him still measured a heavy presence that none could forget. What was that bright beam and warm presence that swarmed him by the hills where Candor's mighty warrior and great shepherd stood secluded in their night exchange?

Curiosity brought the lad to sit upright on the thin gruff cloth as the air became cool and refreshing. The weight of dizziness lifted and his head cleared. His body felt strong and warm, the same energy felt when sipping the creamy milk of the balsam bean. The boy hopped off the matted clothes and sprang loose from the veil expecting Morcial to greet him. Yet he was not there.

The ground beneath the tent canopy was smooth as liquid surface though riddled with wood shavings and stone fragments tipped with dark shades of scarlet clay and dirt. The wall-skins were decorated with writing, drawings of animals, rivers, land and sky. At Aman's feet were several markings carved into the sand. The boy followed the symbols carefully and whispered their meaning.

"Shous ptouhareu ev Ahquah positisou." Aman frowned and meditated on the phrase for several moments.

The boy turned his attention on the clay markings along the interior with probing interest. Tales of Adam's sons and daughters told of the times past. The forefathers of Candor's country and their journeys through Eden. The rituals and practices of men who mirrored the statutes and instruction given by Adam. Aman marveled at the images of strange beast and human shaped beings scattered through the scribes. Various figures painted in crystalline served only to remind the boy of the marvelous light that engulfed him.

Aman grazed his fingers along the wall-skin surface which was textured by deep grooves and thick marks of clay. A beam of sunlight shot into the tent. Seth entered, shaped by the morning sun, gripping a large root from a tree in his arms. The elder paused with little expression before he laid the root down in the center. Silence ensued for small moments. The elder etched the bark and dirt from the wood as Aman stood off timidly. At the elder's back, the boy turned his attention onto the scribes.

"Do not study them long little spirit," Seth commanded softly, "you are too young to yet understand."

Aman looked back at the elder with doubt. Seth continued to carve, expressionless, and made no attempt to look at the boy. Aman squinted with a silent mug at Seth's neck, then turned to read again.

Seth continued, "You are not mistaken by my words young reu... I too know your heart. Yours is curious for understanding. This is welcomed. But to understand these writings there is still much else to learn." Aman paused with a glance at the elder who finally fixed his eyes on the small shepherd. He ceased his work on the trunk, rested his arm on his knee and breathed deeply. "How be in ones so young must we truly place hope, and pray the life of righteousness to bloom? How resilient be innocent faith against such doom?"

# Chapter Two — The Fall of Candor

Seth appeared to measure the boy just as much as Aman measured him. The elder said very little to any, was often so mysterious that he was shunned among the people despite the protection he served. As many gave ear to his words as those who held to the statutes of Adam, believing he spoke no more than the baffles of other elders and prophets. Yet what he dictated was a defined purpose, set not just for the young shepherd who stood before him, but for the entire tribe. And somehow this was no puzzle to Aman, who held wisdom like no other child in Candor.

Seth nodded calmly and resumed his work on the root, "Are you well little spirit?" Seth asked, with more demand than request. Aman nodded. "Head to the *leah*, Elias will meet you there."

Aman obeyed and headed for the thin slit of the skin tent curtain. Yet before he exited, he turned and faced the elder. Seth concentrated on his work, whatever it might become, and the boy was afraid to break that focus. Still he needed to understand the purpose of the drawings that crowded every space of his tent. "Elder, will you tell me at least what the words in the ground mean?"

Seth steadily worked at the root, "As I told, you are yet too young."

Aman sighed with disappointment but would not let Seth's response satisfy him. "Do you even understand all these writings?"

At that Seth shot a sharp glance at the boy. The elder frowned with perplexity and stuck his carver into the ground. He appeared ready to provide Aman with a stern scold for his contest. But after several moments, as his eyes traveled round the tent, he exhaled and answered Aman with sincerity.

"At even my age, little spirit, I do not fully comprehend all I've scribed."

# Lands of Eden

*by M. Gabreyl Scrolls*

Aman looked away briefly with disappointment. "Then why do you scribe all of this, if you don't understand it, how could anyone else?" he responded.

The elder slid on his hind and lay beside the symbols written in the dirt. "We will not always be in this place reu Aman," he stated, "I scribe that when we are gone from here, men seeking wisdom, as you do, will find these writings and symbols and in them our story, our rituals, our lives. And as they too are unable to understand their complex meaning, they might still find simple design in our manners. For that is what is to be understood, young spirit." As Seth continued, he underlined the symbols in the sand with his finger. "In everything there is simple design and purpose."

Aman stared at the symbols as Seth returned to the root with no further word. The shepherd had his orders from the strong elder and needed to head to the leah as commanded. Still he wished to stay longer, to hear more from the warrior who spoke little but imparted much. Yet instead of biding him for more, Aman stepped out of the tent with a meager glance of marvel before he headed for the pasture.

Though the sun shone bright upon the village, the day was still early and no other villager met the morning air for the day's work. As Aman strolled through the village he noticed the little that needed to be done. The wool tents were filled with thick clothes and only a handful of bushels remained to be sown. This would certainly make Hala happy, as she would likely wriggle out of her duties with little convincing. More likely she would avoid the knitting tents altogether and spend the next few days in the fields with her father, away from suspecting eyes.

Grain baskets were piled high and wide inside the herb tents and blushed with fresh fragrance of flavor. The next grand harvest would not come for several hundred days as the fertile fields were fully milled and seeded. Even so, should any work be needed Lathan could not help. Aman wondered if he truly betrayed his friend by not informing anyone sooner of Lathan's excitement and intent upon the Rim. His words spoken more hastily would certainly not stop Lathan's mischief. But might they have given his father and Ephese more time to catch him before the re`em struck? Perhaps Jin was right in blaming him, and perhaps all the others would do the same when they were well.

Elias stood at the stone-fenced pasture gate with his back turned to its entrance. The normal surprise jolt at his back would not be attempted as Aman was too troubled for jollies. Still Elias glanced over his shoulder with a smirk as the boy approached, as if he expected some spring in the boy's step that would entertain him.

When Aman finally reached the elder's side, Elias grumbled immediately to cut quick any words the boy intended. "To the hilltop, quickly." Aman frowned but followed without any question.

"Do you see your herd?"

Aman looked at the elder momentarily, then looked into the pasture where his father's seven sheep grazed the morning grass apart from the other flocks who licked the early dew. Aman found their sparseness peculiar as sheep found morning warmth in huddles, particularly when they where sheared. Elias answered no curiosity and went along in his command.

"Mariah has begun to wean from her mother's side. Only two months ago was she the slight size of my wrist."

Aman smiled as Elias looked down at him with a grin. The elder then sighed and shut his eyes for a few moments. When the elder opened them with a nod, he stared out into the air with a heaviness that made Aman feel uneasy.

"A family needs but six sheep. Mariah has added one more to your count. Your father and I have agreed for you to keep her as your own. You must take her to your father's tent and keep her there. I expect you to tend to her with special care and attention young reu. Ensure no harm meets her, feed her proper and give her much rest. Return to me with her at the dawn of six days from this, when no one is awake. I will remedy your herd each day and check upon your care of her. If you stay with her constant, and bring her to me on the sixth dawn, I will teach you the lesson you have been promised." The young shepherd's eyes lit as Elias looked down at the lad, folded his arms behind his robe then walked back down the hill toward the pasture entrance.

Aman swallowed with hesitation as he watched the elder stroll away. The boy was filled with wonder, there were too many questions and too many matters of excitement for him to allow the elder to leave so easily. He hurried after him, "Elder Elias wait…"

Elias halted and turned with a subtle hum. Aman froze as the elder waited patiently. The boy could not find the words to reveal his wonder as too many images played along his mind. Elias raised his brow and half turned to continue his waltz.

"Wait, elder, please," Aman called as he finally mustered his question. "What happened, what was it that I saw?"

Elias cocked his head and arched his brow. "What was it that you saw, young reu?"

Aman panted, "I saw something with you, up on the hill. It was like a white fire, but it did not burn you and it… What was it?"

Elias smiled and looked at his feet before responding, "What you saw was a being of holy magnificence. And by virtue of being in his presence, you have been hallowed."

Aman's expression grew puzzled. He shook his head and questioned further, "I do not understand, what is hallowed, what happened to me?"

# Chapter Two    *The Fall of Candor*

Elias cleared his throat, turned his back to the boy, and continued on his way. "Return to me in six dawns young reu, I will remedy your flock and meet you at the pasture gate to see Mariah."

The elder then bellowed his call to Jebas' sheep and instantly Mariah came trotting toward the boy who stood with frustration. He looked down at the lamb and sighed. He wondered why the elders were acting so peculiar yet would dare not press them.

Mariah pressed her head into Aman's leg in demand of his attention. With a simple sigh, the boy lifted the lamb onto his shoulder and headed out of the pasture.

The day would see no play from the three delighting children and indeed much rest for the entire village.

\*         \*         \*

Night air was warm with the bonfire heat and basins simmering delightful scents of savory hyssop. The bright yellow and orange glowed over those gathered round the bonfire, where the elder prophet Jodia held an audience. Laborers, the men of the pitch, mason, and hunt were come to listen and enlighten their hearts with ancient teaching. Such was the custom of the village, though this was met with silent grumble among some who perceived no purpose, no explanation in the ways of their fathers and thus desired no adaptation to the old ways.

The night would not follow the same course of silent discontent turned indifference. A seed was planted through the sting of the looming enemy of the border. And from this deception would come a hushed insurgence against the ways the elders taught. Even so, not all was obscure to the father's of Candor.

Ephese sat few meters outside the half circle audience gathered round with listening ears. The father sneered with quiet disdain as he twiddled a twig recovered from the Rim floor where the being of brilliant light met him. The fright of its presence had been forgotten, but its words could not escape his mind. The hunter refused to grant acceptance of the elder's lesson as the others. Instead he found flaw with each sentence and soon headed away in disgust.

His disoriented demeanor was not unseen, and he was quickly met by Dolan and Jin.

"Ephese," Dolan called, "breaking away from the lessons early, aren't you?"

Ephese glanced over his shoulder as the two hustled behind him. "And are you two not breaking away for your concerns with me."

Dolan chuckled, "No, we're breaking away for our concerns of interest. My ears can take but so much before my eyes flatten me with weary."

Ephese hummed, "Well that makes three of us. But you boys should head back before the elders find suspicion."

Jin glanced at his brother then back at the hunter, "Well, according to your account, why should we really worry of the elders' suspicion?"

Ephese paused as the two positioned themselves in front of him. He did not know what to make of their presence, yet would engage them. "You gathered by fire to listen to the elders, then come after me as if I will teach you as them. Do you believe them or me?"

The two paused for a brief moment and glanced at the crowd now beyond earshot. "You told us the other night of the being, seen with your very eyes." Jin responded, "I don't believe either way, but if you've seen something then surely this being would be willing to prove itself to us as well."

# Chapter Two

## The Fall of Candor

Ephese squinted at the two before he took a fleeting look at the audience round the bright flame. Several other men looked back at the three periodically, with attempts to appear attentive to Jodia. Ephese brought his attention back to the boys, "I see others are not foreign to what you have heard from me."

Dolan looked away as Jin folded his arms. The older brother answered, "We did not hold our tongue, even so none we've told have voiced rejection."

Ephese cocked his head to one side before he sniffed and pushed through them to continue to his tent.

"Not all of Candor feels these elders teach the proper way." Dolan hastened, "You've lived for fifty years here, others seventy years and some hundreds. We do as the elders say we should, go as they say, believe as they say. 'Such are the ways of Adam, who pleased the Creator...' and so forth. But must his ways be ours?"

Ephese paused and looked back at the boys who stood unwavering in their intrigue. He glanced peculiarly at Jin who stared back emotionless. "You would believe there is another way, young Benjin? I sensed so much disdain for my words the other night in your case."

Jin nodded hesitantly, "If there is another way, better than that of sacrifice and labor from morning to night, a way that works to give men more from this cursed ground... then I would be a fool not to listen."

Ephese lifted his head with doubt.

"Whether we believe you or not, hunter, you stand before us as proof." Dolan interjected, "Gone into the forbidden forest and returned unscathed. Surely, that adds some account to what you saw."

The hunter inhaled slowly as the heat from the fire began to diminish with the end of the night lesson. He nodded momentarily, "Those you have told, are they willing?" The two nodded. "Gather them. Find more to apprise as you go. In three days I will return to the great bright being as he commanded. Tell men, the promise of their desire, the fortune of Candor awaits us."

The audience disbanded and was quickly making way into the village for the night rest. Dolan and Jin parted and Ephese quickly continued his stroll to Morcial's tent so not to be seen by any suspecting eye. And with that, the seed of deception spread through the village and geared the course of wayward hearts. The days that followed would see many men prepared to follow the bullied blind to the deceit of a vicious adversary.

*   *   *

The fourth dawn passed quickly from day to night. Jebas woke calmly from sleep filled with dark visions and an eerie presence that loomed in his mind and teased with deceptive threat. He gazed blankly into the russet fibers of the animal skin that captured the warm wafts of Morcial's flamed pit. Several feet from him lay the still small boy with swelled scraps wrapped gingerly in aloe leaf mache. A subtle smirk perched upon the boy's face alluded to the gray mischief that the hamstrung hunter dwelt upon in suspicion. Jebas could shake no essence of disruption felt toward the boy as he wandered through jumbled memories and fragmented flashes. His dampened dreams envisioned through the passing nights evoked the terror of the Rim chasm, and produced greater doubt of what was to come.

Nights before, a dream so vivid jolted the unshakeable chief from slumber in cold sweat. In the dream, Jebas stood upon a hill in Candor and envisioned his son running through the camp. While Aman played joyfully, Candor groaned with

# Chapter Two  —  The Fall of Candor

solemn haze. The sun shined a blazing indigo that scorched the earth into crystal steam which reflected rays of violet that stung the eyes like daggers. Aman became lost amidst the fog and Jebas found himself helpless to reach him. As he began to search, there came a hidden force that choked his voice and weighed his body with immovable burden.

A shadow descended with bass that grumbled at the crack of wind. Jebas' eyes beheld a distant figure, child-sized, yet engulfed in smoke. The figure unveiled with sharp sinister perception. His pupils sparkled with delight and upon his face rested a familiar mischievous grin. It was Ephese's son. On his face was a fierce and threatening glare that darted Jebas' heart.

Aman reappeared, few cubits from him. Jebas watched as Lathan charged toward his son. As he pursued, Jebas lunged forward, and attempted to shout, only to be pinned upon his belly. Lathan rushed forward with intrepid speed. A roar echoed throughout Candor and the sky hummed with crimson cover. Lathan's eyes glazed into black and his skin flushed from coral to stone. He became a dark animal with rotted essence. He launched at Aman with predatory intent, claws protruded from his hands, and his skin became inflamed. Aman's screams echoed with helpless horror as the beast descended upon him.

There the dream ended, frightening and with bitter taste. The vision produced a feeble sensation with which Jebas held no familiarity. From that night, the dreams continued with eerie images the hunter could not shake.

He rose from the tormented slumber with not a wince at the sharp pain of his infliction. Morcial's wishes held no matter, Jebas was recovered in his mind and would lay no further. He eased out of the drape to look into the magenta halo of evening. The apricot glow of Candor flames dispersed softly against the night and allowed a starlit sparkled sky. Through the village he strolled but offered no attention of himself or to any other.

# Lands of Eden

*by M.Gabreyl Scrolls*

Greetings were met with a grunt or nod meant to ward away conversation.

Warmer air met his face as he neared the boiling pools of the springs. A common wonder of Candor occurred at early dusk when the bright sands of the banks, which absorbed the light of day, blended with the river and rendered aqua glow that illuminated the east village. No matter how often seen by the eye, the marvel mesmerized men into distant drift.

Jebas placed his feet into the warm water and mused as the glow reflected against his pupil. His mind began to travel, yet he had not sauntered senselessly. Beside him stood the great shepherd Elias, who gazed ahead in heavy thought. The hunter knelt and scooped water over his face and hair.

"Though I look distant, you have my ears," the ever perceptual elder started. Jebas rubbed his chin and gazed into the glow with no response. Yet Elias needed no reply to dignify his assumption, "I know of your journey, Jebas. A man who has gone into the dark forest and seen what you have...You seek answers for—"

"—I do not seek answers from you, elder," Jebas interrupted as he swiped his face again. He slurped a small amount of water through his fingers, spat back into the river and rose with a stern look ahead. "I know the Abba speaks through you, but He can also answer me directly of what I seek."

Elias glanced at the hunter and nodded in agreement then smirked and looked off into the distance. "Still you do have questions. Be my answers the same as our Abba or not, I cannot say. They are answers nonetheless." The elder looked out again in anticipation of Jebas' response. Whether the hunter desired the answers Elias would give, the need to rid himself of questions his mind could not satisfy outweighed the pride he often exuded toward the old men.

# Chapter Two — The Fall of Candor

Still Jebas kept quiet, long in thought and images that swirled in a mind that could make no reason. Elias pressed him, "Perhaps you'll enlighten me of what you have seen. To at least clear your head of falsery."

Jebas responded by clearing his throat, "I have been unable to remember what I have seen. I still feel the fright and darkness, but all I see is shadowed."

Jebas squinted for some time into the bright glow, enveloped in lost memory. He then relayed what he could fathom of the night moments before he entered the dark forest. "The beasts of the vast meadows that stalked us, they chased until the opening of the dark forest. There they held rampage in fear that even I smelled from their flesh. They would not follow us further. Only their howls and barks at the forest went onward. What held them at length is what I now believe should spark our doubts."

As Jebas mused, something came to him and he leaned upon discernment of his own. "You know already."

Elias looked down for a brief moment with no response. Jebas studied the elder's reaction to see his notion upheld. "Even before now you have known. And it is true. Something looms among our borders."

Elias was still and offered no answer.

"This place was tainted by beast and dark animals, creatures of wild… unnatural prowess." The hunter continued through Elias' silence. "And these beings return to lay claim of our village. You know this?" Even while Jebas questioned the elder, he had already deciphered the answer in his mind. Whatever he beheld in the Rim, whatever shook his memory of recall, was indeed something grim and far beyond the essence of any earthly thing ever witnessed. And if such meant the small harm caused upon him, even more must be meant against Candor.

# LANDS OF EDEN

by M. Gabreyl Scrolls

Elias held his response for a long moment and broke without instance of his concentration that traveled the vast meadows. Not until a gentle breeze that ushered sparks from near flames did the elder finally speak. "Few men of today's age give thought to the great evil that has hid long enough among the lairs of Eden. Now on the brink of dark force, Candor stands unaware, a clay bowl to be shattered against stone. If there be a dark force gathering against Candor, these are not the same as seen in days of old. Same in dark intent for the land here, yes. Yet ravenous to dare mount against a land promised to Adam's bond."

Jebas paused and combed the horizon with his glare. "You speak of something more threatening then," he responded with a stern voice, "something that has long since chased the promises given to men." The elder stared into Jebas' discerning eyes without response. "I know of what you speak. And if it is true, who can believe that we of this realm promised to Adam should have no doubt for what threatens?"

Jebas continued, "How long have I heard you elders insist we are simple men? When has promise been kept in the wayward hands of simple men? As was the promise of the Great Garden snatched and now we toil till night for fertile soil. The promise of nations from Adam's loins split as Cain struck his brother with a poisoned heart. Where was Seth's promised dominion as men turned to rebellion and false ways?" The hunter waited for contest to his words yet none came from the elder. Jebas continued, "Men have allowed the venom within to make them neglectful, turned their hands for idle purpose, this is true of Candor, this is true of Eden. And I know this, that nothing comes but a scourge from wayward hands. How is this promised place to be held if the great deceptor comes?"

Jebas glanced at Elias who stared off with down-turned eyes and barely flinched at the allusion to the dark prince. The elders knew and long believed the dark being's existence. Yet

# Chapter Two

## The Fall of Candor

Elias would not possess the same fear as few displayed at the simple mention of his name upon their lip. Jebas held this same spirit.

Elias suffered his mind to soothe the doubt of the hunter, and greater to quell his own of what he dreaded was to come upon Candor's gate.

"What is promised is always the conquering quest of Sëtan," Elias responded with calm, "he will not end until he has fully taken and destroyed what the Alpha has granted us." He looked at Jebas squarely, "In this manner you are true, hunter."

Jebas squinted at the elder and felt the sense of defeat, yet the old man's face held no amount of despair. Deep within, Jebas knew defeat had not and would not overcome Elias. "You must never speak as if you have no hope, hunter. I know this is not of you, it is why you speak with me here, you believe there is more for your land. This is what is needed to keep these people when the deceptor comes."

Jebas lifted his chin at the elder's confidence. "Do you hold onto hope as well, elder," he spoke with a glint, "can you truly admit no doubt of your own for this place?"

Elias smiled. "I have sought hope, prayed and meditated long through my ages, hunter," he answered. "That what is certain to come upon Candor would not. That our Abba would spare Adam's children of evil hand. That has long been my hope. Knowing what will inevitably come, I hope now in that what threatens will not offer full dismay for Candor, That from our people will come greater for all of Eden."

"What do you believe to come from our people?" Jebas pressed.

Elias hummed briefly, "Not what, who… and you know in whom I believe. And have you yet trained your heart for the same trust? It is only your mind that denies the promise in your blood."

The hunter's eyes narrowed, "You speak of my son." Elias did not answer. "I have taught him to learn from you, to hear lessons and seek wisdom. Yet not to become so fully minded as you elders. That is not to be his way." The hunter hesitated briefly. He then turned his body to the elder. "You have intended to give him lessons beyond a child's understanding. Aman is a small boy, yet ready to be filled with so much belief."

Elias waited calmly and responded with caution. "Aman desires to be filled himself, it is his own wish to learn more. In teaching him to seek wisdom, you hunter, have made him seek like none else in the village. Which is found admirable to ones like myself."

"He has not reached the age of understanding," Jebas countered, "he does not know who he is, where he is from."

"He is a child of great promise. You know more than any, Jebas—"

"—I am the son of Jabal, elder," Jebas remarked with scorn. He turned his face in shame and anger. The chief long hid his descent from men and even his offspring so that they would not find taint in their being. None other than the elders knew he was of Cain's line, and none of them scorned him as one dellamy blood.

The hunter shook his head and looked away briefly. "My descendants know only simplicity, not wisdom. Ours is not the blood of promise."

Elias cocked his head as he faced Jebas, who looked back intently. "Jebas, you are a son of Elimelech, of Methuselah, and Enoch. This has been bestowed upon you, and you have bestowed this upon your sons. You have sought Adam's way,

## Chapter Two — The Fall of Candor

instilled such search in your sons. Aman is indeed our son, as are you."

The hunter skimmed the elder's face. He returned to his trance into the glowing river. As he settled his nerves, the elder sighed a deep long breath full of thought. "You know that I believe much of the young reu Aman. And you know why," he broke, "Yes, perhaps I spur him more than I should. But what I believe of him matters little. There is much more trust built in him for you than any other in Candor. There are days soon to come upon him that will test his heart. And if he is to become what I believe he must be for the rest of Candor, then what matters is what you, great hunter, believe of him and have trained him. My lessons for him come only from your intent for him to be wise among men, just as you. You have trained your heart in expectance for him, and must show him the way to follow. For your trust in him will be a reliance upon which he will stand all the days of his life."

Jebas stared back at Elias with calm settling as the message appeared to mend his spirit. The questions slowly scattered in the challenge that the strong hunter faced. What Jebas believed of Aman was just as hopeful, if not greater than even the elders. With no other reason to pull but the prophetic words of the boy's mother did Jebas set his heart to ensure Aman would find his quest and become the great man intended for him. Indeed he had instilled in Aman instruction that he would depend upon all the days of his life.

"There is aim still, to assemble men for what is to come, to warn Candor so that we can keep this ground against the enemy."

Elias looked into the clay and hummed with sorrow. "I know your courage hunter, as those of many others who do not desire trespass upon these grounds." The elder looked away with a sigh, "We have thrived here far long in peace and sanctity. Yet the enemy strikes men's hearts with great fear far removed from sanctity. Such fear that men are froze in his rumble. We elders are not called to lead men so filled." He looked over at Jebas with no essence of confidence in his eyes. "Candor will not stand with men who do not will against a seed which taints their hearts."

Jebas could not answer Elias' solemn words. He wanted to charge the elder with a trust which he could scarcely summon. So mirrored was his mind after those of the elders of Candor who believed men were far corrupted against Adam's way to stand against darkness. Yet he would not allow his doubts, as the others, to craft a heart of retreat. "This is my home, I will not bow my hand to such darkness. In great charge will the elders simply bow against the coming gloom?"

"Do not mistake prudence for fear, Jebas," Elias responded with lifted brow and stern voice. "Those of us who can stand have wrestled against fiends far beyond what the minds of these here could comprehend —."

"— Then stand again elder," Jebas pleaded, "for prudence will not halt an enemy so bent. If Candor is to fall, at least let it fall with resistance of its men, such resistance that we are not chased from refuge to refuge again."

Elias stared in silence as Jebas awaited his answer to a challenge which his ears were not unfamiliar. Yet the elder shook his head. "The men's hearts are far filled with dark seed, the Alpha will not keep His hedge for their continuance."

"And how of what the Alpha will do for Candor do you know elder —"

"— This I know hunter, and question me no longer!" the old man grumbled with fierce eyes. Jebas stared back at him with even stronger gaze. Yet he spoke no further objection. The two turned their attention back over the stilled pools as the wind hustled. Through long silence Jebas finally pressed the elder for purpose.

# Chapter Two — The Fall of Candor

"What then, Elias, does Candor abandon our flourish and flee?" Even the taste of the word troubled the hunter.

Elias sighed with humble spirit, "Candor does not flee hunter, people will spare themselves and let this land become the enemies who prey upon it. There is much better beyond for us. We will seek refuge across the Pison, into the east lands of Havilah, where we will secure Candor and thrive."

Jebas scoffed, "And if we are tested in Havilah with more threat, what then? How are we to thrive if we must continually spare ourselves from lands?"

"The Alpha will spare Candor, we will not need to contend with the enemy there."

Jebas cocked his head and studied the elder who appeared to doubt his own words, "If these men are so tainted that they will not stand with you against the enemy, how will they follow you onto the east?"

"Because there will be nothing left for them to remain."

At that, the hunter dropped his tensed shoulders and released his frown. Sadness engulfed him and he looked off into the distance with dismay. Neither spoke a word for several moments. Each charged inside to fight the coming threat, yet each in full knowledge of the futility of their aims.

Jebas lifted his eyes and sighed long and full of tire. The hunter pondered and suddenly smirked with humor. "My sons complain that Aman holds onto one of my flock by the night." Elias smiled shortly as Jebas looked at him. "You intend to teach him the lesson of the lamb. Is my son to be guarded rightly on his dawn?"

Elias nodded, "Seth will wait among the leaves of the Candora, he will ensure Aman meets no harm."

Jebas grunted and turned his back to return to his camp. Elias pressed again before Jebas trailed away, "You were called to this land hunter, and have served Candor with prominence.

Men who see you as their chief, will also follow you when the time comes. Whatever threat exists round this place, trust wisdom, and seek refuge into the east, for your fate will be grave if you contend with the enemy."

Jebas squinted with a league of frustration that the hunter would need to swallow in relented protest. He stood for several moments more as Elias stole one final glimpse of the horizon, then walked off with no further word. Jebas skimmed the dark as the euphoric glows of the ponds dimmed. Much of his time passed spent in worry before he returned to his tent to find Aman fast asleep with head rested upon a scribe. Under his cheek were his scribbles, *ptouhareu ev positisou*, "design and purpose." Jebas meditated over his son through the night until slumber overcame him. With a sleep that was free of troubled dreams, Jebas reminded his heart to empower his son for his coming day.

## *The Sacrifice*

Mariah continued to poke Aman's ear with her cold hoof while he laid on the warm mud snoring as drool streamed slowly from the corner of his mouth. The sixth dawn had come. The boy had not seen sound sleep in days since he began taking close watch of the small lamb.

Aman held Elias' command to guard the young cub more faithfully than the elder thought. He would not let an eye close until Mariah flopped onto her side and rested on her own. His brothers were not much help to his cause as they began to tease the poor lamb from the moment Aman brought her home. He reserved to protecting Mariah from their bullies by forcing himself to even later watch while she slept. Only after Jebas' return did Aman rest with comfort. Aman could hold no longer

## Chapter Two — The Fall of Candor

from five restless nights, and slumped away with Mariah still baaing at the dim tent firelight.

The boy awakened to the gooey sensation of Mariah's saliva traveling down his neck. His hair was drenched with the scent as she had found comfort in gnawing on the young boy's curls. Aman was disgusted and immediately rose with Mariah. He peeked at his father who rested with quiet breath. Aman threw the veil and hurried to the Candor springs.

The mist of the warm water raised high into the morning atmosphere and glistened with brilliant colors of red and purple as vapor cooled and fell onto the fertile soil. Aman cautiously cupped the hot water in his hands and swiped the pool over his face, hair and neck. When fully refreshed, he peered through the great hover over the river. Deep within the mist, a dark presence existed, blurred in the prisms that reflected the salve of the golden sun. Aman rubbed his eyes and squinted in attempt to cut through the haze. A faint green glow drudged through the fog with a ghostly moan.

"Young one," startled Elias from behind. Aman turned and faced Elias who stood in front of him with a demeanor of command. "It is time."

The small boy glanced once more into the fog. The glow vanished, the hum unheard, and nothing of attention to keep him staring. So he lifted Mariah into his arms and followed the great elder into the pasture.

Another day had come but much of Candor was at rest from the labors that routinely kept the village bustling. The stillness was eerie. Aman followed the elder up the pasture hills. The animals were silent. Some milled with unrest as if something dreary loomed. Mariah even began to moan as the boy held her at his side and Aman could not fight the anticipation of something bleak.

Elias lead with determination, not turning one look at the young lad. He headed down the pasture hill toward the north village tents where the giant Candor totem rose triumphantly to grasp the first rays of the morning. Mariah began to lick Aman's hand with each continuing step as Elias guided them through tall wheat field and finally to a clear flat outside the village tents.

The elder stopped. His garbs glided on the gentle breeze flowing from the Caspian forest in the distance. The morning air crystallized his long sigh for but a moment, then released it into the calm wind. After which the elder stood for several moments, staring and waiting, as if for something to show presence before him. He held out his hand and beckoned Aman to his side.

Aman approached with a gasp which the old man quickly halted with his finger pressed gently upon his lips. Another cool breeze lifted the shoulder-draped locks of the elder's hair. Again he sighed with eyes closed for a brief period, then fixed them upon the distant nothing in prospect of something Aman was becoming too frustrated to wait upon.

Mariah seemed just as impatient from the confusion and began to jostle in Aman's arms. She pushed her hooves into his elbows to pry free. She kicked and spun in his grip as he wrestled to steady her. Elias offered no help and she was steadily freeing herself of the small shepherd.

"Mariah…calm, please." Aman struggled to keep her still as she began to moan. With a swift hoof to Aman's forearm, she was free. Aman yelped as she fell the short distance onto the ground, landed on her side but managed to scamper forward before Aman could catch her.

Elias continued to stare nonchalantly. Aman wondered why the elder made no attempt to call after her. But his concern for the suddenly dazed elder would offer nothing. Mariah was

# Chapter Two             *The Fall of Candor*

his lamb, under his protection, and no one would be more responsible to her than he. He darted after the animal with full speed. Mariah was always a feisty little being, and it showed in how quick she trotted ahead in spite of Aman gaining ground.

"Mariah, stop, tut~tut…tut~tut…" Aman's attempts to call after her failed, just as his attempts to whistle and converse as he had heard Elias do on several occasions in the pasture. She was nearing the forest edge when Aman tripped and fell onto his belly. The boy slapped the ground in frustration then jolted to his feet only to find the lamb had vanished into the forest. "No!" Aman shouted before he took a look back at Elias, who stood with arms folded, unmoved. He shook his head and turned toward the forest. "Mariah…Mariah…tut~tut. Come back!"

The boy began to walk forward as the trees seemed to boast their prowess with grand shadow. Through a clearing the echoes of snapped twigs triggered his senses. He hurried into the woods without regard. He called several times for the little lamb but could neither see trail nor sense direction from her moans.

The forest floor was covered with thick mud moistened from the morning air. Several dead twigs littered the fertile fern floor. Leaves danced in the long shafts of sunrays as they descended to the ground. Aman looked at the canopy above which glittered like a starry green sky. He took the opportunity to grasp a sunbeam in his hand. He mumbled as the warmth of the morning sun engulfed his arm. He called again but his voice only echoed back. But his shouts did not go unheard.

Aman's scent had already carried through the sparse forest as sediment upon river. It found the cold black nostrils and dry tongue of a sinister creature with fowl intention. The boy's voice was all the creature needed to find its prey with ease. Its paws quietly propelled its sneaking body behind trees and away from the boy's view. Its golden eyes were pristine. The beast fixed its sight on the boy's small frame and glossed its fangs with its tongue as it inched closer to Aman's heels. Though poised perfectly for its strike, a simple gash from behind would not suit its predatory nature.

Aman perceived the presence behind him. As he brought his arm from the morning glow, a menacing growl shook chill into his core.

There was an adage in Eden spoken to warn the curious heart, 'Feet spent wandering will only meet hungering eyes.' And no eyes were more insatiable than that of the grim creature that snarled at Aman's heels. Though darkness drove many beasts wild with territorial prowess, the woodlands knew the true rulers. Predators both by night and day, fearless and merciless in carnage, eyes as bright as a fallen star. Their prey heard only the thunder of their growl before demise and all else cringed at the dare of their howls. Behind the small boy lurched the great grey wolf of the wood.

Aman turned and saw the wolf sneer at him. It set all paws with teeth drooling and wild fur clumped with dirt. Its yellow eyes accented the threat as it neared and stood at the height of Aman's chest. Each pounce closer caused the boy to breathe heavily. Few human encounters with the great grey wolf could be honored with recount. And those that were, only incited immense fear among listeners. Aman pondered this as he stared into the creature's heartless eye. And with each thump of his heart was the wolf spurred by the smell of fright.

Aman took a quick step back and instantly slipped into a shallow brown muck. The beast growled in reaction and lunged forward with a start. But it did not attack.

Instead, it toyed more with the boy's scent, strolled over Aman's legs with mouth agape, saliva oozing down its sharp canines. The monster nudged the boy's knee and as if almost

# Chapter Two                                    *The Fall of Candor*

with a smirk from the boy's hesitation, the animal glided its tongue along Aman's finger to tease its taste.

Instinct suddenly set as Aman gripped a clump of mud and lunged it directly at the animal's eye. The beast yelped and sputtered away as Aman pushed himself through the muck onto his feet. When the beast recovered, it jolted after the boy, who was in full sprint.

A wild howl pierced through the chaos as it charged with pace thundering. Its claws flung clumps of mud and dried vegetation. Aman panted heavily as he raced forward. He glanced over his shoulder periodically to see what distance he had created from the beast. He was creating none. He decided to lose the animal in the only manner he knew. As the wolf barked for Aman's halt, the boy lifted his heel, planted it on the trunk of a tree, and with a firm thrust, sprung himself from the bark into a flip that sent him another direction. He raced on for several paces as the sound of the brute scattered. Believing he was free, he glanced back to see if the beast was lost.

He should have known the glowing eyes would not lose sight of prey so simply. A whiff of Aman's fear brought the animal directly upon Aman's path. The boy could yet see the scavenger which lurked nearby. It hid among the tall trees and positioned itself for blind attack. Aman spun and searched as tears pooled in his eyes.

Suddenly, the animal leaped from a fallen tree and chased directly toward the boy. It fumed with each trounce upon the soil. Aman caught site of the animal and jolted off. His feet beat the forest floor with mighty force. His arms threw off the tall olive ferns and thin branches that challenged his escape. Still, with each stride, Aman felt the weight of the swifter, havoc determined hound mounting on his heels.

The beast pawed at his ankle and nearly tripped Aman onto his face. The boy managed a fleet kick into the nose of the beast which caused it to halt and sniff with agitation. It plunged its nose into the dirt and rubbed the ache on the cold ground as it writhed in a circle.

Aman continued forward into a wide hollow of the wood. Around the hollow were several moss-covered fragments of fallen trees which blocked his path. The ground concaved into a center where lime colored branches were shelled together in an oval pattern. Aman rounded the branches and hoped they could conceal him.

Yet the wolf was relentless, and no child could move quick enough for it to abandon its craving. The fiend took siege of the only escape from the clearing, clipped its claw upon the earth and snarled at Aman with a dare. The boy's mouth and eyes were wide with fright. He waited for what the animal would do. With a wild howl, the wolf proceeded into the hollow, leapt over the branches and charged forward.

Aman had no time. The beast lunged at his shoulder with teeth prepared. Aman launched into a lateral spin and tightened his arms against his chest. The wolf's teeth clenched down as it reached the boy. But it caught a remnant of Aman's clothing, and was spun off by Aman's momentum.

Aman landed on his belly, surprised his acrobatics succeeded. He glanced and saw the monster land on its feet. It slid along the damp soil but remained focused on attack. Aman hopped onto his toes and froze as the wolf paced.

Eye to eye, they gazed, both stuck in anticipation. The cool morning wind threw several dead leaves into the concave. Not another creature sounded as the contest stalled. Aman felt every instance of nature upon his brow, the clumps of mud clung to his skin, the tickle of Eden air through his ears, and drizzling sweat which soaked into his clothes. He was gripped with fear yet could not let it unsettle him from the beast's next move. The wolf inched forward with scheme of attack. Aman

# Chapter Two

*The Fall of Candor*

poised himself as the animal snarled and leaned its weight on its hind legs. It grumbled, long and steady with glared glowing vision, hairs sprung at its neck and jaws twitching over its fangs. This was enough warning that the brute was geared to rip the boy to shreds. But Aman would not be scared away again.

" C'mon…" Aman dared the animal as he took a step back to ready his arms. " C'mon!" he dared again as the dog barked with surprise.

Suddenly, the beast hurtled forward. Aman did not move an inch. He held his breath. His heart pounded faster with each foot the wolf gained. He clenched his fist and stiffened as the beast thrust upward, widened his eyes as the animal's razor sharp teeth appeared threatening to bite, lifted his hands as the mouth of the animal broadened with aim at his neck.

Aman shut his eyes instantly, fell onto his back with knees to his chest and thrust his feet into the monster's abdomen. The wolf yelped at the plunge to its gut. Aman rolled back with the weight of the animal applying dense pressure upon his knees. He gathered enough strength to straighten his back and lunged with the full force and might of his legs. He grunted with fear as he fully extended and sent the wolf airborne. It soared overhead and crashed into the nested wood where it howled in agony.

Aman rolled onto his belly and squirmed away as the wolf whined. He still was in no better shape for the exit, but thought he had done enough to allow him time for escape. Once the wolf regained its feet, it found its prey hesitant near the junction and lunged at him in rage. This time Aman dodged in time causing the dog to catch a mouth full of tree bark and moss. The canine ignored the pain, and barked ferociously as it chased after Aman who headed out the hollow.

The small shepherd panted and was ever more frightened as the monster steadied its pace from injury and howled for another strike. He tried to lose the beast in misdirection, but its charge was relentless. The animal no longer toyed and had enough. It would tear into Aman, not for taste or hunger satisfaction, nor any other reason but to end its opposition.

The boy sprinted several feet ahead of the being, glanced at the low branches of the trees towering overhead and decided to get to higher footing. He headed straight toward a tree trunk as the wolf quickly gained ground. When he reached the trunk, he once again planted his heel, leapt from the trunk and gripped a low branch. He used his momentum to swing his body up onto the stem. Shards of bark caught the animal in its eye and caused it to slow. Aman stood on the branch and gripped a higher stem above him. He swung again and wrapped the branch with his arms and legs. The boy clung tightly.

The beast snarled as Aman shimmied along the branch. Aman continued to make attempts to get higher. Several moments passed as the wolf circled below and waited for the boys grip to fail. Tears formed in the boy's eyes as his strength began to fade.

Suddenly, the branch gave way to his weight with a loud snap. Aman careened to the forest floor where the animal quickly cleared to avoid being pummeled under falling debris.

Aman landed hard on his back, but gained enough composure to roll and avoid being smashed by the tree limb. He groaned as his shoulder and leg throbbed from the impact. Yet he released all concern for his pain as it would do nothing for him in the face of the threatening beast.

The boy shuffled toward the tree trunk and looked back to see the wolf snarl with pleasure at him. It delighted in Aman's downfall as if the hunt was complete. Aman's heart pounded as the animal lunged with tease. As the beast neared, Aman attempted to give the beast another kick. But he could not lift his leg for the intense pain around his knee.

The animal sniffed at his belly with its teeth drawn for action. Aman's chest heaved as the animal's cold moist nose slid across his neck, leaving a smear of spit. The wolf's mouth opened wide, with strings of warm saliva that dripped and soaked into Aman's shirt and oozed down his chest and neck. The beast savored the fear with pleasure as it cocked its head and prepared to plunge its sharp drenched canines into the boy's tender flesh. Aman clenched his eyes and shook with silent prayer as cold tears flooded his cheeks.

Suddenly came a sound that rang like a shout, though it broke through as calm and subtle as wind. The beast moved away and stood upright. It looked off toward the origin. "Baa~ah," came the protest again, this time with more force and command than before. The wolf snarled at the small innocent creature, barked with a threat then turned his attention back on the boy.

Aman opened his eyes to see Mariah hop into the clearing and make her third protest. The beast planted a paw on Aman's chest and growled at Mariah again. Mariah stood her ground and moaned repeatedly until the wolf's full attention was set on her.

The monster circled Mariah as she stomped her hooves and panted at the monster. After several moments of impatience, the wolf lunged at Mariah's feet and chomped. Mariah dodged several times as the predator bit repeatedly. Finally, the little lamb scampered away. The wolf howled at Aman, then neglected the small shepherd for new chase.

"Mariah...No!" Aman shouted as he tried to lift himself to his feet. The animal barked viciously as it tracked the innocent lamb. Aman could hear the commotion distance from him and desperately needed to get to his feet. Though intense pain seared through his legs, he managed to limp forward. He continued to hobble as swift as he could toward the chaos.

The barks intensified. Mariah's cries grew stronger. Aman pressed his way forward with all his might. Through the muddy floor as Mariah bellowed loudly with agony and torment.

Then all went silent.

Aman pulled himself over a fallen trunk to see the vicious monster with teeth clenched round Mariah's neck. Tears instantly flooded Aman's eyes. His sorrow was quickly chased with intense anger.

Aman searched the ground, found a thick branch and snapped it over his knee. He raced toward the wolf. The branch hummed with wind-breaking speed as Aman swung with all his might. The powerful swing met the crack of the wolf's ear. The animal released the lamb and snarled only to be hit again on its other ear, a smack that spun the wolf onto its back. In attempt to cease the onslaught, the wolf rolled onto its hinds and lurched at Aman's weapon. Aman swung again, caught the open mouth of the beast with a break that flipped the animal in mid air and sent one of its razors from its mouth.

The impact was so strong that Aman could not hold the weapon and fell to his knees. The animal griped in pain and writhed in circles before it howled into retreat. He waited until the beast completely trailed off. Once alone, he looked at Mariah who lay motionless on the forest floor.

Mariah moaned with each rapid pant as blood soaked the fur of her coat. Her eyes were lazy from the gouge. The boy cried uncontrollably as he placed one hand on her belly and the other under her head. Mariah moaned one final time and licked the center of Aman's palm. As the morning air caught her last sigh, her eyes sealed in pale silence.

## Chapter Two — The Fall of Candor

Aman knelt beside her for several moments and whimpered quietly until the crown of the sun shown through the canopy. He found his way from the forest without any further disturbance.

The morning mist had cleared from the northern grasslands as Aman limped his way across the prairie. He carried the lamb on his shoulder and steadied his weight on the branch used to drive away the great grey wolf. Ahead stood Elias with his arms firmly folded across his chest, still unmoved. The elder's face was marked with perceptive sorrow as if the ordeal needed no explanation. He kept his eyes straight ahead as the boy approached, avoiding eye contact until the final moment the shepherd stopped in front of him.

Aman looked up at the elder with tears that detailed his pain. There were so many questions to ask, so much blame to assign. Why did Elias not call after Mariah, why did he not help the meager shepherd boy in the Candora? And yet ultimately, Aman knew that Mariah was his responsibility. Was this the lesson to be learned? What could be taught from such danger, fright, and sorrow?

Aman waited long for the elder to speak. After moments of meditated silence, the elder sighed heavily. "Young reu, what happened to the lamb of which you took charge?"

Sorrow flowed from the boy's eyes, yet he did not release a whimper. "There was a crazed wolf in the wood, it was going after me when Mariah came and led it away." Aman could barely speak for the regret that overwhelmed him. "She was… the wolf chased after her and it…"

He could not struggle out the words and looked down at his feet. Elias knelt by the lad and lifted his chin with his long finger. He thumbed the streams of tears from Aman's cheeks, gripped his shoulders tightly. "Aman, this dear lamb led the wolf away for the sake of your life. This was very brave of it.

Sad as it may be to have lost her, you have gained much by such sacrifice."

Aman sniffled uncontrollably as Elias held his gaze. The boy wrapped his understanding around the meaning of Mariah's sacrifice. He would not have been spared if she did not take Aman's place. He wiped the back of his wrist across his nose as Elias continued.

"My boy, hear my instruction, in everything that you say and do, in every rising sun and silver moonlit night, be as Mariah was to you this morn. Be of great courage, strength, and willing to give yourself for the endurance of another. This is sacrifice young reu. Make your life thankful for what this innocent lamb has given back to you." Aman nodded and looked away only to have his attention brought back by Elias' warm hand. "Aman, this is the heart you must have. For all your days, remember the heart of a lamb."

At that the elder brushed Aman's shoulders gently and smiled with reassurance. Elias took the lamb in his arm. He took a jagged stone in his hand and used it to clear a lock of the Mariah's wool. He handed it to Aman and instructed him to give it to his father. The elder then turned and headed back toward the village with no other word.

Aman stood for several moments and took a long look at the forest. His mind was littered with confusion and sadness. So many questions riddled and yet nothing could be said to soothe him. He wiped the last tear that would fall from his face that day and headed confidently in Elias' footsteps.

\*          \*          \*

The young shepherd entered his tent with no intended disruption. His appearance caused his father to sit upright. Blood stained the side of the boy's neck, cheek and chin. His

# Chapter Two — The Fall of Candor

clothes and hands were muddy with claret soaked dirt and purple clots. Though the sight was alarming, Jebas remained calm as he looked at him.

"What is this upon your hands and face young reu?"

Aman glanced at his brothers who frowned back at him with a crooked eye.

"He has lost one of your sheep father." Jin trumpeted as he marched toward Aman and sniffed his neck with a scowl. "He kept it here so long, and now he has lost it."

"It is true," matched Dolan, "He brought it here over several nights. Where has it gone?"

Jin sniffed again, "I smell the stench of hound on him, its blood fumes from his cloth. He lost your lamb to the wood and a timber has slew it."

Aman kept his focus on his father through his brother's accusations. Aman spoke nothing, and neither did Jebas, who stared without waver. "Is this true, Aman, you have lost one of my flock?"

Aman waited for a few moments as Jin pressed against him with flared eyes. The boy turned and looked at him, then faced his father and nodded, "It is true father, I have lost the cub, Mariah, to the Candora wood." The boy held out the lock of Mariah's wool which was colored mahogany.

Jin gripped Aman's cloak round the small boy's neck and yanked him rudely, "Reushamim—"

"Release him," Jebas commanded. Jin peeked at his father who stared at Aman with no sign of fury.

"Father, he, who was responsible for the wound upon your leg, who spent our night to chaos because he held his tongue? Now he has failed his responsibility to your possession! You must deal with him properly, as a father does, with your staff upon his hind!"

# Lands of Eden

*by M.Gabreyl Scrolls*

"I said release him, Benjin," Jebas stated with more force. "You do not decide how I am to deal with my own flesh."

Jin stared at Jebas with disbelief and eyes hinting of disgust. He looked down at his smaller brother and seethed before he released his cloak. Jin then looked at Dolan with a mutual glare, hissed and hurried out the tent. Dolan walked pass his father with a brief look in his direction. Jebas answered his glance with order, "If you hold his mind too, then off as well with him, if not, then see how I father my loved sons."

Dolan glanced at Aman who looked ahead without a word. He returned his eyes upon his father, yet he could not keep his eyes on him without shame. He followed after Jin in anger.

Aman and his father kept their focus on each other as if nothing else existed round them. After a long sigh, Jebas finally asked, "Aman, have I not put you in the keep of my flock. Yet you stand stained with my pride. What happened that my cub is lost young reu?"

Aman swallowed and relayed what happened to his father. He refused to allow sorrow to shake him. The tale came with a gentle quiver that did not mark fright, but overwhelming prowess which the boy never felt. "She ran into the wood and I tried to keep her from the wolf, but he found her before I could stop it. So I had to do what I did, to help her…it's just she… it had gotten to her too soon. She sacrificed herself for me…"

Jebas nodded slowly, took the wool from Aman's hand and sighed. "Give me the branch you used to drive away the timber." Aman handed the branch to Jebas who began to scrape away the bloodied bark at one end. Aman watched intently as Jebas scrubbed several layers from the end until the heart of the branch showed with a smooth surface and curved shape. Jebas then took the lock into his hand and began to weave strands together. He tied the woven lock tightly around

# Chapter Two — The Fall of Candor

the carved area, set the branch upright, and looked into his son's eyes.

"Did you study how I have carved son?" Aman nodded. His father then handed him the carver, stood to his feet with a grunt and folded Aman's fingers over the tool, "I have lost a cub to wandering, and the blood of my flock has been spilled so that my son could return to me and not the devour of the grey wolf." Jebas stared solemnly, " because of this, I am grateful."

Jebas strained briefly before he handed Aman the branch and sighed long breathes full of concern. "Travel to the warm springs and clean your face and hands. Take this to the river, and mold from it a staff. This will remind you of the sacrifice you have earned this morning. By nightfall, return to me, for you are no longer a simple shepherd, but called now to your greater purpose."

Jebas waited for but a moment as the boy released his sobs. He then left the tent as Aman meditated further. The boy looked round the tent for a moment before he followed his father's command. That day would see the final hour of the peaceful village.

## The Night Scatter

The day wore and several men ended early their labors as the seed that occupied their minds became the pursuit of their hands and feet. No hint of this seed displayed in these who plotted a course hidden from suspicion. A course stripped from the influence of wisdom, not to be altered even by the doubt of some who fixed their hearts to journey with uncertainty and the sense of a grim threat that was impatient for them within the dark border.

# Lands of Eden
### by M. Gabreyl Scrolls

Shadow thickened round maddened figures halted midst the trunks and root. They seethed in scum and spit with destructive delight. Poison seeped through the realms and called their prey forth from the untouched gates. Gambits beguiled by false ambition in wait of the brooding monsters meticulously meddling with a sting so potent that none within the reaches of its point would prevail. Only needed was the cover of night which would cite their vicious acts.

The plot took birth once the final velvet ray lifted from the totem of Candor. The men gathered quietly at the helm of the southern fields, deceived for the promise of the great being of light. Their exodus was scattered to avoid detection until night fell when their journey met cover. The men convened toward that jagged gateway with a march that resounded like wings. These souls raced across the open country toward the gloomy trees. Among them were several young hunters, scribes, and fieldsmen, convinced easily astray from the old teaching. Dolan and Jin ran alongside Ephese, spurred with pride and distaste of the old way's progression.

Cackles in the shadow fired off rhythmically as the sound of wild animals. Several of the men's eyes widened and heads turned in fear at the warning shouts and growing darkness that stole the vision of the blue moon. Yet none turned back. The Rim was their only aim and nothing would pin their hopes for Candor but the promise and splendor offered from within. Their pace ceased upon the brink of the bleak forest. Several panted with unrestrained fatigue. Ephese, however, agitatedly hastened them forward.

Dolan surveyed the Rim border as the fright that gripped him nights before returned. "Ephese, my eyes and ears do not spare me fear. Listen to the calls around you, around us all." From deep within the enemy fused ear-pounding ravenous howls that vibrated the scores' bones with powerful

## Chapter Two — The Fall of Candor

intimidation. "This noise bids me to return or at least gather myself in guard. Are you certain this is what we must do?"

That night would never again see a more pivotal moment in which a single choice divided a clan among two paths. A choice which could have forever transfixed the ages of Eden, stowed tumultuous battles and curtained a darkness which transcended the simple knowledge of evils.

Ephese stared fiercely into the eyes of those huddled round him with the fate of Candor and destiny of Eden in his voice.

"Forward."

\*       \*       \*

Night descended with a tranquil mood accompanied with bond fires that lit the parish. Villagers were calmed with the melodious chirps of night crawlers and nocturnal creatures, rhythms which often soothed the fatigue of steady day labor. Few noticed the absence of the men, fathers, brothers, sons, love ones gone in the cover of dark, in search of guidance from ways gone aloof. Puzzled minds were chased off, if only for few moments, in the splendor of a calm night that showed no distinction in midst of looming chaos. Still the unsettled hearts, Jebas, Elias, Seth and others met cold suspicion through the night, and geared for the destined hour with vigilant eyes.

As the midnight neared Jebas found his mind troubled for his eldest sons who had not answered his earlier request. He rose to his feet and began to stroll through the village in search of them. As he wandered there seemed a sinister tease in the air which mocked his mind and rattled his bone. The late air saw few villagers, mothers and children, waiting outside wigwams with weary eyes and impatient breath. Jebas gathered perplexity from the gazes. He wandered no further, stood for long moments noticing the grave unrest that unsettled Candor.

When Jebas decided to finally continue his search, it was Morcial who rushed toward him with throngs of distress that would stir the night.

"Chief, I am grateful to find you, you must come quickly."

Jebas followed Morcial through the village where some had succumb to the midnight comfort and left concerns for the missing men to dreams. Morcial hurried Jebas into his tent where the drizzle of spilled balsam trailed from a vacant hammock. The tent displayed no other sign of disarray than the extinguished kindle where the balm doused the flame. Suddenly, the boy held under Jebas' puzzled eye was among the missing. A scene that only thickened his wonder.

"He has been gone since dusk," Morcial stated, "I searched the village for him."

Jebas glanced at Morcial, "His father, Ephese, seek him out and speak with him concerning his son. I am sure he has gathered him."

Morcial shook his head in protest, "His father has shown no place here. Even when the boy was first brought. I only heard his whispers at times outside the tent. But never spoke... and now even he is missing."

Jebas cocked his head with narrowed eyes, "Whispers..."

"Yes," Morcial responded "at night, he whispered constantly. He stands outside the tent near the bed, but he never enters to check upon his son. He spoke into his chest as if he conversed with another."

Jebas looked away briefly, "Did you hear what he spoke?"

"I did not, but since his son was brought here many others have convened with him. Speaking in quiet as he. And these too have been lost to my eyes this night."

Jebas stepped toward the empty hammock and studied it with growing question.

# Chapter Two — The Fall of Candor

"—Jebas," Morical interrupted, "your sons have been among those who I've seen convening with him."

Jebas squinted and began to breathe heavily as he turned and faced the doctor. His eyes were fierce with the blend of anger and concern. Immediately he flushed from Morcial tent and looked over the village. Those whose worry maintained their alertness held faces of urgent call. The chieftain marked each face as he hurried onto his tent. He found Aman, still and sound with shut eyes, curled at peace upon the dirt.

Jebas looked round the tent without any demand, yet much frantic. Missing were several counts of his hunting tools, signs which Jin and Dolan left of their exodus. Distressed, the father threw forth the opening of his tent, paused and looked toward the south bend which bulged with daring darkness. Instantly, he became as those in conflict with the panic. He spun, dropped to his knees and moaned into his hands. He punched the earth, gripped the dust, and threw a handful into the air with a grunt. His muscles shook at the surge of powerless emotion as he punched again and again. The hunter threw out his hands and released with uproar. His voice echoed through the village, shook Aman from slumber and brought many eyes upon him.

Several of the hunters crowded round the crouched chief as he ranted. Aman peeked his head from the tent to see his father bowed in craze. Uriah was the first to calm his shouts with a stern palm upon his shoulder. Jebas huffed as the passion spurred his mind with action. He answered Uriah's hand with a call upon himself.

"I must retrieve my sons," was all he said. Then leapt to his feet and rushed into his tent. Others who witnessed the commotion milled with question. Jebas hurried round his tent and gathered the tools that remained. Aman watched his father's frenzy and did his best to avoid hindrance. After Jebas gathered all he could, he commanded his son to his side. He piled several tools onto a cloth, counted them, then wrapped them together. As he finished securing what he could into the seams of his robe, he knelt by his son and gripped his shoulders firmly.

"Aman, I must go." Aman frowned with mass confusion. "Your brothers have gone across the plain into the Rim as your friend Lathan." The boy's eyes widened and heart began to throb. He shook his head as Jebas continued. "I must go after your brothers this time."

"You cannot, you will not return again—"

His protests were quickly halted at his father's order. "I must go son, but I will return." Aman's eyes pooled with fear. Jebas stared back at him with sincerity in his promise. "I will return, you will wait for me by east springs. I want you to take my tools to the springs. You must clean them properly, understand this?" Aman nodded and the father handed the cloth to his son. He wiped Aman's sobs away with his thumb. "Aman, I will return for you from the wood, just as you did for me. Wait for me in the east, we will leave Candor by nightfall." Though his voice was full of doubt, Jebas gave his command in no expectance of protest.

Jebas held his son's shoulders until Aman finally relented. When Jebas exited the tent he was at once confronted by Seth. The elder stood before him with arms folded behind his back and open cloak which caught the eerie winds of the night becoming restless. Jebas glared at the elder with unmovable conclusion.

"You will not save your sons, great hunter. They have chosen their course."

Jebas frowned with anger and began without any restraint. "If you had known of that which called my sons away, why did you not stand against it?" he countered. "These men spoke seeds for secret paths, now leave Candor, women, sons, and

## Chapter Two — The Fall of Candor

brothers... for an evil you have known of for centuries. What purpose has your held tongue achieved? What purpose has the elders silence served?"

Seth paused as the crowd grew. The commotion was now charged with enough fret that nothing of the gathered chaos could be ignored. But Seth would not answer any motive as he held contrary mind. Nevertheless, he needed to forewarn the reckless action Jebas determined to take.

"If you follow after these men, you will fall—"

"—Enough!" Jebas grumbled, "Do not speak to me of what I will or will not! I know too of the dark beings..." Jebas stared into Seth eyes with boldness, "... my mind may deceive me, but my dreams remember..." he stated with a glance over Seth's shoulder where Elias stood. "... And I will not bow my flesh to that," he snarled. He set his focus back on Seth and continued, "My responsibility is to my sons. It is the elders who have theirs to Candor. Candor might fall, but it will not be at my still hand."

At that, Jebas pushed Seth aside and hurried toward the south bend of the village. The warrior turned and watched the hunter disappear into the shadows cast by the lit fires. He stared for a long moment as the crowd set their focus where the chief exited. Aman stepped out from his father's tent and joined the gazers. A subtle smirk lifted the corner of Seth's mouth. He did not turn as he addressed the crowd.

"Men of Candor, those of you not tainted with fear as your chief, who of you will join him to retrieve your brothers?"

Silence reigned for a short moment. Uriah stepped forward with a quick nod then rushed to his tent to gather his weapons. He was quickly followed by a host of other men, hunters, and scribes who charged toward the southern gate in silent hustle. They left Candor in the night with Seth warning them to listen for Candor's horn. "When it trumpets, go no further for the lost, for such will see your end. Return to Candor for your wives and children, and head with the east wind."

The men would join Jebas in time to search for Candor's misguided with hopes to overcome a futile quest. The elders spoke no other word that night but remained vigilant for those forced to rest in wait of the coming doom.

## The Fall of Candor

The day that Candor fell was no more unique than any other in prior existence. Dawn saw the brilliant orange of Eden's sun glisten through the translucent dew and gleam reflections of rich greenery and golden field. Of those who journeyed into the Rim beyond, nothing was spoken of them. Of Candor's remained, little care was held to the hills and borders, where there quickly gathered a destructive force focused with desolate intention.

No one in Candor saw nor heard the black shadow which loomed that day along far terrain. No disturbance came through the day, and rightly so, as the radiance would not hide the onslaught of the wicked. But the fate of the ground would not to be shaken no matter what course expended. For the day that Candor fell would meet a night terror filled with malice, destined to dismay the hearts of the refuge.

Aman spent the day mending his father's spears and pares in the banks of the cool springs. The air filled with the aroma of warm seasoned bake. Near Aman's kindling, four ripe ruby tomatoes sliced evenly into quarters sizzled upon the smoldering stone. The kindling heated assorted herbs in preparation for supper which the boy monitored while he fashioned the long staff. The staff was hewed from the tall tree branch used to drive off the grey wolf of the Candora wood. He mirrored the scores of his carver to the rhythm of the sizzle

# Chapter Two                          The Fall of Candor

in the fashion instructed by his father. The bō was complete and nothing more was needed on its stem, but Aman was compelled, at his father's command, to yield a long staff with great diligence.

And what he yielded stood tall and thick, an oval rod shaved perfectly parallel to the ground, wound at its center with tightly packed scaffle skin, coated in *konoa*, and smoothed from end to end with precision. The bō towered above the boy, was much taller than his shepherd staff yet lightweight and tuned for him to lift and swing with ease. Its thick diameter and rounded tips provided steady balance, unbending stem, and strong defiance to split. The small shepherd completed his work with a slight notch near one tip which he colored with his scribe and where draped the firmly woven band of Mariah's wool. This was unlike any other crafted even by men of old.

Aman placed his father's tools into the cloth and wrapped them as the sun melted into the horizon. He tied the wool cloth to one end of his staff and hoisted the heavy hunting tools upon his back. The shepherd stared across the waters with a longing for his father. As he faced Candor, an eerie crawl seized his shoulders. The dark of night advanced quickly with a cover that blotted the burgundy glow of the set sun from the sky and cast the village into night. The glow of the garden guard could not be seen in the west sky and a menacing shadow loomed overhead. Darkness set so fast that not even torches had been lit to brighten the night for the villagers. Soon they became aware that something was amiss.

Aman stared into the village with unbreakable attention, eyes wide with fear and heart racing as the drum of something approached. The ground began to rumble as a mounted force in the distance advanced. And yet Aman felt something closer, something upon him that lurked with claws that reached through steamy breath. The boy gave the presence no further

# Lands of Eden  by M. Gabreyl Scrolls

moment and jolted into the village with little care of what tempted.

The rumble increased and some among the tents paused in wait of the furor which grew. Few innocent shrills rang from the tents as small children and women voiced fright at the unknown, unseen danger.

The wrap fell from Aman's pole and spilled the sharpened spear tips as the boy tumbled onto his belly. He crawled toward the wool to gather the tools. At the sound of a clasp from the distance, he scampered away with his staff dragging behind.

Suddenly, the rumbling ceased. The air fell still with thin clouds of dirt rolling over the hills. Candor, now fully awakened, crowded the paths, faces full of wonder at the night disturbance that trounced the peaceful rest with tremor and deathly black. Not a sigh breathed through the long held silence that feigned to clear the moment of impending doom.

A single flare shined from the distance in the Caspian field. Aman peered at the light as several other eyes also met its shine. In sudden succession, the light soared skyward, brightened as it ascended through the night air. Everyone focused on the solitaire as it neared with patient speed. The gleam danced in the cutting wind and began its majestic descent over the central. Its cascade hovered gingerly and revealed a torch which guided a smoke trail like a beacon into the heart of the country.

As all eyes set upon the glow, the village echoed with the resonance of the ram's horn. Though hearts pounded at the blare, all were transfixed so on the spectacle that none moved. Aman whispered to himself with a discerning inner voice. "It is now."

Suddenly, the flame flared with blinding light. Candor shielded their gazes from the radiance. The sky lit with

## Chapter Two — The Fall of Candor

hundreds of flamed arrows ignited by the single torch. These plummeted toward the village in battalion fashion. Chaos followed.

Arrows pierced into the ground, through animal skin, and some dreadfully through human flesh. Flames quickly engulfed tents and flora of the village as the hundreds in witness scattered with shouts of fear and misdirection. Several ran toward the eastern gate only to be met by a rally of flamed arrows flooding in from the dark sky. And yet a second rally torched the south as the distant attack poured from the border. Arrows met targets with intended precision. Pitiful souls writhed in agony as the untamable embers invaded from the heavens. Blazes flooded with relentless rage as arrows stabbed the dirt and splattered flames as liquid. Gusts howled and carried the projectiles further into the village on the dust and smoke that swarmed the night air with unclear direction.

Aman spun from tent to tent as did others who were unaware of any method of escape. He produced no sound of fright though his chest nearly caved from his gasps. His feet raced frantically in strides to dodge the blazing spears. He hurdled flame trodden tents. He sped toward the pasture looking back at nothing as he ran with all might from the falling inferno. Hala darted from behind a tent and slammed into Aman's shoulder sending them both toppling. She wheezed with fright, but was up on her feet in moments, ready to charge off again.

"Aman, what's going on!?" she shouted as she yanked him upward.

Before he could answer, a charge of flames whizzed over their heads and pierced few feet away. Hala shouted with terror as the flames spit over them. The two took cover and fire raced round them. Aman spotted several more inclining directly overhead. His eyes widened. Immediately, the children found themselves hoisted from their feet. The arrows slammed

# Lands of Eden
*by M. Gabreyl Scrolls*

into the ground as their carrier slung them, broke through the wall of flame and carried the children to safety.

The two bounced for several paces as the sound of the commotion dimmed. Finally placed on their feet, Aman felt his body surge, his father glared into his eyes without a word. Despite Aman's excitement, Jebas appeared worn with fret. "Stay here children!" he commanded.

His father hurried into a nearby tent as the two shivered. Moments later Jebas returned with a thick strap tightened round his torso. Dangled from the strap were several dull chisel rocks and small spare spears used in hunt. Jebas carried two heavy pares and loose straps in his hands. He dropped them at the children's feet and knelt before them. He frantically counted the pares as Uriah joined.

"Papa!" Hala shouted hysterically as she jumped into his arms.

"It's okay young one, we will be fine."

"Papa, what's happening? I'm so scared!" Tears flowed from Hala's eyes. Uriah held her tight.

Jebas continued to number the final pares and chisels. "Uriah, six and ten."

"That's enough," he answered. Jebas nodded and handed several to him.

"Aman, turn..." The boy obeyed straightaway and felt the jostle of his father tying one of the straps over his tiny shoulder and round his torso. Jebas strapped two stone pares to the boy's back and anchored them with the boy's bō. The weight pulled on his back, and Aman was forced to stiffen so not to fall.

Jebas spun his son to face him, "Father, I prepared your tools as you said, but I dropped them near the—"

"—It's, okay, Aman. Tell me how this feels upon your back?"

## Chapter Two — The Fall of Candor

"It's a little heavy," Aman pouted.

"Can you run with it?" Aman hesitated but nodded with affirmation. " Good, you must run toward the east gate," Jebas commanded, "Do not let anyone or anything stop you, understand?"

"Father, there too many—"

"—Let nothing stop you Aman, you must fend yourself as you did against the wolf if anything stands against you."

"But Father—" the small boy whimpered with eyes broad and fright filled.

Jebas gripped Aman tightly, tears began to swell in the father's eyes. He was soon joined by fellow hunters Barra and Ezra, his son, who held long spears in his hands.

A blast flared in the distance, yet neither Jebas nor Aman flinched. Jebas sniffed and looked sternly into Aman's eyes, "You are not to be afraid son. You must not be afraid, hear me?" The father broke his hug and stood in front of his son with command. "You are called to a greater purpose young one. As the lamb laid its life for you without fear, so you must be fearless."

Aman panted away his brief tears and swallowed his pout to return his father's look with a determined face. "I am not afraid, father."

"You must not be," Jebas nodded, "you must be brave, run toward the east gate and do not look back. Let any danger along your way meet what is on your back, understand?"

Aman frowned and looked around with question, "Father, I don't know how to use these."

"Tonight you learn," Jebas answered. The chieftain looked upon his son with determined confidence. Aman saw the charge in his father's eyes.

"Jebas, we must go," Uriah pressed with impatience.

Jebas nodded as Uriah planted Hala on her feet yet held her against his chest. "Hala, you must run with Aman, do not leave each other's side. Find your mother and we will find you." Hala whimpered uncontrollably to which Uriah replied with a kiss on her cheek.

The sky sung suddenly with hundreds of descending flames careening through the rising smoke. "Run children, go and warn as many as you can!" Jebas shouted as the flames crashed down. Aman snatched Hala's arm into his hand and for the first time darted off faster than she could keep pace.

\*     \*     \*

Jebas led the four men to the façade of Candor's east gate undetected and untargeted by the wild villains launching their night assault on the grounds. The growing smoke hid them perfectly in the night, though the mass of darkness kept them blind from the dangers encircling the borders. Jebas fought off the shiver caused by the horrendous growls of the dark beasts raging in the distance. He knew no plan nor contrived any method to overcome the enemy. All that was discerned was the fate of Candor, his sons and the potential of mankind rested in his task.

Blazing arrows continued to pour upon the camp in relentless sequence as the ash blanketed the sky. Few torches were quenched as the targets scarred the village with massive flames. The four hurried along in wonder of the blaze that entranced around them. Jebas knew this was only the first marvel that Candor would witness till the first light of dawn.

Ezra and Barra followed close behind with Uriah at the rear guard. Ezra was among the youngest of hunters, equally set apart by his portly shape as by his youth. Yet he was trained well nonetheless by his father, and while the reflection of the

# Chapter Two — The Fall of Candor

chaos was in his eyes, the young man was willing to push through his hesitance for his father and for Candor.

"Jebas, are you certain this is wise? We are mere hunters, not fighting men," Barra warned.

Jebas halted along the dark path. He panted with the other three, "These creatures must know that men do not fear them, even if it is only we who stand against them, they must know."

"How do you know these are creatures and not men themselves?"

A wild roar echoed through the sky with harsh vibration. Strong gusts followed the sound as the moments grew still with eerie silence. Jebas rose to his feet and looked into the sky, eyes extended with amazement. "You saw the same as I in the dark forest," he answered. "These are not men."

The other three looked into the smoke blanketing the village. Suddenly, a wild brute soared through the density and landed upon the ground with a thunderous rumble. Its eyes glowed and body hunched to catch its weight as it gathered itself upright. The being lumbered forward into the firelight revealing its bony black frame marked with a peculiar hump in its back. The scent of the creature permeated the atmosphere with singed stench of rotted animal flesh. The monster howled again as several more landed beside him and surveyed the camp through glowing green eyes.

Ezra began to gasp for air. A growing cry was quickly hushed by Barra swiftly covering his son's mouth. "Do not allow any fear, my son" he whispered with an assuring nod from Jebas.

The beasts halted cautiously yet did not perceive the men's range. Jebas glanced at Uriah who signaled their count in his palm. They were outnumbered by two, and the cries upon the night air signaled the threat of more descending. Jebas waited as the beasts distanced themselves, then turned and faced the others.

"Ezra, you will stay behind me, keep my guard, do not set your eye on the demons, keep them on me." Jebas peeked briefly into the distance before he huddled them again. " Barra you with Uriah. Your hunting tools are your arms, keep them ready…"

Uriah handed Barra several spikes carved from tree stem. Jebas loosened his belt so that he could snap the dull but blunt chisels. "Jebas, once more, are you sure this is wise? The tower may enlighten the enemy of our place here."

"We have no other choice," Jebas responded as he glanced at the demons heading off. "The beacon must be lit, for my sons, for your brothers. Candor cannot flee in such fear." He looked at Ezra whose face revealed great terror. He felt little comfort in the young man's eyes.

"He will not be fearful, Jebas." Barra chimed with a stare of reassurance at Ezra, "Just see that my son meets no harm." Jebas promised as he took a last glance at the creatures in the distance. With the final nod, the men scattered toward the monsters.

The four found hiding in the shadows cast by the billowing fires. None of the beasts appeared aware of them as they neared the east corner. Jebas and Uriah placed their tools strategically along the path as they neared.

The totem stood unscathed by any of the flaming darts. There lie the wonder of how the enemy knew of its torch which could be seen from far off lands. The six beasts set round the beacon where they appeared sent to guard.

Jebas kept his eyes on both the creatures and the totem with decisive measure on how he would scorch the pole. He took position behind a pile of singed debris clouded with rising smoke. Through the dark cloud, he could see clearly the figures. Uriah found his spot in the blinding glow of a bright flame engulfing a tent.

Jebas searched to find Ezra few meters behind, hidden from the beasts' eyes by a mound of branches. He met eyes with Jebas who hoped the young hunter would keep focused. He slid one of the chisels from his belt, wrapped the stone at the end of one of his straps, then began to swing the strap in slow circular motion at his side.

Uriah, who was slightly closer to the beasts, snapped a spear in half and quickly whittled sharp points from the disjointed tips. Both planted their feet and shut their eyes briefly.

Uriah took the remnants of the broken spear in hand as Jebas sped the momentum of his swing. The air round the whirling chisel whined gently. Uriah positioned the fragments overhead, gripped tightly and glared straight at his targets.

Jebas balanced himself with one arm, fingers pointed straight, feet planted and knees bent. He leaned forward and stomped as he released the strap. The stone arched with remote speed as the strap dragged from the projectile as a tail. The targeted beast turned in time to be caught square upon its head by the heavy weight and sent onto its back.

The two beasts in vicinity turned and looked upon the clunked monster. Uriah thrust the spears through the flame that hid him. The two were quickly impaled and fell to the ground in agony. The third jumped to his feet and gripped the chisel that slammed him. It stepped forward only to be quickly entangled at its feet by a second strap tied with stones on each end. The beast fell with a rumble. Jebas glanced back at Ezra with a lifted thumb. Ezra nodded and the two sprinted into another shadow to remain unseen.

The creatures roared out in anger. In seconds the vicinity was welcomed with four more monsters. Jebas found Uriah who stared back at him with exhaustion. The two were caught in mutual thought. They feared they would soon be overcome.

*　　　*　　　*

Aman and Hala surged through the village swarmed with chaos. The flames to the south cast the village in thick smoke which hid the small children and their pleas in diverted commotion. The fires spread reckless darkness that separated parents from children, men from wives and tossed Candor's people to and fro with screams of fright. Even so, the barrage of arrows was only the first scare to descend upon the night.

Hidden in the smoke crept hideous beings settled that Candor would not stand long from the flames. Thunderous roars blasted through the village with rival call. Cries were instantly drowned by echoes that reigned the midnight atmosphere with tremble. Every heart froze and eyes focused on the ash-filled sky.

Aman snatched at Hala's wrist to call her attention from the flashes and sounds amidst the dark plumes. The east gate was close and he was to continue onward and let no fear stop him. But Hala refused, she tugged her arm away and halted the small boy with frightened gaze. "Listen..." she shouted with focus directly overhead.

She pointed to the sky. Aman looked directly above. The sound mellowed into mysterious silence.

Suddenly, a demon tore through the smoke curtain and dived with deadly speed. It landed directly in front of the children with a commanding rumble that shook earth. The creature snarled, revealed massive sharp teeth that dripped with yellow putrid salivation. It hunched in front of the children with branch thick arms spread wide, muddy claws

# Chapter Two  —  The Fall of Candor

drawn at the tips of its fingers and eyes aglow in dim green with vapor rising from its gaze.

Straightaway Hala screamed and bolted from the creature's presence. The beast leapt from Aman's sight, soared through the air only to land again in front of the small girl. It roared with intense anger that singed its entire body with a flash of pale flame.

Hala fell onto her back. Those in vicinity scattered in terror as Hala squirmed at its feet.

Yet Aman stood still. His bō strapped to his back caught his attention. In sudden panic, he yanked it from its anchor, gripped tightly and charged the beast.

The monster lifted his arm with clenched fist. Its flames clapped as the fiend brought its arm down swiftly upon the girl. Hala turned her face in fear of the impact.

Aman shouted wildly. With all mustered force, he plunged the tip of his long staff into the torso of the monster. The bō vibrated vigorously. Yet Aman held tight. Kept his charge and sent the creature rolling.

The beast bellowed as it stumbled backward. Aman kept his eyes on the creature as he helped Hala scamper to her feet. Ahead of them the monster clutched its chest and sneered.

"Pest," it cursed as it stood. Aman frowned in wonder at its ability to speak Eden's language. His wonder was quickly torched as the being walked briskly toward him. Again the boy gripped his staff and pointed the rounded tip at the brute with a hard swallow. A rapid lurch snatched the staff from the small boys' grip and hurled it away.

The bō spun from view. Aman stepped back as Hala clutched his shoulders and cringed. The creature stomped toward them, menacing with snickers as the heat from its thin flame ridden body stung the children's cheeks. Its belly grumbled as it reached forward and grinned with conquest. "Fear me!"

Aman panted mightily with Hala sheltered behind him. Behind them burned the wool tents. In front, the hideous mammoth hissed through glared teeth with nothing more than cruel intention. It cackled crazily and leaned into the young boys face and hissed again, "Fear me!"

Aman turned his nose from the fowl stench of the creature's breath. He closed his eyes momentarily, then looked at its grotesque face directly and replied. "No."

The creature glowered and withdrew with confusion. At that, Hala yanked a pare strapped from Aman's back and thrust it into the creature's eye. The beast recoiled but bucked back at the children in anger. Hala thrust repeatedly which only aggravated the being. Finally, she threw the pare at the monster with a scream. The fiend slapped the object to the ground. Hala threw another only to see the beast slap that one into fragments with a chuckle.

Finished with its game, the animal roared and lunged at the children with full fury. Aman clenched his fist to steady his nerves. Instantly, the beast caught a swift impact to its nose from the forearm of Candor's brave warrior. It snarled in pain before Seth snatched lashes to the animal's chest, hind leg, and back with Aman's long staff. Aman watched the beast take several more whips as the elder commanded his ground. A final swipe sent the beast falling back where it collapsed onto a flame drenched tent. Seth studded the ground with the tip of the bō and beckoned the assailant up who responded adversely with a powerful leap from the flame into the dark cover.

Aman kept his breath as the mighty warrior turned and faced the small children with solemn intent. He gripped the weapon in hand and examined it. "Yours?"

# Chapter Two  *The Fall of Candor*

Aman nodded hesitantly. Seth tossed Aman his bō with a grunt. Aman caught the weapon and stared at Seth, who looked back authoritatively at the small boy. "Continue on to the east hills, and do not look back!"

"My father," Aman pressed, "he is — "

" — Run with the east winds and do not turn. Go!" Seth demanded.

With that Hala yanked Aman's arm and the two darted away.

\*     \*     \*

Uriah moved swiftly behind the blinding bright of the flames. Screams resounded from deeper within the village yet the four did not turn their eyes from the creatures ahead. Jebas signaled to Barra who snapped another spear upon his knee. He snapped a third and sharpened the jagged tips. He placed the spikes on the ground and nodded for Uriah to follow. The two planted their feet and launched the spears through a brilliant flame. The lances sped toward the targets which appeared unaware.

Without warning, one turned and glared at the projectiles. It swung its arms, knocked two off target, and caught the third in its grip with little effort. It studied the spear with mild curiosity. Instantly, its hand flared with a pale emerald magnitude that singed the spear from the center to ends. The ash whisked away as the beast opened its palm.

Jebas swallowed hard and peered through the black smoke. The monster dusted its hand then pointed in Uriah's direction. The two standing at its side leapt into the air with tremendous power and dived directly over Barra and Uriah.

Jebas shouted and jumped into view with his fashioned sling spinning overhead. He tossed one with all his might and watched it entangle one of the beasts round its legs. This sent it to the ground with a crash. Jebas prepared another sling but was quickly slammed with a heavy claw to his chest that lifted him from the ground and sent him flying back. He landed hard on the ground as the beast followed after him.

Ezra was at once crazed and cried out to his father with hasty sprint. Jebas called after the young hunter, "Ezra, no, stay your ground!" The commotion shifted the monster's interest onto Ezra. It hissed at Jebas, then raced toward the teenager who hurried frantically. Jebas recovered, rushed to grab his sling and chased after the demon.

Barra shot a spear into the air with all his might at the careening monster. Yet the spear missed its mark as the beast came upon him. Uriah grabbed the hunter and rushed him from the crushing blow. Barra grunted with cold eyes from the impact and remained motionless.

"Father—" Ezra shouted as the beast behind reached over the boy's shoulder with vicious aim.

Jebas shouted wildly and heaved a chisel from his waist. The object smacked the back of the beings head and shook its attention. It halted and turned.

"That's it..." Jebas responded, "That's it... come get me!"

Uriah shook Barra with no success as the hunter remained dazed. He was instantly whipped at the side as another demon flung him with a mighty blow from its wing. Uriah twisted in the air and managed to land on his feet.

The beast straddled Barra. Spit dangled from its mouth and ooze glistened off its face.

"Father, no!" Ezra shouted. The being hissed at the boy, prepared to strike.

Uriah split the remaining staffs across his waist as he rushed back into the creature's mark. Before the monster could lift a claw against any flesh, he thrust the spikes into its wing,

# Chapter Two　　　　　　　　　　　　　*The Fall of Candor*

removed them and thrust again, catching its leg. Ezra froze as the monster rolled onto the ground and writhed in agony. Uriah planted his foot into its back and forced it away.

Without question Uriah commanded the young hunter, "Do not flee, wake your father and fend yourself!"

Uriah then charged toward Jebas who found himself standing in striking distance of a hideous beast. Jebas rolled onto his side as the creature lunged at him. He dodged every swipe of the beast and spun the strapped stones over head in wait of a precision strike.

"Behind you!" Uriah called, but too late as another demon knocked him flat. Jebas rolled as the creature straddled over him. It raised its fist then came down with all its might at his face. Jebas slid under the beast as Uriah kicked it square at its hind. The creature lumbered forward clumsily yet the force was not enough to drop it. The two paused to see the massive hump upon its back. They frowned in disgust as the beast spun and slammed the back of its palm into the men's chests. Both were sent spinning.

\*　　　\*　　　\*

Seth smirked as he looked into the sky. Another rally of fiery arrows soared toward Candor. A strong gust of wind kept the darts airborne, lingering overhead before they descended upon the village. Several careened directly over the warrior. As they began to make target, a steady row pierced the earth in steady succession toward him. Yet Seth did not move. He took quick cover with his cloak then swiftly flung its drape at the falling flames and swiped them from impact. He then stomped out a flame from an arrow and dared for a second rally.

Volley trumpeted from the sky which was suddenly luminous with pale green flame. Dozens of creatures descended onto the grounds, each landing with rumbling presence. They encircled him and mocked with spit and flared eyes.

" Sefíyai!" Seth said with distaste.

"You will address us properly fleshly one," one of the demons swore, "We are wise beings of heavenly birth!" They hissed and sneered at the warrior and readied for attack. Seth, who stood unaffected, was soon joined by brothers Jodia and Elias, who stepped forward with commanding presence.

"You do not belong here, creatures of death!" Elias stated.

One of the creatures lashed its flame at the great shepherd's feet. "We have our right here, of your own we are brought to this land."

"This land was promised solely to Adam and his descendants!" Elias replied.

" Haaa…" the Sefíyai roared with aggravation, "Your Adam broke the bond, and the promise has passed! Your Adam is as the dust of the field, you cannot use his power against us!"

"Though you will not abandon this trespass," Elias barked, "I will not fear you."

The beast snarled as Elias challenged its ground, "Fear me old man, for this land is ours, and you will be driven from it tonight!"

At once the monsters charged the trio which was simultaneously joined by more elders wielding their arms.

Elias dodged the attacks of the demons which jeered at him with steady patience. The searing heat of its eyes posed no threat to the elder who leapt from the creatures grasp and gained quick ground for counter attack. From his waist, he drew two short staffs, each of one cubits length. He thrust his weight at the demon with weapons equipped. Once within reach, he unfurled a rapid sequence of strikes upon the sefíyai's

## Chapter Two — The Fall of Candor

head, shoulders, and chest. As he landed, he continued the strikes on its legs and finally swept the demon onto its back. He lifted the staffs over his head for a final blow. But the demon countered with a swift kick to Elias' torso that sent the elder tumbling.

Seth found himself encircled with three demons of varying stature. His long bō remained strapped to his back as the monsters deciphered who would attack first. Suddenly, out of the sky came a fourth, mouth wide with fangs to chomp upon the warrior's flesh. Seth clenched his fist, thrust himself upward, and caught the chest of the demon. He spun and slammed the creature onto the ground with the force of its fall. The ground rocked with incredible vibration. At once, all his aggressors rushed, bodies flared with anger. Seth snatched his staff free, spun and plunged its tip into the chest of one. He carried the force of the jab through the creature and laid it flat, turned and snapped the stem of the bō across the back of another brute. Seth mounted several whacks upon the heads of the two remaining sefíyai before subduing them with a mighty blow from his side.

A wild roar preceded a vicious kick to the small of Seth's back that slammed him to the ground. Seth rolled and showed no sign of pain as the beast quickly straddled the staff wielding warrior. The monster grinned with conquest, opened its mouth to plunge its thick teeth into the man, but was instantly gutted and heaved back by a spear. Seth scooted on the ground as another soared upon him. Before it could crush the warrior, it was tackled in mid air and slammed. Seth jumped to his feet to see Jodia pummel the beast with steady fists until it finally relented. Jodia rose and faced Seth with a stern nod.

The two sprung back into battle as the assault continued. The onslaught swelled with mounts that put the defending elders at mismatch in the throng advancing in the dark night.

Dozens broke the plain of Candor's border and began to drive the elder's defense back.

\*     \*     \*

Jebas rushed to his stance as the demon charged ferociously. At his feet lay one of the split spikes knocked away by the very monster threatening him. He kicked the stick up with his foot and caught it in his hand. His eyes shot back to the beast as he braced his back foot. The creature lunged forward and plunged its stomach onto the sharp tip. It groaned and faltered backward. Jebas stepped back and frowned with confusion. The beast then roared and lit with a forceful blaze. Instantly, Jebas was encircled with four demons.

As the monster's blaze simmered, the demon forced the fragment free of its pelvis and threw it to the ground in disgust. The spike singed in olive ash. "I will taste your very flesh tonight, human!"

Jebas was cold with shock at the creature's voice. The demons toyed at him with barks and feigned gouges. He saw hatred in each of their eyes. Their fangs oozed with vicious poison. Claws sprung from their fingers as each seized the moment in charge. Jebas' body stiffened.

Shock struck two of the beasts who were swiftly speared in reverse. Jebas turned to see the others, tangled round their haunches, fall onto their bellies. They landed with heavy thuds and slid away as Jebas rolled to dodge their momentum.

Barra rushed past the commotion followed by his son. Their faces glowed with trepidation, yet they kept watch to spring in defense. Ezra hurried to help Jebas to his feet, as Barra thrust three remaining spikes at the monsters that threatened Uriah. They darted in retreat and Uriah jumped to his feet as Jebas

# Chapter Two — The Fall of Candor

dusted his cloak. The four searched the area and panted heavily. The monster was cleared for a brief escapable moment.

"I told you he would not fear," Barra exclaimed with a glance at his son. Jebas nodded his thanks to the young man who yet held wide eyed worry.

"This is too treacherous," Uriah gasped, "we must go back."

Jebas swallowed and responded with great desperation in his tone. "The beacon must be lit, Uriah," he panted, "if not for Candor, or for our men and brothers…" Jebas lifted an ooze covered spear near his feet and ambled to a nearby flame. "For my sons."

Jebas turned and raced toward the totem, the yellow torch blazed upon the tip of the spear. As he charged, a demon soared toward him, hidden in the blind of the smoke above. Jebas stopped several yards from the beacon and planted his feet. He gripped the spear in his hand and hoisted. The monster landed on the ground in front of him and took immediate charge. Jebas halted, lowered the spear in exhaust, closed his eyes, took a final breath. He thrust the spear forward with the full force of his body.

The spear channeled through the air with wind-splitting speed, steady in its projection, flaring triumphantly with a bright flame that would ignite the totem, until the sefíyai snapped it off target with a swipe of its gruesome arm.

Jebas slumped in disgrace. He fell to his knees and hopelessness engulfed his countenance. The sprite roared immensely. It blasted the celebrated hunter with a powerful blow to the chest that sent Jebas airborne. The sefíyai leaped forward, snagged Jebas' limp body in mid air, and disappeared into the dark cloud.

\* \* \*

# Lands of Eden

*by M.Gabreyl Scrolls*

Aman felt a cold thud that stilled his breath and dropped him to his knees. Hala halted several paces ahead to see her friend struck with bitter fright. She called to him but received blank response as the boy gasped with mind aloof. Many brushed pass the children with careless attention.

Careless was the sense that overpowered the small boy who was frozen with cold abandon. A dark loom gripped his heart with slowing pace, and blanked his vision of the chaos round him. He stared at the south bend with no word to speak and mind full of want. 'Papa…' he thought knowingly.

Hala shook his shoulders impatiently and Aman finally marked her voice. He could yet gather any muster in his legs. And little shock came as the two were joined without any expectation by their companion in play, Lathan.

Hala contrarily shouted with grim glee. She gripped Lathan and hustled him with questions. But Lathan too was in stupor of the wonders round him.

"What's going on, where is everyone going?!"

The small shepherd swooned in confusion as the roved rascal tugged him. Lathan's voice slowly channeled into his ears until Aman was brought back.

"They are running from the village," Hala exclaimed, "there are monsters burning the tents, we must get to the east gate before we are found!"

"No wait, but… where is my father?" Lathan asked as Hala pressed the two to follow her.

Aman spoke no word. He tried to clear his head, swipe his eye of the eerie shadow that covered Lathan's face. Lathan asked again with eyes full of fear. Suddenly, a violent boom resounded as a sefíyai dropped several feet behind them. Lathan shook with fright as Aman turned. The beast rumbled toward them. It roared tremendously.

# Chapter Two

## The Fall of Candor

Elias landed behind the demon and whipped a hard smack against its leg that caused the being to fall forward. "Run children!"

The three scampered from sight without a word as the sprite turned and launched its attack at the elder. Aman hid nearby and watched the spectacle while Lathan and Hala clung to his back.

Elias maneuvered with impregnable poise from every claw of his enemy before he recovered his weapons. With one final dodge, he pummeled the savage with blinding contact across its brow. The demon dropped like mortar and made no further contest.

Elias spat and surveyed the destruction and chaos engulfing the village. The east and south corners gushed with black soot as Candor fell to the flames of the invaders. Men, women, and children cried with panic as they raced from the falling city to the hills. He looked down on the beast which wheezed with a mild sneer across its grotesque mouth.

"Why did you come here, Sefíyai?" Elias demanded, face tweaked with incalculable anger.

The animal began to cackle from deep within. "We answer the call of mark't flesh…" the sefíyai snickered, "you will see this place burn to ash by dawn, son of Adam!" Its dark voice shivered Aman's core with evil echo and vile mockery. In that small moment Aman felt immense fury against the being and desired Elias to end the barbarian.

Yet Elias backed away with weakness that flushed his chest. The elder turned and faced the destruction that hampered the gates. Aman watched sorrow fill the elder's heart. Tears found abundant rage and the elder lifted his staffs to strike the fallen beast again. But with a shout the sefíyai jolted upward. A strong wind followed its exit and Elias was thrust back by the gust. Aman shielded his face from sparks and hurried into Elias' sight.

Elias looked at the small boy who stood afar in cold stupor. Upon both faces was the knowledge of something grim. Though the elder did his best to hide his unease, Aman read no comfort. Before either could answer, three figures rushed from the smoke toward the elder. Elias readied himself and squinted as Barra and Ezra appeared. The men coughed harshly from the smoke that engulfed them. Uriah was moments behind and hacked from the mass.

Elias stood solemn as Barra nearly collapsed at his feet in desperate gasps. The elder helped him to his feet as Ezra stared into the monsoon flame ravaging the tents. "You return from the dark wood so few. Where are the others who journeyed with you in the passed twilight?"

Uriah panted heavily, "Driven mad in the dark forest by the very creatures which trounce Candor this night." The four men looked at each other as the gloom of the chaos weighed upon them.

Elias looked at Aman with a solemn gaze. "What of Jebas?"

The three looked at the ground in sorrow. Only Uriah answered. "Jebas could not be turned from his task... Candor is fallen."

Elias sighed with anger and gazed in sadness upon the eastern sky. The elder riddled with decision as the young shepherd neared. He tugged the elder's robe and looked up. The elder did not respond.

"Where is my Papa?" he pressed.

The elder only stared at the young reu with no words to provide. Aman remained solemn, comfortless and cold.

"Brothers, I must tend to my daughter and wife," Uriah stated. He patted Barra on his shoulder and hurried to where Hala and Lathan stood.

## Chapter Two

*The Fall of Candor*

Barra stood for several moments as Ezra turned and followed after Uriah.

Elias finally answered the stares, "Get to the east hills and be swift. See that no one turns back, for Candor falls by dawn." At that the elder sprinted into the cloud of ash.

Aman was instantly frantic and called after the elder. Barra hoisted Aman onto his shoulder and ignored the boy's cry. He protested greatly and jostled in Barra's arm. Uriah scooped Hala and hurried Lathan away as the boys shouted for their father's with kicks, gouges, and flails that hindered progress.

"We must get to the east young one," Barra pleaded. Yet Aman would hear no reason. He continued to fight and Barra found his arms loosed from round the boy's waist. "Papa!"

With a swift flip, Aman darted from his grasp and sprinted after the elder.

Barra called after him as vicious howls screeched the gray fogged air. Hala yanked at her father's arm and screamed for her companion as the small child vanished in the thick smoke. What he could accomplish was nothing more than ranting attention for the devouring sprites, yet he would not be settled without the calm of his father's hand.

Hala continued to shout and pull, but could not free herself from Uriah's grip. Barra would not move any further as Uriah charged forward. "I cannot leave the child to his own," he called, "I will retrieve him, get to the border!"

"Father no!" Ezra shouted as the ground began to tremble with enormous waves of stomps. He followed after without any notice. Lathan bolted after Ezra and the entire group was scattered with all but father and daughter continuing on.

"Aman!" the girl shouted with tear filled eyes and abundant terror. She cried again and again, yet Uriah spoke no further plea and with daughter in arm left the ground of the village long known as his home.

L ANDS OF E DEN *by M.Gabreyl Scrolls*

\* \* \*

The small boy whined with each trounce as tremors proceeded from the east border. His innocent mind could not perceive the menace most heinous which planted its presence upon the village ground. In the lime of the fire, its heels and hinds glowed from the flames. Its body, shadowed in the smoke, towered unseen and yet its vicious murmur shook the earth as thunder.

Aman froze as the atmosphere flooded with putrid essences of vile and gut wrenching character. He turned in circles at the echoed hisses that stung his lobes and inhaled his sweat. He sensed them, each one of them, invisible eyes set on his heart, five or six pair perched round him with ready devour. The reu could manage no breath, heaved and fell upon his knees, not of fear but release. No single man could overcome such animals that stalked night in herded soot. His father was lost, his brothers were lost, and he was doomed to their same end.

A growl shook his entire being with violent force as the first launched at him. He tensed. But another call of rivaled resonance met with fearless command. Aman rose to see Jodia and Seth hurry to his guard. Elias followed and gripped Aman to his side.

"You should have obeyed my command child!" Elias shouted.

"Where is my father!? You have to find him!" Aman pleaded.

Elias slipped his cane into his belt and clutched Aman's shoulders, "Your father is not here young one," he sighed, "Candor is lost, and we must flee."

Aman shook his head continually and protested with weightless emotion as Seth lifted the boy onto his back and

## Chapter Two — The Fall of Candor

hurried away. The remaining elders followed, but all were halted by Barra, Ezra, Lathan, and several others whose faces showed a mass of trepidation which the elders needed only one glimpse to recognize. "He is here…" Elias answered.

Dozens of Candors people rushed passed them with no relent to their sprint as those flown to the east gate met with unsuspecting terror and doom.

Blasts shook the middle ground as the great adversary mounted his assault on the singed soil. This was the one who took aim to annihilate any further retreat. The one who required no conquest but to fulfill his desire to vanquish all odds. Elias gathered no second decision and urged the men away. "Candor is fallen," he marked with tear filled eyes.

"To the northern plains!" Seth shouted as the people scampered, "and do not look back upon the beasts!"

The men ran swiftly as several demons scurried round them. They each scattered in the same direction and would let nothing keep their escape. Overhead poured the remains of the promised village that by dawn would see no end but ash.

# Chapter Three

# The North Refuge

Morning came with a blue haze beaming through a mist-less sky void of energy and joy. Cold air flowed with scents of wet ash and soot carried on the southern wind, reminding of the village lost to the fire of night. The bright horizon gleamed in the distant east. Yet bleak was the mood of the dawn, and bleak were the minds of these few, dispersed from their homelands into the unknown. Tear-chilled cheeks, heavy heels and drained emotion resounded through a night where mourns were swallowed in exhaustion and sorrow. Lament turned to confusion and ultimate anger, seeded deep in the bellies of these men, women, and children whose eyes held the orange glow of the night with screams of horror. They continued to sprint, to stroll, to slug, to wait, to bloom at the slightest proposition of the threat that scattered them. This, the precise desire of the enemy who stalked the open expanse with contest.

The night saw many escape the deadly clutch of ruin along the north retreat, including Cephas, forger of wood and stone, Apayim and his nephew Melhazur, dark barters known for their greed. Joseph the scribe, who would chronicle much of

# Chapter Three                                    *The North Refuge*

Candor's past for the ages hence. These and others trickled into the keep of Elias and numbered four score and nine.

Elias, accompanied by his brothers Jodia, Seth, and eldest nephew Mered, guided these few through the thick fields littered with dark shrubs and tall ferns onto a vacant field. But none found rest there. The dawn met only sobs and shivers, fear struck hearts, blank stares and grumbles.

The northern tundra brought frosty air and chilled stony grounds unbearably harsh for the small feet of the young sojourners never sent such distances. Neither Lathan nor Aman wanted to display the anguish in their legs, but both tired greatly from the night journey. They followed without protest and much duress from the fear of what might happen if lost from the group. Yet the children among these were worn with no answers and no strength.

Tears, never witnessed among the youth who exalted him, were found in Lathan's weary eyes at the blue dawn when the men turned from the flames of Candor to the shadows of their journey. Quietly, he hummed his longing for his father and sulked in lost memory. Not much was exchanged with Aman, who stood beside void of expression. The two made no attempts to decipher the other's thought, yet between them was a sea of wonders and unexplained mysteries that swarmed the events round them and produced doubt that would be revealed with rifting effect.

Lathan rose in a midst of groans with belly aching of want. He sauntered round the desolate, peering for scraps that might calm his stomach. There were none. Still he continued blindly, until he strolled into Apayim's way. He thumped against the thin shin of the scraggly man. Apayim glared fiercely upon the youth.

"Watch'eh your walk boy…" he hissed. Lathan stared at him with question. Apaymin quickly grew impatient and snatched Lathan's cloth. He tugged the child to him and grit his teeth. "Turn your eyseh elsewhere boy, and be quickeh away fromeh Apayah!" He thrust Lathan away who hurried off without repress.

Elsewhere among them, men began to grumble to the elders who led them to undesired rest. "Are we to be much longer Elias," asked one of the men, "have we distanced ourselves enough from the threats that we afford rest here?"

Elias turned and surveyed the distress upon the men. He glanced upon the path where they journeyed and had no answer for them, offering only his back as he limped away. Not regarding his distress, Seth found him and pressed as well, though with more command.

"We are several nightfall's away from the base of the highlands. If we continue to rest here, we will be caught along the fields in the dark night. Sëtan has shown enough threat in the night that bids us to be off."

Elias softly broke his silence. "If we continue, we will wear ourselves of strength, so even in the midst of more threat, we will be had."

Barra interjected the humble conversation. "Elders, we must find food and nourishment for this crowd. If not for our strength, than at least for these young ones. " Elias looked again over the mass. Dried tears were upon the rosy cheeks of ones too young to have endured the chaos of the previous night. Some disguised their fatigue, though not well, with stern gazes of readiness. The elder responded faintly to Barra, "Who will seek food for them?"

Barra responded quickly, "I know the northlands well enough. There is much *pannea* grain along this path. I will, with my son, gather for the group that we can feed through the day."

# Chapter Three

*The North Refuge*

To that Elias closed his eyes and sighed. Barra hurried off immediately. Elias then addressed Seth, "Where are my brothers?" Seth signaled retrieve to the elders, Jodia and Mered, who walked through the crowd with mounds of sorrow for their people. Their eyes were downcast, yet their hearts ever ready.

Elias swallowed hard and released his tensed shoulders, "Of Morcial and Udell, none of you have heard…" Each shook their heads. "Despite such a night as we have seen, we must believe that they were spared with those who escaped before calamity."

Seth, Jodia, and Mered lifted their eyes as the reality set with further measure of gloom. Seth sniffed, "We must not focus on what might have come of them. Before us exist many choices. There remains refuge for these spared in the night in other lands."

"Where will we go, brother," Jodia asked, "that our enemy will not find us?" The three paused in long thought.

"We will go to the valleys of Orgêeda," Elias answered.

The men remained silent for brief moments, each with question but knowledge that there existed no other course.

"The valleys are four dawns' journey," spoke Mered, "Could we hurry these families so quickly?"

"How willeh we not be hurriedeh into devour," shouted Apayim who eased into the elders' discussion. "Onto the valleys of Orgêeda? You expecteh to move ' tis masseh so from ' tose beasteh in four dayseh? We shouldeh even hope ' tat we willeh not be devouredeh by nightfall."

Elias turned and faced the barter who amassed a small gather of some. "Why not speakeh truth of ' tese beasteh, elders? Tell'eh us what flesh ' tese truly seekeh." Apayim glanced viciously at Lathan, who neared the commotion. The barter set his focus on him long and hard until Seth answered his challenge.

"What is true of these beasts, is that they seek the flesh of us all." His voice commanded back the crowd's questions. "And if we wish to be spared of their rampage, then we must continue on to refuge. If refuge means four days journey, than that it must be. If we keep our stance here, the same perils that spurred you here in the night will return." Seth looked the barter in the eye and saw that Apayim had no response. "We must continue on." Few milled with slight at Seth, but all were hurried onto their feet without question of their pains.

Elias addressed them with reluctant command. "We will eat here for strength, and find our refuge onto Orgêeda."

Once Barra and his son gathered enough pannea grain, the crowd hurried their trek amidst the rigid grounds, set in route to the valleys of the burgundy mounts of Orgêeda.

Sun brought the custom warmth of midday halo and emery hue across the sky. Vast grasslands of the north pine danced with careless winds swirling to and fro as they vanished over the tall sage hills. Round them no creature sounded, the fields whispered the absence of life and offered tranquil moments for frenzied minds.

The northern plain was vacant land, vast and fertile with random clusters of trees scattered distances between the tall green blades. Eerily vacant, with held breath mistaken as peaceful quiet.

Ahead Jodia and Mered scouted the terrain. Lathan stared into the sky nearly entranced in fatigue. A dark speck drifted to his attention. The speck performed an aerial dance of loops, twists, and barrels before it descended and came into recognition. It was a *lobita* beetle, one of the many palm sized winged insects known to pester the crops of Eden. This particular bug was loved by children who would skip these

# Chapter Three

*The North Refuge*

insects as stones across a smooth water surface. The beetle recoiled into its shell when frightened, then, after several skips along the water, would take flight sporadically. Whirling without aim, a lobita would ultimately plummet into the water from dizziness. Not too amusing to the insect but good for endless entertainment among the youth.

The beetle whizzed above Lathan's head and finally rested on his arm. Lathan cautiously positioned his hand above the bug. A quick snatch and the beetle was in his palm before it flew away. He turned his hand over as the beetle shrank into hiding. Lathan stroked its cold rigid shell which was wet with substance. That moment saw the first grin upon Lathan's face. He looked around with excitement for his companion. "Aman, come look quick!" he called excitedly.

Aman sauntered to Lathan's side and stared at his clenched hand. He showed, if for only a brief moment, a rare glint of joyous curiosity.

"Look, I caught a lobita beetle!" Lathan opened his palm and revealed the shiny black shell of the bug. Its mulberry wings flailed quickly, but the insect did not fly off and remained hidden.

Aman gasped excitedly. "Can I hold it?" the boy asked as he reached at Lathan's hand.

Lathan shut his palm and snatched away, "No way, this is mine."

Aman recoiled and looked at Lathan with annoyance. He sighed and stared as the blank demeanor set back upon him. Lathan looked off for a moment. Finally, he snickered with a mischievous grin. "You think we can find some water around?"

"I can find some," Aman said in a soft voice filled with anticipation. They searched the tall green for water surfaces, but there was nothing to be found.

Lathan shook his head as the two met afar off from the group. They both continued to look around but panted from fatigue. Lathan decided to change their aim. "Pick something for me to hit, I bet I can hit anything near or far."

Aman squinted and turned about in search of something. He would not settle for any easy target, Lathan had to be challenged. Upon seeing a boulder a few cubits off, he quickly nodded and pointed ahead. "I bet you can't skip it off that rock over there, it is way too far for you."

Lathan peered at the boulder then inhaled, "Watch this!" The boy focused ahead sternly and squared his shoulders. In rapid motion he hauled his arm back. Then thrust forward and released the beetle into the air. The black shell spun rapidly. Aman and Lathan watched intently.

Suddenly, the object veered off target. The beetle's wings hummed with panicky movement as the insect took flight in erratic barrels. When it finally got its' bearing, the bug opposed its direction and whizzed over the boys' heads and raced toward the mass.

It zipped between the people. None noticed, even with its subtle buzz. Ezra stretched his arms above his head with a wild yawn and, upon completion, became host to the beetle.

The boys hurried forward and watched with wonder as the beetle explored Ezra's back. It traveled up onto his shoulder, halted there for moments, then scurried toward the man's neck before it vanished under his robe. Lathan and Aman glanced at each other shortly. Ezra instinctively scratched his neck, shook his shoulder's and stretched to scratch his lower back. He twisted at his waist and arched his head in a constant squirm against the irritant. The boys chuckled. Ezra squirmed more and more. They snickered uncontrollably and watched as the beetle crept just below the hunter's hairline. There the insect was met with a swift whack.

# Chapter Three

*The North Refuge*

Black goo oozed between the young hunter's fingers. Ezra's face cringed instinctively as he slid his palm from his neck and beheld the crushed, seeping shell. His neck was stained with a slimy dark oval. He reached back again and swept his fingers through the ooze. The hunter flicked his fingers, flung black sludge with disgust. Simultaneously the boys burst out loud into laughter and were soon joined by others who noted Ezra's face.

Ezra, who held his hands away as if they were plagued, turned and looked at the boys as the laughter continued. He cocked his head to one side and sneered before he advanced on the two. Aman and Lathan quickly jolted around the crowd as Ezra chased them. The hunter held out his hands to give them a taste of what they caused. They screamed with excitement with Ezra pursuing ineffectively.

The light mood was short lived as Seth abruptly halted Ezra's pursuit.

"Listen," he hushed as he looked into the sky. The laughter ended. The air hummed with a growing vibration. Seth stepped forward and stared more keenly into the southern sky. The hum intensified and shook the ground underfoot. Lathan and Aman joined the wide-eyed expressions as gusts proceeded.

Seth immediately turned, faced the crowd and ordered, "Our rest here is over." At that, he ran swiftly and commanded all to follow. The entire gathering scampered at the command as the hum trailed.

The noise resonated violently as the sky was quickly shaded. Not one turned to look as the canopy filled with a dark swarming multitude. The sound of wings thundered and caused many to hold their ears in agony.

Aman managed to get a view of the sky as the wind intensified. His heart pounded at the sight of an infinite count of insects making their way above. He jostled with fright as Seth clipped at his heals.

"Let your feet carry you onward young one and do not turn again!" Seth barked.

"I cannot outrun the–"

"Do not turn!" the elder thundered.

Aman protested no longer. The insects zipped overhead with staggering speed. The cover was rapidly overcome with lobita as hundreds careened to the ground with aimless flight. Their rigid shells snagged fibers and scratched skins before they hit the ground with blunt force.

Lathan steadily fell behind. He called frantically but was of little concern in the panic. Only Cephas saw the child. He hurried back to gather him as many sprinted onward.

"Hold," Cephas shouted, but too late. Lathan rushed with all fear in his eyes. The boy plunged into Cephas' wide belly and the two toppled.

As Cephas stumbled a lobita pelted the back of his crown with descending force. Instantly, he was stunned. The boy hollered in agony. Seth turned at the bounding rumble to see Cephas pin the boy under his great weight.

Aman heard the cry and turned. He watched as Lathan wrestled uselessly, halted and cried out for his friend with pointed hand. Seth continued toward Aman, scooped him into his arms and dove forward moments before several beetles grazed the elder's skin. The lobita slammed into the ground where Aman would have succumb to their stings, then took flight again in crazed swarm.

The two rolled with Seth swallowing Aman into his cloak. Aman could not bear the horrific buzz of the insects. The sound shook his eardrum crudely. He cried out in fear, desperate to see what had become of Lathan. In one moment he caught a glimpse of the sky darkened with thousands of lobitas

# Chapter Three                            *The North Refuge*

scurrying overhead. The next he was covered under Seth's robe and commanded still as the elder hurried off.

Tears poured down Aman's face as all he could do was listen to the shouts of fright around him.

Seth stripped his bō from his guard and swiped at several careening beetles that aimed for the crowd. When the moment allowed, he snapped the rod in two and raced toward Cephas.

"Take cover!" he shouted as few others felt the stings of the hard shells upon their skin.

Seth found Lathan pinned under by Cephas' limp body. The two were horded with lobitas. Upon his presence, some flew at him with what seemed deadly intention.

Seth hollered and sliced one stem of his bō against the other with powerful vigor. He sliced again and again until one ignited from a bright spark. A shrill sounded from the insects as Seth guarded his body with the growing flame. Elias met Seth's side and lit the tip of his jō. Once the torches were fully flamed the elders swung them sporadically, catching several insects with the flares as they descended. The lucid substance coated upon the lobitas ignited at the touch. Heat sent hundreds swarming into retreat. Cephas' still frame was cleared as Elias rolled the heavy forger onto his back.

With a final yell, Seth hurled the inflamed fragment of his staff into the colony. Instantly, the dark canopy lit with a burst of blazes as thousands of beetles caught fire. The flames scorched through the swarm in blinding amber that parched the air. And just as quickly as they ignited, the flames dispersed as hundreds of beetles fell to the ground in trails of colorless smoke. Seth shielded his face with his forearm enough to allow him to watch the surviving lobitas scatter. Calm was slowly restored as the crowd recovered.

Aman peeked from under Seth's robe at the sound of confusion amidst the group. Round him were several smoldered shells. He was chilled from the subtle squeals of the agonizing insects inside. He hesitated to touch one and recoiled from the heat captured in its shell.

After long quiet, Aman threw back the cloak and was on his feet. Lathan strolled backward methodically. The boy kept his gaze on Seth who knelt near Cephas. His face was filled with horror from the dark scene. He limped from the ache upon his joints caused by burly forger.

Before any could speak, Apayim rushed Lathan in anger.

"Curset!" The aged barter stood before the boy in the grumpy quick-tempered fashion well known of him. He tore his cloak along his shoulder and walked briskly toward Lathan with intense flare in his eyes. "Curset is he!" The old man spat again, grabbed a khaki stone. "Deh boy, you've done ' tis! He brings deh darkness on us. He must be remov'edeh!"

He planted his heel against Lathan's shoulder and knocked the small boy onto his back. At that, the barter gripped the cold marble and beat the child's back with powerful thuds. He beat again, then stood over Lathan who turned over with tears pouring from his eyes. Aman gasped with fear as the barter prepared to hurl the stone down.

Barra rushed Apayim. He gripped the old man's arm and ripped the stone from his hand. He then flipped the barter onto his back with a grunt. A cloud of dirt formed around the enraged villain at the impact. Apayim snarled, clawed and kick more dirt in attempt to continue his attack. He thrust a clump at Barra, then crawled toward Lathan who squirmed from reach. Barra wrapped Apayim's chest with his arms and hoisted him into a squeeze. Apayim cried out as Barra clenched tightly.

"Enough!" Elias shouted as he ambled over to the disorder. Apayim fidgeted to free himself, but finally relinquished. Barra set the man onto his feet and shoved the enraged haggler away

# Chapter Three       *The North Refuge*

as Elias continued. "We will not have this same character here," he demanded. "You who were driven by creatures of wild emotion act just as they even now. Have you forgotten the way that put you on this treacherous journey—"

"—No Elai'seh" Apayim revolted, " Apayah haseh not forgot wah spellseh put us here." The crazed man hissed and spat at Lathan's feet. "No even teh elderseh, or any man wah end ' tis but he," the barter's long thin finger set on the tearful boy, "he wah end'eh us all if you do no rid'eh us of him."

Seth glanced briefly at Lathan. He studied the eyes of the men while Elias ordered the barter still. Each was filled with doubt and distress from the chaotic events that beset them. There were no words that could quell their worries. The people were overwhelmed by doubt which painted grim hope for their journey. He studied the child with question, yet held his tongue according to his own way.

"Two Hundre'deh years I've seen deh plains of Candor resteh peacefully. Whether I held to deh promise or not, I saw what men believedeh in ' tis land remain true." Apayim turned and faced the others who gave him indiscreet audience. "Only last nigh'teh did Candor finally meet ' tis fate." He turned and looked at Lathan with menacing intent. "When tis child brough'teh deh darkness of deh Rim perils onto peaceful landeh. Candor fell as swif'teh as deh night, and now look how Cephr'ah, our brother, has fallen. Look how we are scatterdeh. ' Tis boy be deh reason. He is full of curset misfit'eh, and darkness hord roundeh any who are with him. All of us here wah meet'eh deh fate 'tat follows if we do not send him'eh on his own—"

"—I will not send him nor will anyone else here," Elias proclaimed. He walked toward Apayim, spoke soft and direct. "We have suffered enough through the night for you to cause this fool hearted thought. Your pains are no greater to demand such hand on his back." Apayim tightened his jaw and looked off for a moment before Elias addressed the gathering. "What you hear of this merchant is not of wisdom, do not give him ear. He is shameless that he would blame this child for Candor's fate, that he would make his hand reckless upon a child." All eyes looked upon the barter in paralleled shame. "What is Candor now but wasted wood and clay? There is nothing for us there. Yet those of you, like this one, who keep your mind on ruins, seek back to where there is nothing." Elias paused with a stern gaze into Apayim's eye, "for such cannot build again the greater refuge we seek."

Elias paused in wait. Apayim hung his head in a fit as the crowd offered subtle grumble. The barter took one brief glance at the boy then walked away without another word.

Seth then turned and faced Cephas who finally groaned from the ache of an arm scathed and bloodied. Long scars and gashes offered a grotesque view for all present. He only appeared dazed as he held away Seth's assistance and rose to his feet under his own strength. The forger rubbed the back of his head where his neck was moist with the throb of his wound. He brought his fingers before his face, then looked at the young rascal with a sharp eye. The glare exchanged bitter chill and distaste that Lathan would soon find common among the men.

Seth broke the silence among all as he watched Cephas surge with inner misgiving. As he commanded, their play was over. The confused crowd dispersed from the chaos in a continued trek toward the northlands. He gathered the remaining fragment of his staff, tied it to his waist, and headed with the crowd. Elias waited as Seth came forward. The elders stared at each other with thick tension between their thoughts. Unlike his older brother, the elder could not fight the misgiving of fate set round them. Yet he allowed none any mark of his mind. Only Elias knew his brother's thoughts. Even long before

# Chapter Three — The North Refuge

the night perils, Seth found suspicion in the boy who escaped the Rim darkness.

Yet neither spoke word as Seth ensured to remove suspicious eyes from the lad. The elders parted with the crowd that moved at even quicker pace. And as they went, there grew gloomy silence of mixed doubt and dissent. What was the hope that lied beyond? This silence would remain viciously unbroken until the fall of night.

## Plots of Evil

Grey ash glided upon the hot winds which carried the scent of singed carcass and wet dung over the murky smoked ruins of Candor. The grounds were veiled from daylight by a thick wall of smoke kept pluming by vicious seraphs who tossed dark soot with arrogance over the ravished soil. The demons fought among each other. Clawed, bit and scavenged over charred remains and broken bones, many which crumbled in their powerful grips. Even with nothing left to destroy, the beasts spoiled tirelessly as swine among scraps.

The grim prince stood upon the scorched hill that was once the oval pasture. Beside him Vestual and Beelzebub, the brute Sarim, cackled proudly over the anarchic scene. Lucifer, however, turned his back to his minions. His face soured with disgust and cringed at each boisterous shout from the beasts. Beelzebub turned as Vestual hummed in Lucifer's ear.

"By night have we, His trodden and broke, o'er claim the vested land of Adam. And proved, who is He to vest the ground or grant the earth? For exist but one prince of Eden, and stands he."

# Lands of Eden
by M. Gabreyl Scrolls

Vestual grinned as Beelzebub jawed with favor. But the two met no response. The prince stared off with distant eye, curled his snarl periodically and sniffed with disgust.

"Wretched earth, wretched ground, wretched air, and wretched fowls…" Lucifer scoffed and faced them, "…all this burned squander protest, futile amends for wretched loss. What good, mindless wretch, are promised grounds taken from ones filled full with pleasures of fulfilled promise."

Vestual hissed at Lucifer's rebuke, but dared not display his distaste for a moment long enough for the feverish adversary to note. Lucifer surveyed the ruins of Candor, "In Adam's bosom rests no land, but pleasures of vested peace. Only in bones carried deep were vests released."

"Bones carried deep," Vestual responded as the prince broke his address and trailed off in inaudible mumble.

Lucifer showed the ages' worth of confusion as he pondered, "How now, with bones carried deep is my appetite awakened? Passed eons of restless travels in dens and damp't caves, in pitch-black burrows, with dust 'pon my belly. E'er my taste was drought and my bowels did rumble. Yet only of sudden I act to pillage? To pillage was all I e'er sought when 'pon this vile earth hewn. Why this epoch… only after these carry deep Adam's bones, long after his feeble blood met His promise set in stone."

Vestual pressed near. "Entreat me," the feign requested, "to your thoughts my prince."

Lucifer exploded. He turned and swung at the demon, catching him with the back of his hand. The thick thud laid Vestual flat where he cowered at Lucifer's feet. The dark prince sneered at him, eyes flared and smoked with anger. "Pick more at intents and in my thoughts and perhaps on your body will remain your head."

# Chapter Three — The North Refuge

"My prince, hold your hand," Vestual pleaded, "We only wish to know your intent, are more triumphs for us to contend?"

Lucifer stomped on Vestual's chest and held him under foot. "You cursed, vile, insolent scab, is this Supreme fooled enough to you for mock`ry? Can *we* wish for the dumb? Come, show me how *we* give it voice." Beelzebub scowled at the prince but made no motion. Lucifer's tease at the brute's mute tongue only seeded greater contempt.

"My prince, please hear us, and hold off your might, we want only more from you," Vestual gasped.

"What more do *you* demand of me? Am I not lord now, am I not triumph't this day, lo days to come as stand I 'pon this knoll triumph't. Have I not torch'd flesh of His creation and singed Adam's loins? There… soot beneath my feet, there… hope as drifting ash. Drag no more upon my intents!"

"But dear morning," Vestual gasped, "Adam's loins remain, scattered, but they remain."

"How do any remain from these scorched ruins?" Lucifer demanded.

Beelzebub placed the massive weight of its dark damp paw on the scales of the monster's back. The sarim's eyes glared at Lucifer's neck with wide shadow. Its eyelids, which closed in vertical fashion, twitched rapidly. Lucifer moaned and lifted his foot from Vestual's frame. The great dragon staggered as if suddenly unaware.

Vestual squirmed frantically and panted as the enraged monster curled his jagged tail above his shoulder. The fallen arch hoisted himself and draped his marred body with his thin leathery wings to protect himself should Lucifer flog again. The commander then glanced at Beelzebub who glared back with a menacing snarl. Vestual shook with fear at the grim visage of the powerful sarim, and with good reason.

# Lands of Eden — by M.Gabreyl Scrolls

What is said of loyalty among barbarians hails from the anarchy of the fallen. The belief that all Lucifer's minions esteemed him after their demise is greatly misguided. Only his unknown prowess, which was greatly feared by these, saw him as champion. Not one fallen being sought him once they were banished from the kingdom. He was greatly hated for the doom in which he led the multitude. And none hated him more than the likes of the sarim.

These once most beautiful beings were scattered throughout Eden after their tremendous plunge. Sarim became the most hideous beings on earth. Deteriorated from the majesty of color and splendor of music produced from their bodies, each became cloaked and scarred in everlasting black. Only Lucifer was spared the curse of infinite silence which rendered their tongues halved, dry and quenchless. Their bodies were never to hone another note or bring perfume to the Trinity's throne.

The violent hatred harbored in each sarim was greater than any other known to mankind. They were foul and barbaric in nature and their anger was unpredictable. The dark angels feared the power of their brutality, and none was more brutal than Beelzebub.

Beelzebub was known to thrash many members of the fallen in the heat of its rage, more often at times of sporadic rampage, which stemmed from the very sight of the dark offender. It hated Lucifer greater than any other sarim or demon among the desolate. Yet it stayed at the side of the prince as a right hand. The demons believed that the great serpent imparted powers to Beelzebub before the mighty fall from the throne. But this was not true. Beelzebub's hatred for men superseded its distaste for Lucifer, a distaste that set it more common with the self-deified fiend than any other demon. Lucifer's temptation of Adam is what spawned

# Chapter Three — The North Refuge

Beelzebub's devotion. Yet the level of its disdain was bountiful. Only time knew the extent of its loyalty.

The mystery of this grotesque sarim was foolishly misjudged by the prince of darkness. His carelessness allowed Beelzebub to continually manipulate Lucifer. Like all sarim, its abilities were focused to beguile the mind. But only with Beelzebub was this power extended upon dark forces.

Vestual shifted his attention onto Lucifer who stared off blankly. "Our volleys of the night, and the flames nigh terrified them to stupor. Still remain scoured bone, for here is that which spoils in lesser years," Vestual remarked.

Lucifer's grumbles struck more fear in the merciless arch. Yet Vestual instantly sung into his cunning nature. "Which was planned first, my prince." Vestual argued softly, "Wonder which is better aim, to take the grace given these few with sumptuous tumult, or hand that given life from them back to Him who created it?" Lucifer seethed with hot flames spurting from his eyes and mouth. Vestual perched his chin at the dragon's ear and moaned with pity. "Ward one-thousand Kanes to slaughter their own flesh, and still will Able's blood cry out from Hades' bosom. So to no good." The crafty demon then maneuvered to Lucifer's other ear and slurped seductively. "Ah, but taint one-thousand Ables with the blood from wandering hearts, and see how few travel to limbo and witness Able's feet. There is our aim dark prince."

Lucifer squinted ahead as the ideals hatched again in his sinister mind. The beast whipped his tail and struck the ground with its deadly venom. The crack echoed over the crowd. His eyes glowed pale green through the dark smoke round his head. Vestual drifted from his shoulder and glinted at the tune he strummed upon the rowdy beast's heart. Beelzebub appeared to smirk with approval at Vestual as the two set their diligence on Lucifer.

All demons present cheered with a mighty roar as abundant shadow overcame the hilltop. Lucifer, puffed with pride, thundered loudly over the minions. "Powers and Dominions, forsaken deities of Heav'n, bend your ear to your lord of worldly realm!" The crowd erupted in cheer. Dark ash tossed skyward blotted the bright rays of a midday sun. This was as the demons desired, as the darkness enticed them greatly. The roars echoed throughout the region before Lucifer continued.

"Eden," he scoffed, "what exists deep within her gulf that can hold immortal vigor. We, once celestial virtues yet oppressed and fallen have not as much as Heav'n lost. Instead, more glory and more dread than those from no fall, who prance His broken throne." The demons hissed and began to mock and jostle. Lucifer raised his claw and calmed them. "Nay, we have not lost Heav'n, what loss is bound will, what loss is tam'd tongue and tempered motion, what loss…" Lucifer paused as his shame overcame him. He trailed again into quiet mumbling. "…forecast and direction, endless divine principality. Peaceful, magnificent Heav'n…loss…lost… for what good comes of evil?"

The crowd was still in wait for their leader to continue. Lucifer brought himself out and snarled.

"No!" The fiends responded with hails of applause and shouting, "Not Heav'n lost, instead we have only Heav'n to gain! And not from Him, who deemed less your Monarch shadowed high 'pon this mound." Lucifer raised his arms triumphantly, "But from these meager vessels.Souls who breathe His life by morning star and moon. These, He's promised our empyreal stage and divvied our share among. And whence did I decree in this, my Haven, that inhabitants should be so graced?"

"Never!" a demon responded with proclaim. Soon others joined in a chant that shook the grounds.

# Chapter Three　　　　　　　　　　　The North Refuge

"Never!" Lucifer rumbled. "And thus, this Heav'n which He has graced them, belongs to none but my hand!"

The demons roared with excitement and spewed fowl scents into the atmosphere as they leaped and soared, some tossed dead animals. Lucifer grinned monstrously as he watched his fellow fallen delight in evil.

Suddenly, the distant north sky danced with a strange shadow and forceful winds. Beelzebub motioned and directed Lucifer's gaze on a grim cloud that slithered over the horizon. Warm wind carried the whine of the cloud over the spoiled wasteland. The subtle sound stilled the brooding crowd and all hateful eyes turned to view the mystery.

Lucifer studied the drift of the cloud and began to whisper to himself quietly. He shut his eyes as his whispers amplified over the hills. None understood what he spoke, yet all where terrified by the dark pattern of his voice.

The dragon's eyes shot open. Instantly the cloud funneled in the direction of the wicked camp. The creatures began to moan with confusion as the cloud drew closer. It channeled with incredible speed and deafening hum over the plains. One seraph spontaneously leapt into the air and was at once swarmed. The demon struck the ground with a quake and agonized as hundreds of lobita tormented him. Panic and chaos ensued as the rest of the legion was quickly overtaken by the shade of insects.

Beetles burst with black ooze as they pelted the callous skin of the creatures below. Their shells stung the beings with as much and even more pain as they had applied to their previous victims. Their speed was enhanced by the dark prince who beckoned them to his feet.

The swarm surged up the hill toward the dark-hearted sarim, in preparation to give him his share of plague. But Lucifer lifted his head calmly, opened his mouth wide and let loose a thunderous howl. A dark chasm formed at the back of his throat and echoed his bellows far beyond. The insects careened into his enlarged mouth by the masses until the entire swarm of tormentors filled the dragon's gullet. Lucifer's roar dissolved as he calmly shut his mouth. He closed his eyes meditatively, inhaled deep and long. When he finally opened his eyes, the sky was cleared of tossed ash and smoke. The cries of the beasts quieted as all eyes set on the grotesque being at the top of the hill.

The prince of darkness surveyed his minions who were frozen in awe. The evil spirits all appeared ready to bend to him with reverence. But Lucifer's face contorted with disdain. He spoke softly to himself, "These I tallied from glory to gloom, their end sealed, act as there exists no doom." The dismal being faced Vestual who cringed behind his wings. "How, Vestual, were these men spread?"

Vestual unveiled himself and scampered closer for the prince to hear. He looked up at the giant sarim with sheepish stare. "To the east ran many to meet poison in my claw," he stated with hissed satisfaction, "yet to the north diverted some others, and those still blithe your Eden's air of Adam's stench."

Lucifer's eyes flared briefly. Beelzebub shook its chains impatiently and grumbled with bass. The great adversary turned to address the crowd once more. "Progeny of Heav'n, sit no longer in darkness here hatching vain empires. This race of man, created less in power and excellence, but favored more of Him who rules above, set your fangs on them. Learn their mold and weakness, tempt at best by subtlety, those who will to join our party, that their God may prove their foe. Still wield ultimate force on this Eden lain exposed, with fierce shadow lay waste His whole creation and possess all as our own!"

The charge flared the excitement of the seraphs and fallen arch's. The demons jostled with cheer. Lucifer turned from them and shrouded his face from Beelzebub and Vestual. A soft

## Chapter Three — The North Refuge

whimper was heard, though neither of Lucifer's hands recognized the sound as a cry. Vestual flailed his wings and requested his leader's command.

The hideous leader turned to the arch and spat a mound of black saliva at Vestual's feet. In the mound squirmed a beetle whose wings were stuck to its shell by the slime. Vestual's face knotted with disgust. "To the north you will head, and take your scores of these. Go, and render intolerable darkness." At his command, Vestual leapt and soared over the crowd. He called fifty seraphs to join him and they were rapidly on their way to the north grounds of Eden.

Lucifer turned to Beelzebub who shook its chains again and pointed to the wasted borders of Candor. "I know great brute. I too engulf the stench of mortals near," the dragon hummed as he stared ferociously into the distant forest. "Whether be on the taste of these flies or gulfs of strong winds, the puny be close. But leave them for the night." Lucifer decided as he reached into his mound of spit and lifted the slimed beetle to his eye. "There is another we must attend."

\* \* \*

From the distant hills of the Candora Forest, the dispersal of the sefiyai appeared as a sudden onset of night. The evil scattered from the terrain taking all darkness with it as the sun reclaimed the midday over the torched remains of Candor. Hidden from their fleeting glances were the sharp eyes of a defending figure driven wild from the passing night. The figure remained hidden under massive ferns that gave him just enough view to know the proper time.

The man maintained his emotion once the ashes were fully cleared of the demons and the spoiled grounds of Candor were revealed. He calmly shut his eyes in confused silence as he was forced to bite back desired tears.

"Lórcephoene..." called a deceptive whisper. The sound jarred his gloom and sprung him from his belly. He slid from hiding and journey back into the dark border to join the company of two mystics that waited for him in further depths of the forest.

Mystics were beings of keen focus and untamed craze made of villainous essence which they used to poison mankind and spur their ravenous nature. They were unseen to the unwary eye, vicious in every facet yet incapable of physical prowess. What mystics possessed was a cunning nature that allowed their cruel manner to be crafted through men. They took the name of whatever men desired to give place to that which comforted. All mystics plotted with the great adversary, and against him. Their desires were for Lucifer's end but for his evil to reign. The plot rested in the shade of men's heart which could grow darker even than that of the dark prince that schemed against them.

"Lórcephoene..." the whisper called again. The man coughed harshly before he called back. They were hid well in the heights of the trees, so well in fact that they caused the crazed man startle when they leapt from branches and landed on either side of him.

The man hissed at them in anger, he set shadowed sight on the malignant misfits as dark drool careened from his rotted teeth. The mystics cowered with howls as he brought his outturned palm upon their heads. He struck one as a father would a disobedient child. Both of them lashed back at him with tiny bites and scratches that barely felt even as pinches to the human who ultimately subdued them with brute strikes. Though the struggle was true, the man finished with the mystics and spoke to them as if the three romped playfully.

# Chapter Three — The North Refuge

"Young sons ignite your hearts to Lórcephoene and pleasure him with your tongues, what desires, what will we have here that has not already begun?"

The sprites spoke no word but only rolled together as animals at play. The man looked into the canopy above where the final seraph left the grounds.

"These skies are filled darker than the morning's last hour with so much swine that my eyes have never witnessed. And set for vulgar infection on relentless course. My body praises them onward to fulfill their pleasure. And yet my heart pulls against them." The man growled and kicked again at the creatures in hatred. "What are your means here? I want the end of such vile beings." The man began to mumble to himself and touched his brow in a mass of confusion. His body trembled and lament finally found his eyes.

One of the mystics seethed and quickly lapped the man's palm as a dog. It left a greasy yellow residue with which the man coated his pale face. He opened his eyes through the strung spit as the sprite channeled through the touch and caused the human to roll his eyes with delight. "After these beings of blood thirst with blood thirst. And even still seek the blood of those on which they whet. How fiendish my sons, will Lórcephoene's hands become," the man responded. The sprites jeered at each other as they regained control of his mind. The other licked his ear and caused him to faint briefly.

"Seek after the north skilled Lórcephoene, draw the blood of these beasts. And there lies the sons of trespass, there lies the child of Jabal, the son of musicians."

The figure groaned with anger and tossed his fist at the creatures only to be swept by them and held down. He fought briefly before he yielded with euphoric snarl and laughter. "Go after the north, after sefíyai and singed wing, after the child whose blood calls to us as his fathers long before. Lórcephoene thus sets his feet on these men, to stain the earth with their fall. Come spears and daggers for we have aim to break flesh!"

He cackled louder and louder until the birds scattered the trees from the noise. The man's faced hued paler as the mystics fiddled his mind onto dark schemes. He rose to his feet and hurried through the wood in the direction of the seraphs, all while growling beastily and ravaging anything in his way.

## There Remains Hope

The elders had pressed the men onward through the tall fields with exhaustion slowing their progress more and more as the dusk settled over the tundra. Night would overcome them long before they reached the last leg of their journey. The pace of their travel lead the people to complain for retire. Their beg was for food, for warmth, for rest, and such grew greatly weary upon the elders ears. Elias relented as the aura filled with garnet glow. Camp was set amidst sleigh stone taverns bordered by sparse ferns and tall pines. The men gathered wood and set boundary for the camp in a circle of small glowing hearths. Centered among them, burned a bright blaze which allowed women and children to keep warm as the men mulled with question.

The blaze of the central fire warmed young Aman and Lathan but did little to quell their bellies of hunger. The pannea grains had become as bites of air to them and only made them long for flavor. The hunters among the men were few, still Aman was greatly puzzled that even those present allowed their stomachs to gripe. None attempted to track a single animal, even as the day was closing.

"Where have the hunters gone," noticed Lathan as he gazed over the camp. His first words to Aman since the early morning only again spawned excited curiosity. Aman looked

# Chapter Three — The North Refuge

round the camp and noticed too that the very ones whom he was requesting of action were missing. The two boys immediately set themselves to search and began to stroll beyond the firesides. The clay taverns offered wide reflect of the camp yet could not help the boys find their way.

Their ears caught whispers that stemmed from a fern pasture hidden from the fires in moonlight glow. Aman stepped into the clearing only to hear the grunt of one hunter who stared back at him with annoyance. The two then searched the ground to see others lying upon their backs with their eyes glazed with fatigue. Perhaps entranced by the plum evening capturing the sky from the glowing orb retreating west. They all exhaled long slow breaths into the moistened air, almost rhythmically, as the sun vanished in a scarlet haze. Lathan glanced at Aman who shrugged with baffle.

"Lathan, Aman," Barra called with breathy resonance, "on your backs you two." Aman frowned and looked at the hunter who beckoned him to obey with a stern nod. The two boys then lay on their backs but continued to look on with confusion. Lathan glanced at Aman and winked before joining the growing chorus of exhales among the men.

A tiny tickle made Aman snap his hand to his ear. He plucked his lobe and the itch was gone. Soon another tingled his nose. He sniffed and picked as another buzz reached his other ear. Suddenly he found himself twitching and swatting as his skin welcomed the bites of several m☐konops. They began to whiz round him and indeed round all the men in excited fashion.

Both boys squirmed with irritation. "Be still," Barra demanded. Aman and Lathan quickly covered their faces to prevent the little flies from biting their cheeks. Aman stiffened intensely, trying to ignore the stings. And both remained puzzled at why the men lay on the ground growing in hunger.

# Lands of Eden                               by M.Gabreyl Scrolls

Yet soon the answer would come. Soft squeaks echoed from afar off. Aman rolled his arm from his eyes and looked into the mauve sky. Another round of squeaks came, this time a bit louder and much closer. Aman heard the sound of wings clapping against the wind. His eyes darted about but he could see nothing. Suddenly, a small dark winged animal squealed just inches above his head. It swooped with ivory teeth flaring and a shrill call vibrating through its black tongue. Aman was geared to jump but quickly found his mouth covered by Ezra. "Be calm, or you'll frighten them," the young hunter demanded.

But what were they? The sky filled with dozens of these tiny winged rodents not more than the size of the prairie moles of Candor. The light of the crested moon revealed their brown course skin as they filled the atmosphere with chirps that scampered within arms reach.

As more gathered, Barra whistled, sounding the call to action. The men skillfully plucked creatures from the air in response and filled their arms with as many of these creatures as could be held. Some removed their robes and caught the creatures into a wrap.

Each man leapt to their feet and snagged more from the air. The hunters chuckled with joy as the chaos calmed with the spared creatures squeaking away into the caves. Ones caught cheeped uncontrollably as each was placed into a large sack to be taken to the central fire. Aman and Lathan dared to near the commotion as the men patted each other with triumph.

"What are these?" Lathan asked.

"These," panted Barra with bellowing chuckle, "are our food for the night young ones, the Creator has provided for us," he said with a smile. Aman frowned with a twinge of disgust. "Oh no, wait till you taste one, not appealing in

# Chapter Three — The North Refuge

appearance no, but Ezra here, my son can make a delicious cheirpto churn."

"Cheirpto..." Aman questioned. The name itself meant 'winged hand' and offered very little in way of appetite.

"Yes, or as we like to call them, 'air rats of the north,'" responded a nearby hunter who noted the boys' confusion.

"You see young ones," Barra continued, "the northlands are quite stony and coarse, so there is not much animal life here. But these caves, the cheirpto have lived here always. They do not mind the cold, moist air of the nights."

"Why did they all come here, what brought them?" Aman asked.

The nearby hunter laughed, "Cheirpto always fly during the night, looking for food. They eat small insects, so we attracted the insects to attract them."

"How did we attract those insects?" Lathan asked.

"The grain," Barra answered, "pannea is full of sweet nectar. M☐konops love nectar and smelled it on us when we laid on the ground for them. We attracted the insects, and so attracted the cheirpto."

Aman grimaced with sickness, "So we attract the m☐konops to attract these air rats?"

"Yes!" Barra responded with excitement.

"And we're going to eat them...the air rats?" Lathan mocked.

"Yes," the hunter smiled with a nod, "Why do you think we've been eating pannea all day? Ah, sweet grain, good for energy. Your father, Aman, he discovered these grains and taught us much of their..." Barra stalled the hunter as Aman looked away. The man paused and smirked with guilt as the small boy tried to hide his longing.

But Barra knew. He smiled assuredly and patted Aman's head. "You will not go hungry tonight young one, don't worry.

Ezra will make your meal right and you will enjoy." With that the hunter walked off and joined his son. The two hurried to the squirming sac. Ezra reached into the sack and joined the men who wrestled the creatures to the camp.

"Air rats," Lathan continued, "your papa eats air rats?"

Aman swallowed and glanced at Lathan, "Well, at least we will not go hungry. I'm a bit sick of pannea. Let's go and have some...air rats." Aman said with a cringe.

Lathan chuckled in a form that had grown distantly rare to the young boy through the course of the day. Aman joined and soon the two were laughing through the early evening as the food was being prepared.

\* \* \*

As the crowd gathered round the flames for the meals being prepared, the four elders sat apart from them in meditation. Elias in particular set his gaze on a distant northern specter where there seemed to be a call upon his spirit.

Jodia, Mered, and Seth were more restless in their thoughts, eager to find their place further along the flatlands where their enemy could not overcome them. More so eager to stand and subdue their enemy's march. Their eyes were not too old to see the bleak destruction intended by fiends that hissed along their footprints. Never had an enemy trounced the staffs of elders. Theirs was always given the mark of victory and forced retreat in dark droves. None returned. Until now. With a raging fire in rifted eyes that armed quest for limb, life, and lung. Their enemies were declared for man's heart, and nothing would stand against them.

Mered leaned his weight against a large boulder where Elias also rested his old bones. Jodia scribbled in the clay clearing as Seth stared off in not so distant thought.

# Chapter Three

## The North Refuge

"There is a mass scatter into the south sky," Jodia began. "If we do not move onward, these men will be scattered again in few dawns."

The fires cackled in the distance, accompanied by the feigned laughter of doubtful men, as the four nodded solemnly in agreement.

"These men will be scattered nonetheless," Mered responded. "We journ by day and rest at night, while our enemy blots the sky so that they might march continually. Their masses are all around and they will not cease their march upon us." The young elder glanced at Elias, "Unless we stand against them."

Elias sighed and stared off without response. He closed his eyes and pressed his face against his jō. His lip quivered with meditation and soon the elder began to mumble. He desired no other ear to give his whispers audience. However, Jodia and Mered heard him thoroughly. Old prophecy passed down from the very lips of Adam marked Elias' tongue.

"Ch☐tum ev abbas essum…" he began with disgust, "null yev sileo pah adamo." This meant *'the accuser is a devouring lion, and there is no rest for mankind.'*

Jodia and Mered gazed at the elder who sat in defeated manner. Elias simply continued in solemn tongue, "He will stand above them, robed in black with eyes of smoke and vile tongue. He will despise and revile them with wicked feet and wandering tail. Yet at his toes they will rejoice as swine to scraps, as fowl to crumbs of spoiled cake. Dispersing them with the command of his voice they will lift the sky of light with wings of skin. Shadow will follow their path. They will plunge the earth with pale flame, they will bark with vicious fangs and spit fire through the land." Elias finished the prophecy and looked into the sky with misery. The elders stood silent for a moment as a howl whined from the caves.

"But still I urge you," Mered responded, "for yours is given a swifter hand and swifter feet by He who is greater in you than your adversary." Mered stared down at his broken uncle sincerely. Elias turned and faced the young warrior who knew there was more to the words of Adam. He spoke the proverb with courageous eye. "The man with whom He dwells, what is there for him to fear? When these and far worse created in earth, in air, in sea...when they threaten you, even so I say it is better for you to stand 'gainst them with sling and stone, than to flee by the name of He whom created all things."

As the father of mankind aged, Adam saw his offspring grow more in the fear and deception of things that took dark forms and threatened common life. The father of mankind spurred his sons and daughters often as he aged, to remind them of the dominion of the Alpha. Mered, who was too often brash in his approach to Adam's way, still kept much of Adam's teaching in the close reaches of his heart.

Mered was the youngest of Candor's elders. He was the son of Cainan who was Enos firstborn. Thus, nephew to Elias and Seth the III, yet as a brother to Jodia who was few years older than he. In appearance he looked no older than the hunters, and even younger than some as his face and hair was free of gray. Yet he was fierce among the warriors. Brave and skilled with his staff. But untamed and impatient with aggression that was rarely marked with full thought. These very words repeatedly touched the ears of Mered who in his youth guided a poor eyed Adam through the vast pastures of Candor. He witnessed the father, in wonder, speak with animals, command fruit from earth, and do many miracles granted to him from the touch of the Alpha. Adam directed such marvels that only left a young Mered filled with desires for power and wonders, and caused his hasty hand. Only in growing days did the man become the elder who realized where Adam's strength stemmed.

## Chapter Three — The North Refuge

"We are greater than these creatures uncle, you cannot fear them."

"I do not fear them," Elias replied calmly, "yet still I cannot shake a troubled heart. As fierce as our hand is against the demons, we have never faced such a force. The senseless attack by night was not just the rampages of vile creatures which we have thwarted in times passed." He turned his attention onto Mered and Jodia. "The great adversary united many under his command, and here we are, driven from our place. How now am I to see us, to see these men against such enemies, without any arms? How can nothing but defeat lie for us again?"

The three stood silent, each picturing the slaughter that might have taken place at the hands of darkness. Not one of them could keep their eyes from shifting to the southern sky. Only Elias let his attention shift occasionally on the far off sparkle which the others did not appear to notice.

Seth finally spoke. "Defeat for these does not lie in the hands of the fiends that chase them." The elders all turned to him as he continued, "It lies in the fear within this camp…the fault among these men."

Elias glinted at Seth with question, "Of what do you speak brother?"

Seth stepped into the clearing with a long sigh. He glanced at Mered and Jodia briefly, then looked into the concerned eyes of his elder brother. "I speak of this boy whom we continue to keep our tongues held."

Elias stared in firm fashion. Neither man blinked but the two allowed long tension to build between them before either spoke word. Each elder was indeed holding their thoughts about the small boy Lathan, who through each elder's denial was not considered the spawn of Candor's scattering. Their hopes that the men of the camp would ignore the harsh thoughts of some against the boy were dwindling in their own doubts.

"Why should this boy be of any concern?"

"You know why, brother." Seth answered with glance at Mered and Jodia. "What child, what man, what being has come from the very perils of the Rim forest, where dark beings have long been abundant, without scar or scathe? How could such wonder not exist when such poison has found all others who have ventured there? Some men already question this...those that know. And as they spread his story, how long before everyone here questions the boy?"

Elias frowned at his brother with disappointment, only to find Mered and Jodia's eyes turned away in form that they too held his pattern of mind.

"Do you not question?" Elias responded coldly, "Do my brothers now follow the heart of such men that would lift a hand against a child?"

"No brother," Jodia quickly answered, "Yet what Seth bids holds warrant. I hear as some of these men beginning to whisper with doubt." Jodia paused and looked at Seth who kept his focus firmly on Elias. "Indeed we wish no hand upon young Lathan, yet his presence might be growing dissention among us, and perhaps it is better if one among us spurs him onto the north apart from the crowd."

Elias frowned greatly and rubbed his brow.

"Must we be defeated so easily?" Mered questioned. "Must we continue to flee at the will of our enemies. We could fare our men much better against these sefíyai. If we teach them. If we arm them the way our fathers armed us. Even with this child along, arm them so that their fears will not be so great they will not stand against the coming enemy."

# Chapter Three

## The North Refuge

"These men will not be taught to fight," Jodia responded. "They have forsaken our voice for ages and quarrel among each other. We cannot have our trusts in any of these men."

Mered frowned, "Then we must have our trusts in the Alpha, brother. Seth, Elias, do as we elders have before."

Jodia shook his head quickly, "I know what you believe, young nephew, but we cannot do as before. Men's hearts are too far removed for the angels to stand with us."

"How do we know?" Mered responded. "They are not men as we, the Alpha is not a man as we. They will not see these men in the manner we have. We must request them to stand with us again—"

"—And if this boy is tainted, if darkness exist among us, how will the angels stand with us?" Jodia softly reasoned. "They are too fearful to follow us into battle even if we call upon the hosts." Jodia looked at Elias as Mered sighed, "You know as I that we cannot spur the hosts or these men to stand with us."

Elias bowed his head as Mered conceded to Jodia. He turned and again faced the distant specter that continually called his attention. He sighed and shut his eyes.

"What ceases us great warriors of Adam but fear, that we see only dark disdain for these men found no means in truth? And have so quickly measured and claimed them not worth defending? This has never been our spirit, for we were not given a spirit of fear, and taking such only dooms us further into ruin and misery."

Elias turned and faced his brothers who each nodded in shame of their inner doubts. Elias continued, "Whatever taint there be with this child, how much greater is the Alpha. Whatever doubt looms among these men, how much more is His promised provision for Candor."

Seth lifted his chin as he noticed a glimmer of hope in his elder brother's eye. A glimmer which he had been searching for since the early dawn of day. "If any of our thoughts be true," Seth calmy spoke, "Mered's ring most of our course. There should be no further action but to seek what the Alpha lays before us. And perhaps, prepare these men. If not to stand against the sefíya, that at least to defend their families as each man ought to do."

Mered nodded at Seth and shifted as if ready to move. But Seth spoke solely to Elias, as if he knew the call upon his brother's heart.

Elias looked again at the distant specter and hummed deep within his chest. "I will seek the face of the Alpha in the night and make request of the angels to stand beside us against the coming enemy."

"I will accompany you," Mered stated to which Elias raised his hand in resistance.

"No, you must remain here."

"Remain here?" Mered responded. "Our stillness is what has spent us from our camp. I want to be along, to know what the Alpha prepares and to prepare myself and these men."

"You must remain here nephew. I know your heart, but do not let it exceed your mind. These men will grumble with more doubt if they notice too many of the elders missing. What's more, the enemy is quick upon this camp, and such quarrels will see us scattered again in the dark. I must take this task alone." Elias set his focus on his brothers. "We must rest in His promised power as we have before. For when has the Alpha not spared men of His heart from the snares of Sëtan. Rest here in this place, guard the camp. Indeed Mered and Jodia, gather the men and ensure they are ready, should such perils attempt to claim us before the dawn. Seth, remain here and pray over them and me. I will return in the morning."

# Chapter Three — The North Refuge

At that the elder turned and exited the clearing to make his way. His brothers remained momentarily before each dispersed to keep vigil over the camp. Each meditated with prayer and hope that nothing would try their hand in the night.

\*     \*     \*

Air rat tasted just as it sounded and hardly harnessed any of the boasts of its cook. Yet the boys ate with no hesitance as their appetites suppressed reaction of their taste buds. Aman filled his cheeks as he listened to the men amidst the camp regale tales of old Candor before the growth of its civilization. Each offered short lived joys which went over with humble laughter that diminished in the cold north air. They spoke of the great monsters that riddled the land, they spoke of the fights of the elders, their travails and triumphs that spawned Candor's resilience. They spoke of beasts rumored to roam the lands of Eden and wonder flowed from nearly every lip at these tales.

The elders spent much of the night charging these men in the protection of their women and children. Aman watched their reactions as Mered encouraged them that there was nothing of the enemy to fear and that refuge would soon come. This seemed to cause more worry and hope for something that would calm their troubled hearts. They hoped, but knew, even without word, that their end was upon them.

The boy milled through the camp and found Seth, who sat alone far from the central fire. The elder stared ahead with complex expression. Aman approached slowly though Seth knew the young shepherd came. The boy sat beside the warrior and yawned briefly. Seth looked at him with a squint, then looked out again through the cover to where the sky blended with the dark corners of the land. Aman waited a moment, then held out a morsel of food placed on a twig. Seth grunted and looked at Aman strangely. After a long stare Aman found something on the elder's face seldom found by any. Seth grinned.

"Your bone needs more nourishment than mine, young spirit, eat."

Aman paused for a moment, shrugged, took a chomp of the charred meat. He crunched slowly, cringed and protruded his tongue. After filling his belly to satisfaction, his sense of taste was quickly catching up to his appetite. The boy grimaced briefly but managed to swallow down the meat without a gag.

After a few more moments of silence, the boy looked at Seth long and hard. "How did you know that fire would chase away the beetles?"

Seth grunted with a twinge of impatience but humored the small reu. "I was not always an old warrior young spirit. Like your father, I learned much about the animals of the land."

The elder's response was sharp and filled with demand to be left unbothered. But Aman stared more to which Seth turned slowly and glared back. The boy saw through the annoyance and questioned again.

"Elder, are the stories of the others tell about Candor true?"

Seth glimpsed back at the central with exasperated sigh. Revealed were men huddled together in farce laughter, their eyes full of repressed fear, and faces pale with concern that made them appear unified. Seth clenched his teeth for a moment then looked back upon the boy. "What stories do they tell?"

Aman settled beside the elder, "They say that Candor was a place of dark beasts before we came. They say that animals with claws and fangs were there and that there was a mighty behemoth there. It claimed Candor with its tusks." The elder hummed slightly as Aman went on, "But they say that the

# Chapter Three — The North Refuge

elders before us, they fought them bravely and beat them. That is why they returned nights ago. To reclaim their land."

Seth groaned calmly, "Do you believe these stories?"

Aman shrugged, "I don't know, I believe some of them." The boy paused with long thought, "I saw you fight last night, only…" Aman was reminded of the night. How Candor was defeated by the crazed creatures. How the elders could not hold back the animals and spare his father. "Some argue that the elders will fight again and defeat them the next time so that all will be returned as it was before."

"But you do not believe it." Seth responded.

Aman could not shake the fright of the dawn, the creatures' howls echoed in his mind, their eyes pierced his memory with wild recall, and their voices flustered his stomach with fear.

"I believe that the Alpha promised the land to Adam." Aman answered with a look for reassurance from Seth. " But why couldn't the beast be defeated as before, if the elders fought them, why did they not defeat them in the night? Why couldn't my father fight them, how will I know he is okay if even the elders cannot defeat them now?"

Aman whispered softly with want in response that mimicked that of every man who pretended to boast by the camp fire while they held ready retreat from the dark dissension. Seth, however, would have no ounce of patience for Aman's doubt.

"If you have tears, leave them for sorrows, not for uncertainty. If there is wonder of your father, what reason is there to weep? If there is hope in his breath, what good are moans? There is not certainty of loss for Jebas, end your tears for you are not so young to know your fears will amount to no gain," the elder stated as he tossed a pebble in front of him.

Aman looked at the elder who stared off sternly, his fierce eyes admonished the boy to sniff away the lump in his throat.

# Lands of Eden

by M. Gabreyl Scrolls

Torched shards of wood floated by and Aman slumped his shoulders with head bowed. Seth sensed the boy's despair and meant no harm in his rebuke. Not long after the boy grew silent did Seth answer his cold ere with warmer conversation. He pulled his broken staff from the strap round his waist. He began to draw in the dirt.

He moved the dirt round until the figure of an animal appeared in the ground. He encircled it and glanced at the boy with upturned brow.

"What is it?" Aman asked.

Seth smirked and continued to drag his cane in the dirt until the animal became more recognizable.

"Re`em?" Aman pondered.

Seth lifted his staff and turned it over to reveal an old deep groove notched at the tip of the wood. Within the groove was a dirt-clumped blond braid of a horse's tail.

"When I was a boy, my father expected me to tend the *ouct* he owned. I learned from him to clean and feed them with great care," the elder stated with a smile. "A time came when my great grandfather demanded me to care for a small foal, not more than days old from its mother. I was to bathe it and keep it warm from the winds, keep it apart from the other young oucts who bullied. One night while I rested in the pasture, a re`em came upon me to devour the foal. It raged? greatly, but I would not let it sense any fear in me. I fought it. But even so I was but a little boy, and the re`em overcame me. It carried the foal from the pasture leaving me only with this braid from its tail."

Aman stared at the staff as he reminisced his frightful morning with Mariah. Seth then produced the boy's finely crafted bō from his back and held it upright for the boy to view. "I have yet returned this to you young reu, and I will in time. For now, will you allow me to hold onto it?" Aman

## Chapter Three — The North Refuge

nodded as Seth chuckled. The elder continued as Aman admired his weapon.

"Shepherd, what do you see on the faces of these men gathered round the camp?"

Aman glanced over his shoulder at the elder request. He examined the men closely for as long as the elder allowed. Without any response the elder answered his own question.

"These men muse much of Candor. But there is no amount of joy in their muse. They consider so much of what they have lost in the night. So much of what they do not have." Aman turned and faced the elder who looked firmly into the camp fire. "They focus so on loss, that this is all they see becoming of us here." Seth turned his attention on the boy who could faintly look into the stern elder's eyes. Yet Seth lifted his chin, "Fear is what destroys hope, their fears grant that none of us will ever reclaim Candor. In their eyes, you see no essence of comfort, no scent of hope." Seth handed Aman his staff but ensured the reu kept his eyes on him. "You have already overcome such fear, even so much in the Candora wood. Thus you are not called to have such eyes, young spirit, or to have such doubt. Your father would not have this, nor will I. If Jebas is the hunter I know of, he will not be so easily done by such creatures. Rest assured young spirit that he searches for you, and will return as he promised."

The elder stared long and hard at the child before he looked off in thought. Aman smiled in full reassurance. His father was indeed a great hunter. He could not allow doubt to take presence over his thoughts.

Aman glanced again at the men and studied their faces, eyes wide with unsteady rhythm, forced smiles from forced laughter. Aman frowned as he could yet understand how their worries could be calmed in midst the past nights and vicious howls that echoed round them. The boy held trust in the elders unlike any other in the camp, and found his worries easily erased in Seth's confirming gaze. Yet, why Seth could gain no relief of others even while they boasted of the elders feats puzzled him. And even more he wondered why their fright was scorned.

"The men say that the elders have done many great things, if this is true why do they still fear?"

Seth hummed with soft bass before he answered, "Never have any of these believed in us the elders. They speak only of what they wish. They portray our valor so that their hearts might be quelled. They portray our greatness and expect to have us return them to their commonplace. This is not the way. We are men just as they. We can offer them no greater reward than they can grant themselves." Seth looked again at the boy, "We deserve no boasts."

The elder raised his eyebrow to see if the small boy understood. Aman offered another shrug.

Seth continued, "There is nothing accomplished by your hand when your expectance is kept on another. But when you put your hand to task, do you not find your own worth of praise? These men would not praise us so when they saw us do nothing, yet they recall what we have done in times past and suddenly they praise us in expectation. How much more could these men praise themselves if they put their hands to do what we have taught through centuries, if they stood against the creatures of the night as we have always done..."

Aman frowned still wondering why the elder belittled the men's acclaim. "Elder, you can do greater things against those creatures than others here... I saw you fight the beasts. I saw all the elders with my eyes. Even if they put their hands to fight, they would not be able to do what the elders can."

The old man paused in the lad's adoration but quickly told him proper. "This is not true young spirit. What you saw, was

# Chapter Three

## The North Refuge

men do what was is gifted for them to do. This was not of our own strength. I have been gifted with skills that far surpass the abilities of many, but such does not make me greater than any man here. Only He who gives me strength is great through me."

Aman appeared disappointed but Seth continued to explain. "Hear me, Aman, and understand this through all your days. Great things can be done through any man." The elder poked Aman's staff as he stated more, "Great things have been done through you." Aman looked up at the elders esteem. "We are each of Adam's blood and of Eve's womb. The same that is done through me can be done through you, but only if you keep trust in He who grants strength. This is why fear must never reign in your heart, as these others. Fear keeps you from being called as warriors, keeps you as one who relies on the strength of others, like these here rely on we elders. You are called to greater means."

The boy nodded with set interest on the elder's word, but Seth found himself taken back by the revelation of his own expectations in the small child. He paused briefly and studied the young shepherd's eyes. There lies the heart which drew Elias to place his hopes in him. The elder nodded with discernment and faced the child with engaged attention.

"Young spirit, you will do great things, as the elder's, as the warriors of old. I believe this of you." Aman gasped unnoticeably and felt his heart beat with surge. "You must not allow yourself to be any lesser. Even in this, do not allow any to boast of you. Place their hands of expectance with the Alpha, for each man was given his ability for simple design and purpose."

Aman's eyes lit with hope. "Shous ptouhareu ev Ahquah positisou," he recalled.

Seth grinned at the small child with patience.

"How great a reward it is," Seth continued, "to know that each one is gifted for a purpose. And how great is the young spirit that sets his mind to use his gift for this purpose."

Aman smirked and played in the dirt with his finger for a moment. His curiosity continued to play at his heart as his father's voice returned to him. The boy mulled for several moments thinking about gifts, the talents of his brothers' and friends, what Jebas told him of his mother, what his mother believed of her unborn child's calling. His swirling thoughts brought him to an encompassing question. "Did you know my mother, elder?"

Seth cocked his head and inhaled the cooled night air with the vision of reflection. "I knew very much of your mother, little spirit," the elder responded.

"Your mother had many gifts," Seth spoke with a voice so in tune with that of the boy's father. He looked away for a still moment and stroked his cheek. He looked down at the woman's offspring and a firm nod followed. "Mariah's hands were most gifted...never idle in any of her days. She could mold anything from the clay, the stalk, and branch...a gift I believe you share with her, young reu."

The boy smiled.

"She was a servant, her pottage was like no other in all of Candor, and she learned many means for the animal hide. She was fair in beauty, and gifted with much comfort for her sons and your father."

Aman looked calmly at his hand and wondered how much it resembled that of his mother. He guessed at what many things she made with hers and a smile spread from cheek to cheek. "What other gifts did she have?" the boy asked with greedy curiosity.

# Chapter Three — The North Refuge

Seth continued with a long sigh, "Above all, she possessed a gift that made her cherished by many. A wisdom to know the gifts of others."

The small shepherd delighted in hearing about his mother whom Jebas rarely discussed without tearful eye. Mariah was seen as a woman after the very heart of Eve. Though very young, her mind was filled with much instruction, and she patterned her life in the way of the elders. She was the daughter of Elimelech, adopted by Methuselah and thus, by right, princess of Eden. Aman, her only son, thus inherited the direct bloodline of Enoch through his mother's lineage. And such made him as treasured as Mariah. Her spirit was so cherished that upon her death the elder's of the village mourned for three score days. Yet in their mourning the elders found solace in the promise that her gifts would continue on through her womb.

As the boy continued to think of his family, his face grew grim. He looked at the elder with repressed sorrow. Seth responded without needing ear of the boy's mind. "Young reu, have you heard of the day of your birth?"

Aman shrugged to which Seth sniffed with a long stare into the distance.

"On the day of your birth, your father came to the elders in the heart of night. The time had come for you to leave your mother's womb. I believe Mariah knew that day what would be required of her. And when the time came, not a tear fell upon her cheek or wail from her lips.

"Upon your very birth, your mother said 'This is a day of joy, for a pillar is born to Jebas, who is blessed among men.'" Aman remained still as Seth spoke. "She named you 'du Lana,' which means his faith will be great, and he will be given much. And your father called you 'Aman,' which means he will be required of many men."

# Lands of Eden — by M. Gabreyl Scrolls

He gripped the child with firm reassuring eyes. "You see little spirit, upon your mother's very lips were promises to be fulfilled in you." The boy inhaled long breaths and felt the warmth of Seth's truth. "Young spirit, take not upon you the sorrow of your birth, your mother loved you, as has your father. Upon your first breath she proclaimed this.

"As I have said, I too know your heart, you seek great strength, faith, and wisdom. There can be no sorrow for any in your existence, for within you are many things which will require much, for you are called and will be much for all of Eden in your days."

Aman returned Seth's firm warning with a face full of sincerity and readiness. The boy felt warmth in the aged warrior that was sorely needed in midst of the peril prevailed and dangers to come. Seth grumbled softly with a command, "Now then little spirit, your bone needs more nourishment than mine, eat on so that you may have your strength for the morning."

Aman then grabbed the twig on which the chierpto was charred and took another bite. The boy gnawed and rolled his eyes in disgust. Seth watched the boy's reaction with held humor.

"Is this really the food of the hunters in the field?"

Seth smirked, "Chierpto, indeed young spirit, thus I am thankful I set my course to become a warrior."

"If that be the case, then I surely set mine for the same." Aman spat the morsels from his mouth and walked away quickly. Seth watched the small child vanish behind the vast light of the campfire. He turned his attention back on the night sky and repeated the proverb calmly.

"In ones so young we must truly place hope, and pray the life of righteousness to bloom. How resilient innocent faith will be against the threatening doom." As the fires dwindled, the

# Chapter Three

*The North Refuge*

elder knelt upon the ground and prayed as requested until the morning.

## The Message

Far north of the men's camp lay a tall bush of *eyviedi* trees shimmering in the soft night wind with star beams from sapphire moonlight. Eyviedi's held sturdy, man-sized leaves with glossed silver surface that reflected light over hundreds of cubits when the trees were numerous. These few provided dim blue light, but light nonetheless, along the fertile root soil for Elias to find his way along the night expanse.

Elias milled through the foliage of the vast leaves and wide tan trunks unknowing of a celestial guide which approached softly to avoid alarm. It mingled amidst the shadow of the leaves and crept quietly upon him. The being was the source of the bright sparkle that engulfed his attention. As Elias journeyed through the field, its luster grew overpowering. He entered a clearing admist the eyviedi ad was caught in such a mass of sorrow and confusion, he could not even bear his surrounding before the lone being was upon him.

A thunderous presence forced him to his knees and he shook from the being's aura. The eyviedi leaves streamed the sweet scents of fig and honey, scents which struck the man with pleasant alert. The dark sand warmed as light surrounded the elder and leaves swirled with a soothing wind which hummed heavenly idiom that he could not understand.

The being shielded its torso with vast wings that scattered the light of its body and allowed Elias to view its face. Before him stood the Archangel Michael.

The arch inhaled a deep long breath and voiced his presence with great resonance, "Eld of Candor, hear my voice

# Lands of Eden

*by M.Gabreyl Scrolls*

in your own tongue. Why bend you upon your knee to Michael of the Arch's? Cloaked perplexed and confound you kneel. With lifted eyes and upon your heel hear my words. For there is none like the Alpha."

Elias rose and squinted through the harsh light to view the angel. His face beamed greatly and caused the man to shield his eyes with upturned palm. Michael waited patiently for him to hearken to him. Elias yet recognized him from the overpowering essence which emanated from his body. This very essence was caused by the presence of the Trinity, which when upon the celestials caused them to radiate with emasculate light and at times caused the rumble of horns to echo through their voice. Custom was for the elders to clothe angels with robes and blankets to cover the radiance until it diminished, which rightly occurred through long sojourn among Eden lands. Elders were also to prepare meals for the angels to consume. Though not of hunger, as holy beings never lacked. These customs were performed in gratefulness to the Alpha who communicated through them.

"Can you not greet me with cape for my eyes, or cover for my wing? Can you not prepare the warm pot for my belly?"

Elias held his tongue in fright, unable to answer Michael's request. The arch groaned from the sense of shame that stemmed from him. "Your men are far from your land. You have no clothes or meal at even your feet to offer your own," Michael continued, "I know of where you have come, I know of where you intend to find refuge." Michael's voice began to rumbled with greater sound as he spoke the very message of the Alpha. "How now is that which was promist waft as ash cross skies and foreign lands? And these wanderers stand bewildered as if your course follows no hand. So easily strayed into his threat, and that which was given is snatched away in the early night."

## Chapter Three                                    The North Refuge

Elias remained silent for several more moments, yet Michael's brilliant eyes pierced the elder for thought and demanded explanation.

The elder finally stepped forward, "Messenger, I am here with my brothers. Seth and Jodia, and Mered son of Cainan the elder. We are men who have fought, with much strength, those who have come to taint our lands. Yet our ground was scattered in the night by a vast host of villains which we have not contended with in any of our days. We are small in men from Candor, and few in fighting. We could not stand against such a mount and were worn here through the night on our way to refuge."

Michael's voice calmed as he looked Elias in the eye. His face was full of disappointment. "Have you not known, better for you to stand 'gainst these with sling and stone in hand, than to flee by the name of He whom created all things."

Elias bowed his head. "Messenger, the men are hunters, scribes, and field hands. They have never followed in Adam's way and their hearts are thick with fear. They could not fight, and we could not arm them against these sefíyai in time. Thus we fled to seek further refuge among Eden's land."

Michael simply repeated himself and said, "The Alpha gave to you the land of refuge, it was of Candor, and will only be of Candor. No other refuge exist that will spare you your enemies hand. For of what has Eden made refuge for one sealed to the blazing lakes of Sheol. Not rock or mount, or cliff cried out to crush has Midnight kept far the Son. And since none exist for he, who wiles and violence rages, so too will Midnight never let men retreat to shade.

"Eld of Candor, was this better for you, has fear turned full your hand, or rid your empty stomach? I speak not of what your heart has already known. Not of their fear have you fled, but of your own. And such has cast these men to great loss.

Was not your charge the same as what was given to Enos your father, to your brothers, and to Seth, son of Adam? How then did you so quickly measure the thickness of Candor's fear to turn your heart cold to them?" Elias frowned from the unexpected rebuke of his motive. He lowered his eyes as Michael hummed, "How grave is this for you, eld Elias, whose eyes 'pon vacant threat turned way true Dominion, and moved by fear to your own empty hand."

Elias felt sudden shame and doubted to offer further word. He slumped inwardly and kept his face from the lifted arch. How well he knew the way which Adam demanded of all his sons.For them never to fear the face of their enemy. Such fear would only mean continued doom.

"Messenger, how grave yet will this be for I who have sought instruction in much and turned my hand at so few choices?"

The archangel squinted with disappointed gaze and gave no answer to which the elder lifted his voice in pity. "Messenger, how grave yet, for such men who have stood in Adam's way, who desire only to serve the Alpha?"

Michael opened his wing with charge and lit the grounds with abundant light. The luminance revealed the might of the arc. His broad chest flared with impenetrable strength. His arms were thick with muscle and he bulged with great power. The feathers of his wing were combed in silk white. The vision was so powerful that Elias was again forced upon his face. The angel commanded the elder onto his feet as he folded his wings to cover his shine.

"Do not question what is just eld, I speak not of reason, only of command. Of fear you lead men away, such fear can only meet the fate of what it has spawned."

# Chapter Three — The North Refuge

Elias stared for long moments at the angel who gazed upon him without further reason. The elder paced briefly in silence, and returned to plea with the archangel who folded his arms.

"Messenger, I know that with He who sent you, we have stood against such a mount."

Michael stared back at Elias without a word, the elder waited before he voiced his request with greater resound. "And with He who sent you, we can arm these men, train and teach them for the great battle ahead."

Again Michael did not respond as the wind whisked with the heavenly whisper of unearthly language.

Elias finally raised his eyes to affirm his appeal, "Angel of the strong order, we desire to claim back that land which is promised, to arm these men and defeat the coming mass, to call upon the host of the Alpha to stand with us, and end the enemies hand against Candor."

Michael closed his eyes briefly. When he opened them, Elias was caught in his stare with ready affirm. Yet the angel's visage held nothing reassuring as he repeated his message softly. "Speak slow your heart, eld, let not your actions be hasted from your tongue. I speak not of reason, only command. Do not question what is just. Fear is not intended to reclaim what's promist. Fear has lost Candor into night fires. And fear will return upon these who will not find refuge."

Elias stared long at the angel with not a word coming. He finally fell to his knee in sadness. Michael looked at him sternly as the elder lowered his shoulders. Soon the rumble returned as Michael channeled the message of the Alpha. "Yours is not intended to lead these men, Elias, I have seen your heart, you have judged them and stoned their ears to your voice. I have searched them, these scattered here, you have allowed them to become too full with fear to stand against the great adversary."

"But messenger," Elias suddenly pushed, "we can hold back this massive barrage." The elder panted and paced at Michael's feet. "What is there for us, for Candor's men? We must not keep our hand defenseless."

Michael thundered back with regret, "Son of Enos, there will be no grace given for your defense against what comes. I have searched and found not strength enough, these men are not meant for what the Alpha intends."

Elias shook his head in disbelief. "This cannot be for Candor, there must be refuge for these men."

Michael answered again with force, "There will be no grace given for your defense against what comes."

Elias continued to plea, "Truly there must be more, we have held to Adams way, we have lived in peace among men. Are we not loyal to the Alpha's hand? There are but so few, how will He not usher any of us to refuge, or allow us to stand against the enemy? What of the promise to Adam's bossom? What of Candor's continuance?"

Michael boomed abruptly through Elias pleas. "Why do you question me, am I not just enough in my ways. It was you who allowed fear to spur these men away. Now look what you have spurred them to, and you continually question, as if blame stands here."

Elias fell on his face from the tremendous power in Michael's voice. The elder whimpered softly with his eyes turned away. Yet Michael lifted him to his feet and spoke calmly. "Elias, indeed you and other men have tarried in the way of majestic Sovereignty, and your request has not been ignored." The angel smiled briefly as the elder looked up at him. "The Alpha has seen hope through those who exist among you. He has favored the shepherd child Aman, whom you have blessed with your hand, whom has been blessed by the hand of

# Chapter Three — The North Refuge

Methuselah, and the hand of Enoch. He will guard him in midst of the flames that will beset your camp."

Elias nodded slowly, "And who will usher Aman to safety? He is just a small boy."

"This will rest in another's hand," Michael answered with abundant bass.

Elias grew quiet as Michael looked down upon him. Michael appeared to close his eyes and meditate for a brief moment before he focused upon the elder with great sadness. Elias shook with sobs at the arch's eyes and raised his eyes to the sky. Without any question he felt the cold confirm of his own grim fate.

"Elder, there comes a great darkness upon your men, even as the night reaches the west. Grace will not be given to your defenses, your men will not prevail. Even before the time, your men will turn against one another and against the elders of Candor. The will fear and depart your side with wicked aim. Yet even more, before you have reached the helms of the mounts will you be faced with the evil hand of the Ya'goviah and be scattered again. Though you plea for them, this will be His just chide of Candor, for He must purge wickedness among Adam's people.

"Am I commanded to hold but few upon the brink of dawn. And before the morns first light, those ushered behind my wing will be spare unto Orgêeda. Few will there be eld, and many will there be that fall into the hands of darkness."

The elder swelled with anguish and could not fight his beating fear for what was intended for the small camp of men across the realm. The south sky appeared darker than any region and lurched with the clawing presence of the approaching throng of sefíyai. Michael noticed the shadow and moaned at the sense of fear stemming from the camp afar off. The arch unveiled again with his wings spread wide. The light blinded the distant shadow and nearly caused Elias to collapse in stupor. Michael then held to the message he was to carry.

"This is the message of the Alpha, Your enemy tarries among borders, but this night are you spared their reach. Sit and eat of the fruit of this tree, and eat of this wounded ram." At his quaking word the floor at Michael's feet was clumped with large olives, and grains. A mighty ram limped from behind a trunk and fell at the powerful presence of the angel.

"You will see your men scattered again, only you must not fear. Eat and fill your strength, then rise and make arms from the leaves of these branches. And take food for your men that they may have strength against what comes. And make for each man arms so that they may fight against your enemies. They will prevail, but for only a time. When Candor is overcome, those who escape behind my wing will be spared. We will not fight, but shall hold back your enemy until the light of dawn. Those who remain must flee to keep guard of the one in whom hope lies."

Michael's voice quelled, "Do not tarry here long, guard yourselves and be found on further plains."

Michael flapped his wing with a mighty thrust and instantly ascended to the sky, the gale of the angel's flight caused dozens of leaves to break from the trees and gather round Elias' feet.

Elias fell back onto the woodland floor. He rolled and buried his eyes into the dirt in long sadness. The night wore with great meditation and no further word from the messenger.

In the quiet, Elias filled his belly with the fruit and meat given to him from the Alpha. There he knelt in sobbing prayer until the morning.

# Chapter Three

## The North Refuge

## The Abomination of Pfíax

Along the southeast bend of the Gihon lie a damp murky region reviled in the tongue of every man though charted only by one. This was among Cain's first wandering pains, where upon the very set of foot he found the gloomy moor cursed and called it "Pfíax," for it was full of ash.

The Pfíax moors were vastly fertile though little vegetation grew. In part due to the sun shielded skies caused by the numerous fire rivers which singed existing plants sprouting from the soil. But of most from the grim dweller who inhabited the chasms as caused the earth of Pfíax to grumble with anger and sorrow. The morning skies saw only the red haze of a setting sun and the hint of violet in warmer mornings when the ash dispersed. But the terrain was cheerless, which made it all too inviting for the banished fiends of heaven.

Hideous creatures were spawned from the influence of the demons that traipsed this place. These creatures were among the beasts that threatened mankind in earlier times and faced the harsh staffs of emboldened warriors who saw to their exile as well as the exile of their creator. Each was birthed from the monstrous heart of the loathsome sarim, Avaddon, who claimed Pfíax as its dark home and sole domain.

This maniacal being possessed a commanding presence among demons upon their landing on earth. Its eyes torched black fire and it snarled fumes of red smoke which carried the scent of blood. Its skin was as cragged coral of onyx hue with fissures that howled with smoke and horrendous quake as the being stirred. Avaddon was a demon of immense size, greater even than Lucifer, and bound with massive chains that rattled as thunder across the sky. Yet it possessed a recreant nature and greatly enticed many of the fallen to his side, as this was truly their desire.

As with all sarim, Avaddon could not speak, but terrified men and even some among the fallen angels with its brutish presence. Upon every ground Avaddon set foot, paw, tongue, cheek, or belly, the land was obliterated. Its very essence shriveled fruits, killed leaves and sapped roots dry. To man's benefit, Avaddon was a slothful monster who wandered seldom and only destroyed those that neared it.

Avaddon perched itself under the cliffs of a deep chasm near the Pfíax bank and glared intensely at the fire seeping from the walls. With it were few minions, among them, Sariel the seducing arch who was known as the key in the spawning of Avaddon's creatures, and Betheal the fallen arch whose wings fell to the sword of Michael during the battle in the Heaven. The red glow of the west horizon reflected off the smoke halo that filled the sky. Avaddon shut its eyes and kept them shut until the entire glow vanished from the above the chasm. Upon opening them, it shuddered with alarm at the sight of Lucifer glowering over it.

The deceptive prince assumed the dim lit form of his former self which, though weak, still lit the arena with ghostly glow. He was flanked by Beelzebub, who sneered with pleasure and licked its fangs as if prepared to devour any who came close. Sariel and Betheal were also jolted by the dark master's appearance yet held their ground without evidence of fright. Lucifer towered over them with a face as fierce as a saber.

Avaddon squirmed into an upright position as it rested its back against the cliff wall. Its eyes were wide with anger and the brute quaked with restrained vigor that appeared set to rip the self-exalted prince of his existence. Lucifer's brazen approach yet commanded Avaddon's respect and caused cautious reaction among all who scowled the unwelcome deceiver.

# Chapter Three — The North Refuge

Avaddon opened its mouth and produced an evil hiss that morphed into an ugly bellow. Instantly the cliff plateaus were flooded with fallen angels and grisly creatures of its dark progeny. Shadow further eclipsed the chasm walls where they crowded with anticipation. At the sight of Lucifer, the beings cackled with threats and menacing jeers. Few clawed at the air as if to dare him onward. Lucifer simply surveyed them with hateful gaze and spat.

A second grumble from the monster echoed as its paw found its place upon Betheal's back. The fallen arch's eyes widened with entrance and he began to speak, "What purpose have you here, in my domain, bright Midnight and eclipsed sun? Do you dare grace my sands to meet your promised end before the set time?"

Lucifer scowled back as the gruesome sarim sneered with mockery, "O' how wretch'd lays this abhorrent fiend, 'pon banks forsaken black, as dismal so of earthly hallow that no elix' of kingdom could be even scarce reminisce of you. Have these malignant seeds high 'pon these cliffs, or that ash'ed sky above, or brooding blood of aimless men tainted even the tongue of this once graced Sarim?"

Avaddon howled as it pressed its palm against Betheal's back and channeled its response. "Has relent seized this foolish dragon so, that even in fires and escapeless doom, he forms his face for hope in what has past? Why hold onto that face, this image which you will never regain? How pitiful this lesser light engulfs you!"

Lucifer snarled with annoyance and replied, "How miserable 'tis once lofted Havan, whose light did seed abundance. Now touches fruit, or taste the meat and only eats of pestilence. Null minded sarim. How be it king? Of what follows you, save destruction?"

# Lands of Eden

*by M. Gabreyl Scrolls*

"Of what follows you at all, Lucifer," Avaddon grinned with a rattle of its chains as it hissed. "The earth has yet to see the great prince rest. You lay, only to add more dust upon your belly. You vile, wicked serpent! And what great plan did this prince have that cursed him this way? How did that fare viper? Turn man against his creator and he would serve you. Ha!" The animals and demons echoed the laugh for a brief moment as Avaddon mocked. "No throne exist for you! So despised is this great, magnificent, morning star that even us, once believers of him, detest the disgust of his smell and guise! Be it as seen now or as he really appears. Great and powerful Lucifer, prince of naught, and Sëtan to all!"

Lucifer instantly roared with tremendous anger, his eyes shrouded as black a cave and his visage grayed. At once the dim light of his being faded and caused the fallen prince to cast an eminent shadow. He clutched Betheal's entire torso with his hand and thundered with tumult. "Vile arch of no worth, learn well that none else control your tongue!"

Lucifer hurled Betheal with all his might into the cliff wall. The impact shook the cliffs so greatly that many of the dark creatures crowded on the plateau fell into the crater. Each being present hollered with rage and jostled feverishly. Still none dared approach the prince who dared them onward with snarled teeth. Sariel drew his crooked sword and silenced the chaos with the clap of his wings.

"I hail you, prince of the morning," the arch challenged with the tip of her sword, "for your might bounds far beyond even leviathan reach. Even so stand I 'gainst this breach 'pon this shore hence clinched and reigned under that palm of our lifted beast named Destruction. Ere vast your power, 'pon these sands plant your feet and see you power shed. Test not the Destroyer's strength here, for such will see your doom, and as unseen came so unseen go and leave Pfíax with our mayhem."

# Chapter Three

## The North Refuge

Lucifer roared again and swatted Sariel with his palm. Avaddon then lunged into Lucifer's chest as the dark prince assumed the form of the red dragon. All the demons present shook with fright at the chaos as Avaddon clawed the dragon's chest with ferocity. Blood red smoke surrounded them as Lucifer wailed and the crimson of its scales dyed with decay.

The dragon would not be undone. It gripped Avaddon with its tail to restrain the gruesome monster claws. The lizard then sunk its teeth into the destroyer's neck and pulled wildly.

Avaddon screamed with pain as several of its minions rushed toward the chaos. Beelzebub quickly halted them with a vicious roar that shook the ground with massive tremor. The cliffs freed rocks which tumbled into the arena with mighty crashes. Many beings were crushed under their weight. Only Betheal continued forward with Sariel's sword. He plunged the end into Lucifer's tail.

The red dragon bellowed with agony and recoiled. Avaddon, freed from the clutch, lifted the dragon and hurled him into the stones that littered the chasm floor. Beelzebub turned and gripped Betheal in his fingers and began to slam the crippled arch onto the ground repeatedly until Betheal ceased movement. The brute then turned its aim on Avaddon. Despite Beelzebub's might, it would be obliterated by Avaddon who charged the brute wildly.

Beelzebub prepared itself with rage only to be smashed into the chasm floor. The destroyer began to beat Beelzebub with its chains and roared with laughter.

Suddenly, the dragon rose and the fright grew. A swift swing of its massive tail brought down Avaddon's attack. The monster was slammed to the floor with paralyzing might. Lucifer pummeled Avaddon with repeated whips of its tail until the being silenced with broken breaths.

# Lands of Eden

by M. Gabreyl Scrolls

Lucifer glared intensely for several moments at the remaining beings with restrained hand. As the beast surveyed the multitude of demons and mutated creatures geared for its torment, the crimson creature appeared to recognize its doom and thus transformed back into the glowing form as he appeared.

Avaddon panted steadily as its miscreants appeared to lurch with recharge. Yet Lucifer planted his foot on the sarim with a brutal stomp. The prince then spoke over Avaddon's agony with careless mockery.

"That this chasm'd, fruitless ground is comely of detested swine dost wrench my bowls of matter. With even less disquiet and grown delight, Destroyer, do I purge you of unholy abhorrence. For cursed are these of no natural form, not of Trinity's majestic mold, and cursed are you to play His hand and relish this soot as a kingdom. How swift the chains of the great Abyss approach you. For this be known, touch not that which He touches with blessed hand, and defile not what the Trinity has made pure."

Avaddon trembled at Lucifer's reproach and many of the surrounding followers moaned with fright. The prince lifted his voice and proclaimed to each of them, "Nigh lies the plum for this condemn'd sarim which fiends so ill adore. This Destroyer be your king? Then come see what king's services incur."

Lucifer then inhaled a long howling breath that shook the chasm with fierce winds. When he exhaled, his eyes thickened with hypnotic sable and his face blackened with spiny pelt. Razor-end teeth jut from his jaw and his visage emit such darkness that the sky was blackened and only he and Avaddon were visible.

As his roar echoed, the sound of clapping thunder grew from his gut. All the demons present pinned their sight on the

# Chapter Three — The North Refuge

powerful prince whose mouth widened to great size. From his belly spewed thousands of pale locust, each with glowing sparks trailing their flight. Horns encircled their heads and shimmered with faint gold light. Long strains of hair strung from these horns hissed with a wind which trumpeted as a stampede. Slender tails with jagged white tips that carried venom protruded from their torsos. The insects squealed with agonizing clatter through their jagged teeth. Shells made of cold metal clanged as brass against their wings. The cave walls echoed with their intensity. These were the lobita, swallowed by Lucifer and altered by the dark hatred in his belly.

The locusts surged from Lucifer's mouth and swarmed Avaddon who wailed with agony. They gnawed at its flesh and sunk their tails into its body like daggers. The creature howled horrendously and rolled from the pain. The demons round the crater watched the spectacle in terror, yet Lucifer looked on with delight and laughter.

"Behold you wrechted spawns of this unholy rogue, employ your destroyer, king Avaddon, lord of the flies!" Lucifer mocked again as he hoisted the sarim over his head. "Lord of the flies…lord of the flies…" He carried Avaddon to an edge in the chasm where the fire river poured from the walls into a shallow pit. "Be you servers of Avaddon? Then into this Abyss follow destruction!"

Lucifer then hurled Avaddon over the edge. The sarim plummeted into darkness, all the while rearing with agony from locusts' sting. The chaos ended with a mighty shout from the cruel dark angel. The sky returned with the halo of smoke and the demolish of the chasm could be surveyed by all present.

Silence reign in the crater as Lucifer approached Sariel. The great beast grinned with triumph and brash as he knelt by the wounded demon. "Be that empty abyss your fall? Follow there your king. Nay? Then speak my dominion and be spared."

The villains seeped into the chasm rapidly. Each advanced upon Lucifer with caution. Lucifer glanced round anxiously as they neared. He commanded the fallen arch again. "Speak dominion and be swift, lest I rend your body as your king!"

Sariel panted with fear as Lucifer grimaced over her. The dragon's claw leered above her belly "I…I hail you…morning star…I hail you my prince," she stuttered.

At that, the beings halted in shock. Lucifer snarled and stood upright with a stomp and pounded his chest. "I am your Avaddon, detested swine, and in my keep you will obey!" His voice resonated so all the minions of the defeated sarim heard. His words were of command and challenge to any that dare, but none would.

Lucifer commanded Sariel to her feet. "You meaningless wing, you take the charge these abhorrent things, be off with tem onto the east. And do not find your hand against mine."

The fallen arch quickly gathered the hideous creatures and hurried toward the flatlands of the east where Vestual snuffed the remaining village. Lucifer desired no further toy and nothing more than their end. "If any scent of human flesh there, return to me with only limbs." The prince's final command halted Beelzebub in the process of ripping Betheal with its teeth.

"Let him along brute, for this fool arch purpose serves. Let him be known as Belial, for such who challenge me be just as worthless."

The chasm was cleared with yelping and howls. Only Belial remained as the night set over Pfíax. Once the crippled arch woke, he wept for the loss of Avaddon. Lucifer would come to regret Belial's life as the arch vowed that night to war against the prince and would soon amass a great following of fallen angels against him.

# Chapter Three — The North Refuge

## *The Rebellion*

"Come back here you vile snape!" Lathan shouted as he pounced on the ground only to have the rodent slip through his fingers again. Early morning came with quiet entrance and none stirred from their sleep, save the brazen rascal. "That's my food!"

Lathan scurried about trying to grasp the prairie dog that snatched his chierpto from his palm. The rodent long eyed the food of the men and planned against the least threatening among them. The food was not enjoyable enough to chase after, but the simple principle of injustice is what urged his chase. The rodent's small legs wiggled rapidly in fear from Lathan. It lead him in several circles, chased up tree bark and back almost in its own jolly at the missed tackles and lunges of its chaser.

Lathan was no more amused than some of the men who were tired from the night, now having to put up with the boy who stepped over them and kicked sand near their resting areas. After several squeals and numerous shouts from Lathan, the commotion was halted as a sharp stone struck the rodent and pierced it to the ground.

Lathan gasped and froze where he stood with eyes set on the prairie dog. A trickle of blood pooled round the poor creature that lay stiff under wrap of the stone. The boy kept his eye on the animal until a coarse old hand gripped its tail. The rock was hoisted with animal impaled at the boy's eye level.

"Can'teh keep hold your meal'eh boy?" the gruff heartless voice came.

Lathan breathed with steady fright as he looked into the pale yellow eyes of Apayim. The thin framed hunter gripped the boy's morning meal in his right palm as he waved and teased the slain rodent in front of the boy. He chomped into the chierpto wing that rightfully belonged to Lathan with careless insolence. Chewed slowly, perhaps feigning to enjoy the bitter melt which seeped from the corners of his mouth. After a humming swallow he steadied the jagged rock directly over Lathan's nose.

"Maybe you should eat'eh deh duss of 'tis pest'eh flesh," Apayim said as he flicked the pup with his bony finger, "`tis migh'teh fill your dark belly betteh." Apayim slung the carcass at the boy's feet. Trickles of blood sprinkled onto Lathan's face. "Or perhap'seh by 'tis stone, 'tat taint within your loin'seh be remov'edeh."

Apayim guided the flat edge of the sharpened stone threateningly along Lathan's gut, "Maybe 'ten you'll keep hold your meal'eh?"

The boy shook fearfully. His eyes pooled with tears as Apayim's hot breath smacked his face. The barter's intentions, whether genuine or deceitful, were vile and cruel for such a young heart to endure. Looking on were the ever watchful eyes of the elders.

"Apayim, draw back your hand," Seth spoke with command and thunder.

The lanky barter shot a glance at Seth from the corner of his vision, grit his teeth and hissed at the boy before he stood upright and placed his spear end against his leg. Lathan panted for several moments before darting away. The elder walked toward Apayim with his jaw set and eyes fierce. When he neared the man, he stood with visual restraint in all of his joints.

"Apayah meanteh no harm of 'tis boy," he paused with sinister sneer, "even whileh his vain course with deceiteh for us."

Some began to gather behind the barter and join in glares of intimidation at Seth. The elder ignored them and focused

# Chapter Three — The North Refuge

keenly on the barter. The two faced for silent moments before Mered stepped between them.

"How heartless is this man of great age," Mered slighted, "that he would threaten a child again with such distaste."

Lathan set his eyes on the lower statured elder and sniffed, "Heartlesseh," he mocked, "rather to have Apayah's hearteh removedeh, than scorchedeh as 'tis boy whom 'deh elders hold for our doom. Look roundeh elders, wat do you see? How many 'mong 'tese men hold not my voiceh of Lathan's darkness."

Several more crowded behind the reveling rebel who set the accusing eye upon the elders. Here lie the seed of dissent geared to rift the scattered hopes and, even greater, geared to wage havoc between the blood lines of men.

"For my threateh, Apayah apologizes. Even so do we seekeh 'deh child be banish't." At his word some began to nod and reveal their turned hearts of fear. Many within the camp mumbled in subtle argument. Overwhelming agreement surged through the crowd.

Mered answered with grave distaste. "You fools! Are you so torched in fright that you would cast a child to the field? Foolish that you think this boy has brought this upon you. The great adversary preys upon you in all of Eden, whether here or there, he seeks to devour such hearts as yours who ignore his threats for the sake of this child. Well then, let it be this, that if any of you dare to grip him to be taken away, it will be through my cane!"

A rise of grumbling erupted from the men who snarled at the elder's challenge. Yet none would dare indulge in sight of Mered's resolve.

Elias was returning from the wood and spotted the commotion. He hurried toward the camp as Mered dared the men again. He gripped Mered's shoulder and tugged with anger. "Of what heart is this," the elder called. His voice quieted the men. He thundered louder, "Of what heart is this?! Are we such brutish men now...set from our place so that we might tend a seed of slaughter and end ourselves even before our enemy has done us?"

Apayim spat back with insult. "Of wat hearteh are tese elders to commandeh us where to go. An enemey comeseh for 'tis child. We do not'eh wish to be scatterd'eh again!"

Though filled with chaos and clash, the men were struck without word as the elder answered. "Of what Apayim speaks is true. Indeed there comes a dark cloud upon us." The people moaned in fear, yet the elder thundered louder to hold their complaints. "A cloud of devils, just as what came nights ago, comes for all of us. Beast of vengeful flame and mighty brute that come to rend our bone. Even now they stalk us, hold peace along dark borders in wait of night when they will be hidden from our arms. Should they just come for this boy... or for the darkness in your hearts, which we are *all* faulted? Is it one child they seek? No, for these devils come for your fear!"

Mered bowed his head and stepped away in Elias' deeming eye. The elder turned and looked upon all the faces as he continued his charge. "They seek your doubt...and the fleet of your feet. To them your fear is as kindle to their flame. This is why they pursue you without relent. Not this boy. Your fear is why you will not stand against them. The Alpha will not spare you even if you send this boy from your eyes. There is no other aim for us but to continue onto Orgêeda, where there is refuge for your weak hearts. These disputes profit us no time or hope. If you desire to be spared of the coming cloud, end your moans, and continue on."

"Continue under Elias' word," Melhazur interrupted with objection as he came to the front for all present to hear."and you will see your bloodeh spilt on the earth." The man jeered at

# Chapter Three — The North Refuge

the elder. Melhazur, along with dozens of others, faced him with determined poise against his lead.

"What will you men have then?" Elias responded.

To that Apayim chuckled and pressed the sharp stone against his cheek. "Removeh 'tis taint, elder," he answered as he plucked a lock from his beard with the jagged edge. He glanced at the pointed rock, then at Elias, "one way or another."

The elder could sense the vicious intent in each of the men who backed Apayim's fear. Elias was so gripped by the cold hatred which bloomed from them that he shuttered with fright. He saw the shadow within their eyes.

"Away from us, you whose blood boils with that same darkness that slew Able. As your predecessor, wander, marked a vagabond, for you have no place among Candor."

The men flared with anger, "You speakeh such against us elder," Melhazur ridiculed, "why musteh Candor prey victim of this boy's misfit?"

"And those of you among this crowd," Elias continued with no regard to Melhazur's voice, "whom so let this boil of Cain surge your thoughts, than be with Apayim and Melhazur as waste in devils' toy."

"Continue with 'tese elders," Melhazur returned in mirrored form to Elias command, "whom leadseh even with deh knowledgeh 'tat darkness chases him and deh scourge of Candor will end'eh you."

"Away all you sons of murder, return the taint of *your* hearts to him whom tools you." Elias cursed Apayim and Melhazur with firm word. The elder turned his back to them and commanded all to turn their eyes from the greed and bloodthirsty barters who continued to rant. The gathered seethed with mix of anger at both the elder's rebuke and the dark heart of these men. Few hummed with slight acknowledge as Elias set his eyes onward. At slow pace, they disperse with few who chose to leave the fuss to decided ears of others who remained motionless with earnest choice.

As more departed, Apayim snorted and restrained his nephew's rant. He glanced at the men who remained with him and chided. "Deh be one here 'tat walkseh with Cayains blood and deserves 'tis curse. Deh curse 'tat equals him, 'tis my prayer it not be vanquishedeh before lives be lost. We willeh go nephew, only we will spareh our people of 'tis boy's taint. Of you who wisheh less upon your flesheh, be with Eliaseh and other foolseh. You who willeh not standeh for vile blood, come under my handeh, for such willeh be an endeh for us to meeteh upon 'tis boy."

At that Apayim tossed the spoke on which the chierpto was charred, spat in Elias' direction and walked far from the camp's sight. Melhazur quickly followed with fierce glare at those who remained. Cephas cursed and joined the men taking their turn from the north refuge. And with him went more than a fourth of the others, many leaving behind their own children in cold, selfish motive.

Elias paused after several moments as the crowd continued on in Seth's lead. He waited in pain to see if the men would return, even while he foreknew that they would not. Just as the archangel warned, these men turned against Elias. How great his fear transformed these men from once peace filled and loyal to disputing and tumultuous rebels. He inhaled solemnly with shut eyes and mind shaken by the dark dismal seed upon them. As he released sorrow with long sigh, he rejoined the crowd which continued on in silent gloom.

\*        \*        \*

# Chapter Three                           The North Refuge

Quiet mood molded the mass of still faces full of worries yet repressed in knowing or undesired response. The ground offered softer footing and wider range for the men and women to span their journey. Children, many unsure of any other aim, itched for play, yet assumed the monocle of their guardians. Far ahead the tip of the mounts peaked. Their base would soon be reached and the course onward would demand more strength.

Lathan found his eyes constantly watched by questioning spirits. He knew even the elders were not free of their worries, as dissenting wonder shown among them by blight silence.

And even Aman offered him no rest, fleeting glance after glance without word. Lathan had his fill of their suspicions.

"What do you want?" he blurted at Aman. Aman halted and stared at Lathan with question. Lathan paused and glared back at him with his face reddening. "What do you want, reushamim?"

Aman held dozens of questions, yet he said nothing. He continued to stare much to Lathan's increased distress.

"What do you want? What are you looking at me for?" he shouted in greater annoyance.

Still Aman gave no response, stared longer with eyes wider and more puzzling. Lathan flared back at the small boy with mounds of rage building. He pressed Aman for reason again. As Aman gave no response, Lathan fell upon his own brand of release and shoved the shepherd's shoulder with a grunt.

Aman simply stared back without movement. Lathan shoved again with more force.

"Come on! Let me show you who is the bravest and strongest!" Lathan dared as Aman adjusted his feet so not to stumble. "Come on!" Lathan challenged again. The two stood apart for several moments until Lathan balled his fingers and punched Aman's chin with his fist.

The impact stung with ringing affect upon the boy's ears. His cheek felt numb and he fell into the dirt and moaned.

"Hey!" shouted Ezra who saw the commotion. He rushed toward them. Aman's pain was short lived. In fury, he rose and bolted his shoulder into Lathan's gut. He tackled him to the ground then punched ceaselessly while Lathan guarded.

The two continued to scrap until Ezra set them apart. They pressed to fight further and scuffled round the young hunter. Elias met both their hinds with a swift whip of his jō. He clipped their heels with the weapon which swept them onto their backs.

The elder frowned at each of them with disappointment. Many round were held in shock as Elias silenced them. Lathan, however, continued in his anger. He shoved Elias' short staff, leapt to his feet and jut his finger in Aman's direction.

"It's your fault, reushamim, it's your fault!" he shouted. Aman glared back with enraged panting and heaving chest. A thin knit of blood seamed from his lip. "Everyone thinks it's me, but it's you!"

"Young lad," Elias thundered, "you will be calm!"

However, Lathan would not succumb. "No! Just leave me alone… everyone…stop looking at me…just leave me alone!" Lathan then ran off before any could seize him. However, not many attempted to halt him at all.

Elias started after the boy, yet Seth intervened. "I will see to him," the elder said in warm tone. Elias squinted at Seth in wonder yet Seth was sure, "You must keep to this camp, continue on and I will retrieve the boy."

Elias waited for but a moment and agreed. As Seth jogged after Lathan, Elias faced Aman with cold dissatisfied eye.

Aman stared back in shame and answered without question. "He hit me first."

# Chapter Three
## The North Refuge

"We will speak on this young reu," Elias hummed to which Aman bowed his head. Elias' demeanor made him feel as if Jebas was standing in front of him.

The people were shaken from the fuss and Elias commanded them to rest for but a moment. As many plopped onto the ground, the elder offered large morsels of food from his gather amidst the eyviedi. They ate eagerly. Though Apayim's final word found no stronger root among these who remained, doubt came with greater strength upon the visage of Elias who spoke no word of the message to his brothers. Such chilled uncertainty foretold the doom to beset these few.

\* \* \*

Lathan sprinted onward becoming a distant speck of difficult catch for Seth's keen yet still old eyes. The boy found the shallow passage and hid amidst the bark of an evergreen cluster to avoid the elder whom he knew followed. As he entered the flora, wild shrieks caused him to press his hand against his ear and moan briefly. The shrieks were followed with cycles of ghostly whispers that echoed through his thoughts. And suddenly, the boy knew something was amiss. His mind was clouded with visions which mocked and cursed his rejection. Shouts and aches swarmed his ears in dizzying distress. The boy spun randomly with his eyes shut to what was round him. The voices grew more forceful with ridicule and hatred. Lathan's moans rose to audible heights, yet no one came to aid him. The boy clenched his fists and prayed for help in wonder of why his agony was ignored. An intense clasp of the dark whisper brought him to his knee, and instantly the voices were erased.

Lathan slowly opened his eyes, released his ears and found himself returned in appearance to the damp reaches of the Rim.

# Lands of Eden
*by M.Gabreyl Scrolls*

Round him were cast shadows that crowded him with choking influence, and his hard breaths only spurred pressure to shut his eyes from distinction of what lurked for his blood. An invisible something, encircling from every escape, hummed its hunt, reminiscent of the dark force of the Rim that struck the canopy black and met his eyes with eerie hollow. Lathan complained with shouts and sprints that spent him no where. Laughter slapped shouts still with trembling mockery.

The boy paced with frantic heart, unsteady feet, wobbly gut, and broad gaze over heightened shoulders. A vicious bark darted him in mad untamed dash that met impact with the trunk of a tree. Lathan fell onto his back with eye set on a spinning cover. As the daze cleared, he shook fiercely from the yellow, blood-littered eyes that glared back at him.

"How'seh deh head boy?"

Lathan attempted to scurry, but was quickly gripped into Melhazur's clutch and lifted to his feet. Lathan jostled with frenzy, scratched at Melhazur's arm, while Apayim rolled his eyes with pleasure. Melhazur tossed the boy onto his back. The evil within the men chuckled as they crept toward him.

Lathan leapt to his feet and plunged his fist into Melhazur's abdomen. The man bent over with mighty coughs. Apayim laughed hysterically as Lathan ran off in senseless screaming.

"Comeh nephew, he is justeh a boy!"

The two chased after Lathan who found more men blocking his escapes. Soon he was encircled with no where to run. Each of them sneered impatiently with fists clenched for action. Apayim entered the center of the circle, gripped the child's cloth and lifted him from his feet.

The boy cried but was full of contest. He kicked the crazed man's legs and knees while Apayim slung him recklessly to quell the boy's fight. "Is 'tis your papa's teach, haseh he show'neh you to fighteh your elders?"

# Chapter Three

## The North Refuge

At that, Lathan yelled with fury, lunged at the barter and sunk his teeth into the flesh of his neck. Apayim shouted with pain as Lathan bit down and grumbled with unearthly sound that echoed through the leaves. The sneers of the men who encircled him diminished. Suddenly there seemed even more to the darkness within this boy whose blood they thought they could tease. Lathan's eyes became as night and his skin paled with foggy shadow. He released his grip and snarled at Apayim in animalistic nature. Apayim hurled the boy down with a strong slam. The barter gripped his neck with disgust as the boy remained and fell back. Now Lathan turned into the predator, ran no further and dared the barter onto his feet.

"He is tainted indeed!" one of the men yelled in fright. And in that same instant, many of the men bolted away in fright as Lathan rushed Apayim with a roar.

"Uncle!" Melhazur shouted as he stepped in front of the boy's attack. Lathan slammed clumsily into Melhazur causing him to land his temple onto a root and be knocked unconscious. Lathan, however, was only shaken for a moment before he faced Apayim again. Yet he turned too late as the barter beat Lathan's back with a stick and hammered him motionless. His eyes returned from darkness and he rubbed his head with pain. Apayim, shaken but unmoved in his taste for redemption, quickly pounced upon Lathan and growled just as wildly at the child.

The evergreen cleared of those who threatened the child and all but Apayim and Lathan remained aware. Above, the pines bowed as if to cover the horror that was to come. Apayim ripped the cloth from Lathan's sleeve and hissed with discontent. "Apayah willeh' teacheh you boy!"

The old man sunk his rotted teeth into the boys forearm. Lathan screamed with tears and whined as the man gnawed and twisted. Lathan kicked himself away and howled in agony, writhed with clenched eyes as blood seeped from the bite.

Apayim laughed hysterically and straddled the child. Lathan tried to inch from reach with each shuffle. Apayim nudged his shin into the boy's side causing him to grunt.

The barter then drew a dagger from his waist and toyed it from hand to hand.

"See 'tis boy," he hissed, "'Tis be what Cephas madeh for your hearteh." Apayim laughed crazily then glared down in solemn flare. "You have broughteh 'tis spell, 'tis darkness on us," Apayim roared and gripped the dagger in one hand with its point facing Lathan's neck. "You must be remov'edeh!"

Lathan shut his eyes the instant Apayim thrust downward. The barter shouted with insane rage set to pierce the child's flesh.

Suddenly from the midst of the chaos came a growl that trumpeted with command and shook the crazed man's focus.

Lathan opened his eyes to see Apayim tackled onto his back with a powerful plunge. He looked with tremendous shock as the figure hovered over Apayim in menacing fashion. Apayim looked up and panted in shock as he lay under strenght of the figure. He set his eyes and gasped.

"Jebaseh…"

\*       \*       \*

Pale with static was the small boy upon the moment Seth's eyes found him. Lathan clutched earth into his palm, dug deep ditches at his sides and stared hollow to all signs of presence. Eyes wide and wet with fright as he breathed with slow rhythm. Upon closer look, Seth found his face sprinkled with sprays of red. Mud clumped to the crimson moisture on his fingers, the same which stained his clothes as scarlet. The elder spoke his name softly and met no response, only Lathan

# Chapter Three                                    *The North Refuge*

continued to stare with emotionless expression and eyes set steadily, upon the body.

Seth guided his eyes to take in the boy's vision and nearly shivered at the grotesque sight. A puddle gathered round the waist of the body of a man who lay upon his back, no hint of life. His body was marred ravenously with deep long gouges stretched from chin to chest, shoulder to loin. His eyes held shock, saw pain, and breathed fear.

Seth turned and looked again at Lathan who remained motionless. The elder gripped his shoulders and lifted him onto his feet. "Young one, we must not remain here, the night is coming soon."

Lathan finally removed his eyes of the body and looked at Seth blankly. The boy spoke no word, turned and began his way from the forest. Seth stood for brief moments before he gathered the body and followed.

## *A Dismal Escape*

Magenta sky mended above with call for rest to these who were greatly weary of their quest. Their journey was long and ached their bones with tire and soarness. A pleasant perfume of *agonya* flower caused very few to remain steady on their haste.

Agonya grew along the flat grounds of the Orgêeda base. The pollen of their seed flowed toward the mount summits as fog and dyed the soil of the mounts the hue of sunset sky. High among the hills, the stone of the mounts captured waters into cool pools which rippled shimmers of light, bright as the night stars. Such caused the realm to parallel the night and mystify wanderers often lost to the Orgêeda valley. Such was the cause of slower pace and groan for rest.

# Lands of Eden — by M. Gabreyl Scrolls

Jodia and Mered were found along their distanced scout. Elias knew from their faces that they too were weary, and with night setting, they could not rightly scout the hills. Elias sighed with impatience knowing the journey needed to reach its end until the morn, knowing the morn would see but few spared onto the valleys.

"We will rest for the night," Elias stuttered with sorrow, "Have the men make fires round the camp, command them each with these torches that we all must keep watch in this unhidden field."

"Elias, you have not spoken of the message from the Alpha," Jodia pressed with concerned visage, "and trouble marks your eyes. What of His message should we know?"

Elias inhaled long air and stared through Jodia without answer. He turned his focus on Mered, who awaited his word. But the elder could not give them the message of gloom and simply looked through them into the camp with further order. "Have them eat of the food that I have gathered from the wood. There will be enough and even more to replenish them. Keep watch through the night that none stray from the camp."

The elder turned his back to his brothers to see Aman facing him. Elias looked at him long and steady. Aman stood in expectance of scolding, but the elder bowed his head and strolled away without a word. He secluded himself from the camp in long prayer and hope against what he knew was to come. And such would be the elder's way through the entire night.

The final night of Candor's existence in Eden began in subtle silence. Unlikely calm among past villagers who tasted hope just beyond burgundy borders. Left was only a hasted journey through cliffs and over peaks that would open to refuge. This hope brought smiles, brought sighs, brought relaxed eyes in spite of the warning to remain vigilant. Yet

# Chapter Three — The North Refuge

these moods would meet eerie disruption in the wild appearance of gloom. For this night would see the vicious threat of the fiends within the Ya'goviah.

A distant rustle embarked a swift moving approach from the back circle of the camp. Mered took his place in front of kindles and focused with hand set on his staff. The flames hindered his view, shadows were cast where his eyes searched. Still he was every ready to be swift with attack. As it neared, however, Mered removed his hand from his staff and lifted his head in question. The approaching figure was the small young lad, Lathan.

The boy's eyes were wide and blank as he walked in unsteady rhythm through the fiery paths. He came near, his face revealed scars and clumps of mud soaked in red. Mered's heart thumped with quicker pace as the boy sauntered past, expressionless. Some grumbled with question as the boy strolled without a look at anyone. He brushed by as if blind to any presence of another, and plopped onto the central ground where the centered flame torched for warmth. He spoke no word.

Mered turned to see Seth trailing behind in similar appearance yet focused glare on the boy. He carried what shown as a limp animal carcass upon his back. As he joined Mered, he spoke with eyes remained on Lathan.

"Where is Elias our brother?" he requested.

Mered frowned and looked back at Lathan whose back was turned to all but the flame. He looked back at Seth, "He is apart from the camp, meditating. Why do you seek him?"

Seth looked at Mered and shook his head, "Lathan must be taken from this place and ushered to refuge apart from the others."

Mered cocked his head, "Elias will not want us parted if he is to lead us to the refuge, why do you speak of this again?"

Seth knelt and laid the weight onto the ground at Mered's feet. The elder gazed with shock as Seth rose. He looked sternly at the body for a long moment. Then just as Seth, he turned his focus on the young lad with firm brow. Gazing into the night sky were the dead gray eyes of Apayim, whose body was rent with scarlet wounds brought upon him in the glade.

As Mered stared on with no word, Seth repeated his command, shielding the fallen barter from the eyes of few others who noted his return. Mered snapped from trance and answered Seth. "At such a sight these men will thirst for the child's blood. I will take the child from here before he is found. Inform my uncle of my follow of the camp by morning, that I will stay amidst the vast borders and guard him until I have reached the gates."

"Of what causes such grey color upon your cheeks nephew," Elias interrupted as he and Jodia neared. Their eyes drew upon the covered frame and the two slowed with cautious watch. Elias knelt and removed Seth's cover of the body. Upon the sight he moaned in pain. "We must not allow others to view this horror," he stated as he rose. "We must take him from here, now, and let no one catch sight of this."

"We cannot all remove him from here without the rise of suspicion among the men," Jodia responded. "Such would not be wise, as even a dark cloud comes upon us. More will turn if they cannot trust us."

Elias looked to and fro briefly, "Then I will take him now, apart from the camp, and I will prepare him for burial."

The elder knelt again and sprinkled dirt over the cover. He tucked his fingers under the weight and prepared to lift.

"And what of this child?" Mered questioned, brining Elias to a halt. "If we do not remove him from this camp, how much less dissent can we expect that will end in bloodshed such as this."

# Chapter Three — The North Refuge

Elias held his breath and searched the ground for answer. He shook his head again with grave concern, "Should his presence truly matter so much?"

"Indeed it does brother," Seth responded. Elias rose and stared into his brother's eyes as if unprepared, though he knew Seth's mind. "These men have readily turned upon us in their minds, these who remain have no belief in our ways. And simply remain in hopes that we spare them from these demons who charge. When refuge is found, how soon they will turn upon us, upon this child, upon each other. Whether tainted or not, such hands should not be brought against a child."

Elias looked steadily at Seth who remained forthright in his belief. Jodia and Mered gazed at the elder in solemn wait for response. Elias bowed his head and nodded slowly before he finally answered.

"Then it is decided, I will gather Apayim for burial, and when I have returned, my brothers will guard these youth and these women from this place in the night and follow the path unto the gates."

The others looked at Elias in question, "Uncle, how are any of these to be moved in the night?"

"It is hard to track, I know Mered, as the mounts shine as night themselves, but you and Jodia are great trackers. And you must guide the path of the camp."

"And what lies for the men of the camp, will they continue on, after our light or trail by the morning?" Jodia asked.

Elias sighed shortly. The others looked with concern and instantly knew, from their elder brother's face, what quickly approached from the skies. "The time is come upon this camp, even tonight it comes. These men must be armed to stand against the beasts. And as you each have charged me, I must stand with them, so that this enemy knows we do not fear to fend ourselves.

Jodia shook his head with confusion, "These men will not fight, and we will not flee while you fend them alone elder. You must have our staffs on course as well."

"This is how it must be, Jodia, I will stand with these men against what comes, but you must gather with your brothers onto Orgêeda."

"No," Mered rebuked, "Without our arms and these simple men you cannot fare. By the time of their attack, how do you expect to continue on by the dawn?"

The elder stared long and hard at his youngest kin who focused back with readied eyes. Seth lifted his head and answered plainly, "He will not continue on."

At that, his brothers looked at him in full note of Elias' sorrow. Despite the elder's resolve, they each knew within that Elias expected no hope for refuge of Candor, and that this was perhaps the grave message held by the elder's troubled tongue. The three bowed their heads with watered eyes as Elias knelt again by Apayim's body.

"How long have we aged men written upon our hearts the truth of man's darkness? Yet we still, as Adam, stand with fruit stained hands pointed away as if we are blameless. This child is not to blame for the beings that fell Candor by night. Darkness was invited to Candor long before those perils. And these by men who set away their hearts to Adams way, who grew ill of instruction and truth, who believed peace was theirs through earthly pleasure. Even we invited this enemy through the age in stoned hearts toward their folly, and now we seek it to leave us be. But where Sëtan is invited, he refuses to be exiled."

The elder faced his brothers with sorrow filled eyes. "I have allowed such fear to try my plot and these people have suffered loss because of me. This is the message of the Alpha, and though I might not meet the refuge of Orgêeda, I will not

# Chapter Three

## The North Refuge

allow a child to meet any fate at the hands of men because of greater fear. Nor will I allow devils to torment innocence."

Elias looked up at his brothers who stared back at him with discernment. He whimpered, yet briefly as the three lifted the aged man to his feet and stood beside him, firm in resolve of what they knew was his course. Each hoped to find him beyond the valley gates of Orgêeda, each knew that such might not be.

"Who will lead these men when the sun has reached the sky?" Elias asked.

Without decree Seth answered, "I will lead them."

Elias placed a hand on Seth's shoulder and gripped tightly as the four elders huddled in quiet. "Brothers, you are men who have stood with me against mighty perils, against beasts of hateful cry and evil heart. And with even greater fiends marching upon you, have you resolved to remain fearless and reliant as Adam has taught us. Keep this way in you, that you do not allow fear to halt your hand, and even more, let no fear halt the hands of those who are to become. Spur them to stand as you have desired long before, and when the time comes, they will fight, and your faith will be restored."

Elias gripped each of them tightly as tears flowed from his eyes. "If I am not with you by the dawn, spare these people onto Orgêeda, and remember me in your chronicles. That I am Elias, son of Adam, and I served the Alpha for all my days, and walked in Adam's way as my fathers before me."

Elias spoke no further word, removed his waist of his staffs and handed them to Seth. He then hoisted Apayim's thin body over his shoulder. He disappeared in the night with full promise that Seth would spare the remaining hope of Candor from vengeful tirades of devils and men thirsty for destruction.

\* \* \*

# Lands of Eden

*by M.Gabreyl Scrolls*

Elias trekked far from eyesight distance of the camp and laid Apayim onto the ground with a calm grunt. He could still see the glare of the fires enough to find his return in the night. He spent long moments in meditation as he knelt calmly with winds passing in subtle chill.

As he gripped dust from the earth to sprinkle upon Apayim's brow, his spirit was tilt with sudden unrest. A dark hold was upon him and kept his mind from meditating. He opened his eyes and could no longer see the blaze of the camp fire in the distance. An intent presence blocked his sight.

Subtle sobs found his ears. He inhaled softly, squinted with discernment, glanced in each corner of his eye and nodded with affirmation. He sensed them. Gathered round him with brutal intent. Breathing heated rage from their lungs. He sensed them, slumped with a sigh and answered their aim calmly.

"You have returned in the cover of night, just as evil hides in shade. Will you be so shamed in your actions upon my flesh that it must be done in the dark?"

"What actions do you call us for, elder?" called a voice from the dark.

Elias smirked and shook his head, "I am no fool in my old age. As I called you, you have followed the mind of Cain, sons of murderer and ill repute."

"We are'eh of Adam's blood," hissed another quivering tone, "we deserve none of 'tis curse which you have spoke upon us."

"Then if of Adam's blood, behold your brother, Melhazur, let your face be kissed by the moonlight.That we may both mourn your kin with embrace."

Melhazur stepped slowly into the moonlight and revealed his scar-wrenched face menacing with crazed, venomous

# Chapter Three  *The North Refuge*

purpose. He stared long and hard at the elder with brow curled of hatred and cheeks wet with sorrow over his uncle. He spoke no word. His eyes were dark and aloof. Nostrils flared and jaw set.

Elias waited upon his knees as he stared at the barter. Hearts pounded, shivered in still breaths. Suddenly the elder was struck from behind and thrust down upon his face. Dirt clumped into his eye and lung as the second strike came with greater vigor.

Elias rolled onto his back as the strikes continued. The elder moaned with eyes toward the sky. "Let these bones rest here, and have my soul taken to Abel's side. My Alpha, keep your promise, guard my brothers, guard young Aman, and restore Adam's way among men." The elder sighed his final breath as the cool night air chilled his body.

\*    \*    \*

Seth shook with chill and shot a sharp glance to the distant field. He glanced at Jodia and Mered who too stared in the direction with question in their eyes. The three stood instantly and strolled in direction of the field as the remaining men slept.

Searing winds brushed their faces with shrill whistle. Each elder frowned in expectance as dust clouds rose before them. Seth tightened his cloth round his waist as Mered removed his bō and Jodia clenched his fist.

The whistle grew with screams as a torch jetted toward the men. Mered leapt forward and caved the flaming arrow to the ground. He turned to face the others who glanced beyond at what lurked.

A thunderous roar sounded again at the men's backs. Seth turned and was instantly plunged at his waist by a dark being.

He gripped it tightly as it rolled him several cubits then lifted into flight.

The entire camp panicked as a second shout came. Jodia and Mered returned to the camp as another beast rampaged through the slumber with wild howl and fearless emotion. It leapt round the men who ran in startled scatter. Many were pummeled with vicious blows that sent poor souls helplessly airborne. Yet a third came and teased the men with mighty bounds upon every attempted retreat. And suddenly the night rest was shattered with dozens of demons traipsing from above.

The men began to hurl clumps from the ground and stones they found at the beasts only to see them greatly aggravated and spawned with more aggression.

"Do not be afraid!" yelled Barra to his son as he charged one of the fiends. He gripped broken fragments in hand and began to beat the demon upon its head with mighty strikes. The demon lunged at him only to find its assault met with thick moist bark. Ezra came to his father's aid and crowned the demon with a club. The monster stilled before them and all who witnessed were silenced in awe.

Barra grinned at his son in victory that was short lived. The animal hollered angrily and planted Barra with a stomp. Ezra cried out and was caught by the sprite's arm and sent away stumbling. The villain pressed its paw upon Barra's chest and leaned heavily. The hunter wheezed for air as the hellion snarled over him.

"I am going to crush you!" it grumbled as a subtle snap surged agony through Barra's bone.

Jodia sprang at the demon and tackled it to the dirt. He immediately began to beat the beast's torso with his fists and forearm. Mered joined the fight and fended the panicked men with trumpeting whips from his long bōs which stunned

## Chapter Three                       *The North Refuge*

several creatures onto their heels. Jodia wrestled his match over his head with little effort and tossed it with a mighty grunt through the chaos onto its sadistic sidekicks. The demons fell clumsily over each other as the elders fought off their attack.

Ezra moaned with growing anger and joined the elder's fight, finding supernatural strengths the young hunter never felt. He beat many beasts with his club and subdued them all while urging the men to stand. Suddenly, the men who watched the onslaught were empowered and began to fight as well as the enemies descended. Found near the central fire were the sturdy arms crafted from the eyviedi leaves by the elder Elias. The men, women, and children gathered them and instantly swung relentless against the plight of these beasts.

Aman and Lathan shuffled from the chaos with shouts of fright. A monstrous growl bellowed from above as a sefíyai set its sights on the children. The beast landed in front of them with deafening thud that knocked the boys onto their backs. It raised its claw to swipe at the boys. But each flared back with anger and scampered from reach. The two found boulders and struck the demon's legs. They scampered for more, finding a massive boulder which each carried into the sefíyai's gut. The force brought the beast onto its back in writhing agony. Yet theirs was not enough strength to subdue a beast so great. The demon launched the boulder from its chest and clawed the boys with one single blow.

The sefíyai then raised its eyes and called to the air. Instantly, the boys were encircled with brutes that gathered senses and snarled with angst at the little ones who dared them onward. Without notice there landed a beaten accomplice at their feet with a heavy thud. The demons frowned in confusion until Seth pounced upon the demon with his knee. He balanced his weight with upright stance on the animal's chest.

Sharp silence held the tense anticipation in which extended pupils and deep breathes gazed upon flamed eyes and hungry drooling fangs.

Vicious roars snapped silence stray as the demons charged again only to meet the relentless hammer of Aman's staff wielded in Seth's hands. He drove the beasts back until they and he were no longer seen. The shouts of the struggle echoed from their distance.

The boys stared as a vast smoke quickly engulfed the camp in darkness. A cold calm haunted the air as the two watched in question of what was to come. A low grumble answered from the distance and flowed with horrid screams of torture. The boys' eyes were wide with fright as they listened to those within the smoke shout with terror. Howls ensued as children cried in panic. Their voices dispersed into the sky as demons hoisted child after child from the camp.

Suddenly, a demon sefíyai rushed from the smoke with body blazed in green. It hurried toward the boys with body stretched. Neither Lathan nor Aman moved, frozen in fear as the monster approached. Yet the demon was slammed as Mered descended from the smoke and came down upon the animal with a heavy club. The two gazed at the sefíyai as Seth broke through the smoke and raced toward them.

"Young ones, with us, quickly!" Seth commanded.

Though the demons were held with courageous fight at the hands of elders and hunters alike, this was only a trickle of the dark multitude marching into their rest. The moon glinted its last glow from the horizon and dawn was fast approaching with violet haze in the eastern sky. As the fighting continued, the sky smoked with dancing ash for descending into the chaos was the vile venomous wing of the fallen arch Vestual.

His wing wailed with agony as he pounced upon hunters and spat warm poison into the eyes of women and children.

# Chapter Three

## The North Refuge

The dark angel moved through the men with incredible speed, breaking their clubs with effortless gouges and tossing them as chaff. It laughed with satisfaction as it conquered the men with seemingly no need of the sefíyai's help. Those who dared challenge Vestual only met the ground as the demon tore through them without relent.

"Flee the grounds," hollered Jodia who chased back attacking sefíyai as few men managed escape from the cloud. Still Vestual pressed without care for their retreat. He brought blows upon any who glinted for a moment at the rampage to their backs. As it came closer, Seth turned and launched at the fallen arch with rage. His long staff pointed square at the demon's eye, ready to impact with triumphant strike. Yet the elder was swatted several cubits by the arch's strong palm. Seth landed and moaned in pain, only to find the seducer swiftly straddled over him.

Vestual pointed his crooked sword over the elder and thrust downward with jeering eyes. Seth stiffened.

At once Vestual's blade was halted by a brilliant pallid hand. The demon stumbled from the push and its face lit with surprise at who stood before him. Seth looked too at the figure, who was Michael the Archangel. He glared at the scuffling beasts with great power.

Vestual scoffed and bellowed from deep within his chest. The shadow of demons rushed toward Michael with torture as their aim. But the angel opened his wings. The grounds were instantly flushed with light and the entire attack was held. Vestual fell backward and hissed angrily as Michael lifted Seth to his feet.

The angel looked sternly into his eyes. "Your men will no longer stand, but the dawn is upon you, get to the refuge of Orgêeda."

Seth replied quickly, "I must seek for Elias, my brother."

# Lands of Eden

*by M. Gabreyl Scrolls*

Michael bowed his head and hummed, "The eld Elias will not be found. But you have been chosen. You must get to the refuge, do not turn an eye until you have seen the light of dawn. Or Candor will be lost to these grounds forever."

At that, the Archangel was mounted by Vestual, who sunk his teeth into his wing. Michael commanded Seth to go onward without even a wince at the fallen arch's clench. Seth stared for but a moment before he was off without question. He called the few who survived the terror to follow, as Michael was quickly joined by two additional angels who held back the Ya'goviah with the command of their wings. The hosts turned their backs to the retreating men and flooded the dark creatures with incredible light, so abundant that it allowed the people to see the land of refuge ahead of them. Yet the light vanished once the men distanced themselves far enough from the chaos. The ground thundered as the demons pursued.

"Do not turn back!" Seth shouted as the enemy's arrows flooded the sky. One man turned with pause and was instantly struck by a flaming arrow. Seth shouted his command again while others stopped in awe and fear. Dozens fell, one by one, from the falling flames and only those who did not turn were spared. The thunder grew louder and closer, and fear gripped the fleeting hearts. Yet they sprinted onward without cease and with evil snapping at their feet. They could hear the threats and sense the tongues of the enemies salivating for their ruin.

Suddenly, the sky shot with the luminance of the sun. Behind them, the villains howled with anger and scattered from their pursuit. Seth turned to see the cloud of smoke lift to the sky as the demons disperse without further trounce. He kept his eyes on them until all was vanished.

Behind the elder, panted survivors worn with morning terror. He looked upon their beat faces and was filled with tremendous sorrow. Seth stood for a long moment of shock before he collapsed to his knees in anguish.

# Chapter Three

## The North Refuge

"So few," he moaned as tears streamed upon his chin, "…so few."

## The Remnant of Candor

Wide boulders pillared the passage which only appeared vacant of watch. Along the gate were several guards hidden amidst the cliffs and roughs. Though benevolent in nature, these Orgêeda guards were poised with pristine aim upon any who approached their gate. And yet, none of them could concentrate such aim so greatly upon these piteous few who drew near.

The dell was heavy with moisture dyed from the stone. Above, the sky was heavy with the drifting mist of the mountain waters. The troop beheld the mauve fog in awe as they neared the vast golden reefs of the valley entrance. Only Seth, Mered, and Jodia ignored the splendor with grief ridden faces.

Seth strolled to the gate and rapped the wooden log against the border. Its sound echoed round the arena as the elder backed away and stood before the troop.

The enormous reef moaned with mild vibration as it opened to the elder. Out stepped five men garbed in layered gossamer made of strong fibers. One that led them adorned a pale purple smock over his shoulder. His chin was brush with

# Chapter Four — The Remnant of Candor

thin gray beard and the dark strands of his hair mingled into long locks that draped his neck and chest.

The man stepped directly in front of Seth, studied the group with question, then looked at the elder with uncertainty.

"What is this dismal sight upon the grounds of my gate?"

Seth swallowed and looked at the man squarely, "We few, have journeyed from afar, and seek refuge among your valleys."

The man turned his face slightly with down turned brow. "Those who seek refuge here, can only find it with peace upon our borders. So, of where have you been ridden which finds you seeking refuge, what unrest continues for these, so weary of strife stand here?"

The men's eyes watered with sorrow as Seth held his tongue in long silence. The man cocked his head in apparent empathy as Seth answered.

"Before you stands, Barra and Ezra, sons of Moaz, Joseph, son of Hiddel and Atyah his wife. Leah and Jesse, the daughter and youngest son of Titus. Lathan…son of Ephese… Aman, son of Jebas. Jodia, son of Enosh, and Mered, son of Cainan. Our land has been removed from us, our men scattered through Eden, Orgêeda our only refuge."

The elder looked briefly at the ground, then stared forward confidently at the man and stated his vow.

"I am Seth the third, son of Adam, son of Seth, and son of Enosh, my father. We are held to this land, to the truth passed down from Adam our father, to the Sovereignty that has spared us to this gate. Let any enemy that comes upon us, and every enemy of the Alpha, be fallen by the strength the Creator has instilled in these, the remnant of Candor."

## About the Author

M.Gabreyl Scrolls is a young writer with a heart for Biblical history and anthology. Gabreyl began penning the **Lands of Eden** series in March of 2003 and has spent extensive amounts of time researching the history of Adam's bloodline, as well as, genealogical documents referenced in the Bible. While this book series is fiction in nature, the story keeps in sync with historical chronology and often includes facts and references to individuals and events otherwise unknown and scarcely found in religious texts. *Lands of Eden: The Remnant of Candor*, the first novel of the series, was originally begun in the fall of 2006 after the completion of Books II and III in this multi-chronicle story.

## About the Publisher

Leeway Artisans is a publishing company that has been operating out of Maryland for close to five years. The company boasts innovated fiction and non-fiction that is fresh, revitalizing, and inspirational to readers nationwide. The publisher can be found on the web at www.leewayartisans.com or via mail at:

Leeway Artisans, Inc.
P.O. Box 1577
Laurel, MD 20707

For additional information, email us at info@leewayartisans.com.